LADY MACBETH

LADY MACBETH

A NOVEL

AVA REID

DEL REY | NEW YORK

Published in the United States by Del Rey, an imprint of Random House, a division of Penguin Random House LLC, New York.

DEL REY and the CIRCLE colophon are registered trademarks of Penguin Random House LLC.

Grateful acknowledgment is made to A. S. Kline for permission to reprint "The Lai of Guigemar" by Marie de France, translated by A. S. Kline, copyright © 2019 by A. S. Kline. Used by permission.

LIBRARY OF CONGRESS CATALOGING-IN-PUBLICATION DATA
Names: Reid, Ava, author.
Title: Lady Macbeth : a novel / Ava Reid.
Description: New York : Del Rey, 2024.
Identifiers: LCCN 2024010495 |
ISBN 9780593722565 (hardcover) | ISBN 9780593722572 (ebook)
Subjects: LCSH: Gruoch, Queen, consort of Macbeth,
King of Scotland—Fiction. | Scotland—Kings and rulers—Fiction. |
Scotland—History—To 1057—Fiction. | LCGFT: Historical fiction. |
Fantasy fiction. | Gothic fiction. | Novels.
Classification: LCC PS3618.E533 L33 2024 |
DDC 813/.6—dc23/eng/20240422
LC record available at https://lccn.loc.gov/2024010495

International edition ISBN 978-0-593-87481-3

Printed in the United States of America on acid-free paper

randomhousebooks.com

1 2 3 4 5 6 7 8 9

First Edition

Endpaper illustrations by Mary Metzger
Book design by Susan Turner

For Sarah, Tricia, and Sam

She turns and looks a moment in the glass,
Hardly aware of her departed lover;
Her brain allows one half-formed thought to pass:
"Well now that's done: and I'm glad it's over."

—"The Waste Land," T. S. ELIOT

She, like a faerie for her beauty;
By the cloak he now seized her,
And to his castle swiftly led her
Delighted to have found a lady
So immeasurably lovely.

. . .

Now I must tell you further of,
That one lady he could so love:
The lord took counsel of a baron
And thus the lady did imprison,
In a grey marble tower, perverse
Her fate; days ill, the nights worse.

. . .

No man or woman comes there,
None beyond the wall doth dare.
An old priest with white hair
Holds the key to door and stair.

. . .

A woman light in her manner
Will long resist every prayer
For she wishes none might see
Her wield her art too openly.

—"Guigemar," MARIE DE FRANCE

CONTENTS

DRAMATIS PERSONAE

ROSCILLE, ROSELE, ROSALIE, ROSCILLA, the Lady

HAWISE, a handmaiden

ALAN VARVEK, WRYBEARD, Duke of Breizh

GEOFFREY I, GREYMANTLE, Count of Anjou

THEOBALD I, LE TRICHEUR, Count of Blois, Chartres, and Chasteaudun

HASTEIN, a Norse chieftain

MACBETH, MACBETHAD, MACBHEATHA, the Lord, Thane of Glammis

BANQUHO, Thane of Lochquhaber

FLÉANCE, Banquho's son

DUNCANE, king of Scotland

LES LAVANDIÈRES, witches

CHANCELLOR, the high priest of Scotland, a Druide

LISANDER, LANDEVALE, LAUNFALE, LANVAL, the elder son of King Duncane, prince of Cumberland

EVANDER, IOMHAR, IVOR, the younger son of King Duncane

ÆTHELSTAN, *rex Anglorum,* king of the English

SENGA, a handmaiden

Attendants, Messengers, Servants, Soldiers

GLOSSARY

ALBA, Scotland

ANJOU, a county of France (adj.—Angevin)

BLOIS, a county of France

BREIZH, Brittany (adj.—Brezhon)

BRETAIGNE, Britain

BREZHONEG, the Breton language

CAWDER, a territory in Scotland

CHARTRES, a county of France, ruled by the House of Blois

CHASTEAUDUN, a county of France, ruled by the House of Blois

GLAMMIS, a territory in Scotland

LOIRE, a river in Brittany

MORAY, the seat of King Duncane

NAONED, Nantes, the capital of Brittany

A NOTE ON NAMES

In the murky setting of eleventh-century Scotland, language was complex, evolving, and malleable. The world of medieval Britain does not have the sort of rigidity that modern-day convention often impresses upon it. Everything could change at the drop of a hat (or the thrust of a knife). Institutions were precarious; titles and rights were contested. The various names for each character reflect the different languages that would have been spoken at the time, even though many of them are dead or moribund today. As much as it might make for more straightforward literature, I chose to jettison the idea that one culture or one language had a totalizing grip on the world.

LADY MACBETH

ACT I

THANE
OF
GLAMMIS

ONE

"**L**ADY?"

She looks up and out the window of the carriage; night has fallen with a swift and total blackness. She waits to see how she will be addressed.

For the first days of their journey, through the damp, twisting, dark-green trees of Breizh, she was Lady Roscille, the name pinned to her so long as she was in her homeland, all the way to the choky gray sea. They crossed safely, her father, Wrybeard, having beaten back the Northmen who once menaced the channel. The waves that brushed the ship's hull were small and tight, like rolled parchment.

Then, to the shores of Bretaigne—a barbarian little place, this craggy island which looks, on maps, like a rotted piece of meat with bites taken out of it. Their carriage gained a new driver, who speaks in bizarre Saxon. Her name, then, vaguely Saxon: *Lady Rosele?*

Bretaigne. First there had been trees, and then the trees had thinned to scruff and bramble, and the sky was sickishly vast, as gray as the sea, angry clouds scrawled across it like smoke from distant fires. Now the horses are having trouble with the incline of the road. She hears, but cannot see, rocks coming loose under their hooves. She hears the wind's long, smooth *shush*ing, and that is how she knows it is only grass, grass and stone, no trees for the wind to get caught in, no branches or leaves to break the sound apart.

This is how she knows they have reached Glammis.

"Lady Roscilla?" her handmaiden prods her again, softly.

There it is, the Skos. No, Scots. She will have to speak the language of her husband's people. Her people, now. "Yes?"

Even under Hawise's veil, Roscille recognizes her quavering frown. "You haven't said a word in hours."

"I have nothing to say."

But that isn't entirely true; Roscille's silence is purposeful. The night makes it impossible to see anything out the window, but she can still listen, though she mostly hears the absence of sounds. No birds singing or insects trilling, no animals scuffling in the underbrush or scampering among the roots, no woodcutters felling oaks, no streams trickling over rock-beds, none of last night's rain dripping off leaves.

No sounds of life, and certainly no sounds of Breizh, which is all she has ever known. Hawise and her frown are the only familiar things here.

"The Duke will expect a letter from you when we arrive. When the proceedings are done," Hawise says vaguely. Half a dozen names she has for the Lady, in as many tongues, but she has somehow not found the word for "wedding."

Roscille finds it funny that Hawise cannot speak the word when, at the moment, she is pretending to be a bride. Roscille thought it was a silly plan, when she first heard it, and it feels even sillier now: to disguise herself as handmaiden and Hawise as bride. Roscille is dressed in dull colors and stiff, blocky wool, her hair tucked under a coif. On the other side of the carriage, pearls circle Hawise's wrists and throat. Her sleeves are yawning mouths, drooping to the floor. The train is so white and thick it looks like a snowdrift has blown in. A veil, nearly opaque, covers Hawise's hair, which is the wrong shade of pale.

She and Hawise are of age, but Hawise has a husky Norsewoman's build, all shoulders. These disguises will fool no one; even the sight of their shadows would reveal the ruse. It is an arbitrary exercise of power by her future husband, to see if the Duke will play along with his whimsical demands. She has considered, though, that perhaps his motive is more sinister: that the Thane of Glammis fears treachery in his own lands.

Just as Roscille is a gift to the Thane for his alliance, Hawise was a gift to Roscille's father the Duke, for not having sent ships when he could have sent ships. For letting the Northmen retreat from the channel in peace, Hastein, the Norse chieftain, offered the Duke one of his many useless daughters.

Roscille's father is so much more beneficent than Hawise's boorish pirate-people. In Wrybeard's court, even bastard daughters like Roscille get to be ladies, if the Duke thinks they can be put to some use.

But as Roscille has newly learned, she is not useful to her father because she can speak her native Brezhoneg, and fluent Angevin, and very good Norse, thanks to Hawise, and now

Skos, out of necessity, even though the words scrape the back of her throat. She is not useful because she can remember the face of every noble who passes through Wrybeard's court, and the name of every midwife, every servant, every suppliant, every bastard child, every soldier, and a morsel about them as well, the hard, sharp bits of desire that flash out from them like quartz in a cave mouth, so when the Duke says, *I have heard whispers of espionage in Naoned, how shall I discover its source?* Roscille can reply, *There is a stable boy whose Angevin is suspiciously unaccented. He sneaks away with one kitchen girl behind the barn every feast day.* And then the Duke can send men to wait behind the barn, and catch the kitchen girl, and flog her naked thighs to red ribbons until the Angevin spy / stable boy confesses.

No. Roscille understands now. She is useful for the same reason that the Duke's effort at disguising her is doomed: She is beautiful. It is not an ordinary beauty—whores and serving girls are sometimes beautiful but no one is rushing around to name them lady or robe them in bridal lace. It is an unearthly beauty that some in Wrybeard's court call death-touched. Poison-eyed. Witch-kissed. *Are you sure, Lord Varvek, my noble Duke, Wry of beard, that she is not Angevin? They say the House of Anjou are all born from the blood of the serpent-woman Melusina.*

Greymantle, lord of Anjou, has a dozen children and twice as many bastards and they always seem to slip into Wrybeard's court with their pale hair, sleek as wet-furred foxes. Her father would not have been shy in admitting to have had an Angevin mistress, though perhaps Greymantle would have chafed at the accusation that his line could have produced such an aberrant creature as Roscille. But the Duke said nothing, and so the whispers began.

The white of her hair is not natural; it is like draining moon-light. Her skin—have you seen it?—it will not hold a color. She is as bloodless as a trout. And her eyes—one look into them will drive mortal men to madness.

One visiting noble heard such rumors and refused to meet her gaze. Roscille's presence at the feast table was so unnerving that it scuttled a trade alliance, and then that same noble (le Tricheur, he is called) carried the story back with him to Chasteaudun and made all of Blois and Chartres shrink from having future dealings with Wrybeard and his court of tricky fairy-maidens. So Roscille was fitted with a gossamer veil, mesh and lace, to protect the world's men from her maddening eyes.

That was when her father realized it was in fact good to have a story of his own, one that could neaten all these unruly and far-flung fears. "Perhaps you were cursed by a witch." He said it in the same tone he used to proclaim the division of war spoils.

This is the Duke's telling of it, which is now the truth, since no one is any the wiser. His poor, innocent mistress bleeding out on her birthing bed, the oddly silent child in her arms, the witch sweeping through the window and out again, all shadows and smoke and the crackle of lightning. *Her laughter echoed through every hall of the castle—for weeks afterward it all reeked of ash!*

The Duke recounts this to a gathered audience of France's nobles, all who may have heard the rumors and been spooked out of arrangements and exchanges. As he speaks, some of Naoned's courtiers begin nodding grimly along, *Yes, yes, I remember it now, too.*

It is only when all the nobles and courtiers are gone and

she is alone with her father that Roscille, not quite thirteen, risks a question.

Why did the witch curse me?

Wrybeard has his favorite draughts board before him, its latticework of black and white made dull with use. He arranges the tiles as he speaks. Dames, the pieces are called, women.

A witch needs no invitation, he says, *only a way of slipping through the lock.*

No one knows exactly what a witch looks like (so in fact everyone knows what a witch looks like), yet they can all agree, it sounds like the sort of curse a witch would give: the shiny apple with the rotted core. *Your daughter will be the most beautiful maiden, Lord Varvek, but one look into her eyes will drive mortal men to madness.* Roscille understands that this explanation offers her better prospects than the alternative. Better to be witch-cursed than witch; better hagseed than hag.

But—

"What, are you Roscille of the Thousand Questions?" Wrybeard waves his hand. "Go now, and count yourself lucky it was only le Tricheur who shook like a dog's leg at the sight of you, and not that Parisian imbecile with all his warmongering vassals whom he cannot keep to heel."

The Parisian imbecile goes on to start wars with half the other duchies and is then excommunicated twice over. This is how Roscille learns that any man may style himself *the Great* even if the only achievement of his life is spilling a dramatic ordeal of blood.

Her father teaches her to abandon the habit of asking questions, because a question may be answered dishonestly. Even the dullest stable hand can tell a convincing lie if it is the difference between the end of a whip and not. The truth is found in whispers, in sidelong glances, in twitching jaws and clenching fists. What is the need for a lie when no one is listening? And no one in Wrybeard's court suspects that Roscille is capable of listening, of noticing, especially with the veil that hides her eyes.

Roscille of the Veiled Eyes. They call her this in Breizh and beyond. It is a far kinder epithet than she has any right to expect, being a witch-marked girl. Yet she does not wear the thin veil now, not with Hawise. It has been pronounced that women are not afflicted by the madness that her stare induces in men.

Thus the marriage has been arranged on the condition that Roscille arrive by single carriage, with only her handmaiden as company. The carriage driver is a woman who handles the reins clumsily, as she has been taught to drive only for this specific purpose. Even the horses are mares, silver-white.

Roscille realizes it has been a long time since Hawise spoke and that the handmaiden is still waiting for a reply. She says, "You may write and tell the Duke whatever will be most pleasing for him to hear."

Once she would have written the letter in her own hand, and paced the room considering how best to relay all the details of the Thane's desires, the treasures that he left unguarded, ripe for Roscille's senses to plunder. *Here is how he speaks when he believes no one is listening. Here is where his gaze cuts when he thinks no one is watching.*

But that letter is to a man who no longer exists. The Wrybeard who sent her away is a man Roscille does not know. Still, she knows the things that will please this other man, as they are the same things that will please any man. The Duke will want to know that his strange cursed bastard daughter is an obedient broodmare and a docile pleasure slave. She understands that these are the two fundamental aspects of wifehood: Open your legs to your lord husband and bear a child that will mingle the blood of Alba with the blood of Breizh. A marriage alliance is only a temporary bond, thinly woven, but if Roscille is good enough it will hold until a son comes along and yokes the unicorn to the ermine.

The unicorn is the proud emblem of Skos, all its brutish clans finally and grudgingly united beneath one banner. And it is said that Lord Varvek is as canny as a weasel, so, not one to let an advantageous epithet go unremarked, the Duke put the barb-toothed creature on his coat of arms.

Before, Roscille would have claimed her father's epithet for herself, too, a trait seeped from his blood into hers (is the daughter of an ermine not an ermine, too?). Now she wonders—is the weasel truly clever, or are its teeth merely sharp?

The carriage clatters and strains around a series of narrow turns, up the cliffside, the horses panting hard. The wind is flat and smooth and uninterrupted, as if it is being piped in through a pair of bellows. And then, shocking and sudden, Roscille hears the dragging pulse of the sea.

Naoned, the city of her birth, sits inland on the Loire; until traveling to Bretaigne, she had never seen the ocean. But this is not like that snarling gray channel. The water is black and muscular, and where the moonlight catches the small crests of the waves, it shows a pattern like a serpent's belly. And the water has a steadiness that the wind does not: The surf crashes the rock over and over and over again with the rhythm of a beating heart.

The graces of civilization spiral outward from the papal seat in Rome, that bright jewel in the center of everything. But the light of the Holy See dims with distance: Far from Rome, here is the world's naked, primitive darkness. The castle of Glammis hulks over the cliffside, vulgar and bleak. There is a single long parapet, running parallel to the edge of the cliff, so that the whole wall is a straight, sheer drop to the water below. What Roscille at first thinks are crosses are only arrow slits. There are no carvings along the barbican or the battlements, no etchings to protect against pale Ankou, the spirit of Death, who drives his creaking wagon of corpses—every parish and house in Breizh must have such ornaments, or he will come— but perhaps something else keeps Death at bay in Glammis.

Stop, Roscille thinks. The word falls in her mind like a stone. *Please, no farther. Turn around and let me be gone.*

The carriage rattles on.

THE BARBICAN GRINDS OPEN TO the courtyard. There is a man standing within it, just one. He wears a gray square cloak and a short tunic, tall leather boots, and a kilt. Roscille has never seen a man wear a skirt before. Wool stockings keep his knees from the cold.

At first she thinks it is her lord husband come to greet her, but as the carriage draws closer and then halts, she sees immediately that it is not. One thing she knows about the Thane of Glammis is that he is large, as large as a mortal man can reasonably be. This man in the courtyard is by no means small, but he does not have the mountainous stature reported of the Thane: He is ordinary. He has hair the color of a roof's thatching, sun-stripped yellow.

Hawise dismounts the carriage first, then Roscille. The man does not offer his hand to help her, which is terribly impolite by the standards of Wrybeard's court, and Greymantle's, and every duchy or county ruled by the House of Capet. Roscille stumbles a little bit, and she hasn't even donned her bridal gown.

"Lady Roscilla," says the man. "You are warmly received."

The walls of the courtyard might as well be made of paper, for how well they prohibit the wind. She has never been so cold in her life. Even Hawise, with her hardy Norse blood, shivers beneath the veil.

"Thank you," she says, in Scots. "This is my handmaiden, Hawise."

The man frowns. At least, she thinks he does. There are so many furrows on his face—the marks of battle or the marks of age, Roscille cannot tell—that she can barely read his expression. His eyes dart to Hawise for a moment, and then back to Roscille, though he does not meet her gaze. He knows the stories.

"I am Lord Banquho, Thane of Lochquhaber and your husband's right hand," he says. "Come. I will show you to your chamber."

He directs the driver to the stables and then directs Roscille and Hawise to the castle. They go up through twisting, half-lit halls. Many of the torches are gone, and there are only black scorch-marks to indicate where they had once been.

The abrupt absences of light make their shadows warp and judder against the walls. Now the wind's howling is hushed, yet from the floors there is a strange rasping sound, like the scrape of a ship's hull against the pebbled beach.

"Is that the water?" Roscille asks. "The sea?"

"You will hear it from every corner of the castle," says Lord Banquho, without turning. "After enough time, you will not hear it at all."

She thinks she might go mad before her brain learns to omit it. This frightens her more than any ignominy she might—she *will*—suffer to her body, that her mind could be so reduced, turned to pulp like grapes crushed for wine.

Even her father's cold relinquishment of her cannot entirely disabuse Roscille of her oldest habits. To soothe herself, she returns to them now. She observes.

Lord Banquho is a warrior; there is no doubt about that. Even when he strides, he keeps his arm crooked, so that his thumb may occasionally brush the hilt of his sheathed sword. He will draw his blade in half the length of a heartbeat, she knows.

This is nothing new—Roscille has lived among soldiers, even if the Duke's men have the decency to leave their weapons behind when they are in the company of women. She notices that the brooch which fastens his cloak is small and round, and made of base metal, not silver. It is something that will rust quickly, especially in this briny air.

Banquho stops in front of a wooden door. It is gridded with iron. He says, "Your chamber, Lady Roscilla." He is hard on the *c,* making it into one of those braying Scottish consonants.

She nods, but before she can reply, Banquho removes an iron key from his belt and opens the door. Her empty stomach shrivels. This is a bad sign, that her room has a lock which can only be opened from the outside. She does not even indulge the hope that she will be given a key of her own.

The room itself is a wardrobe, a candlestick with three prongs, and a bed. There is a large pelt draped across the floor, dark and thick, its head still attached. A bear. Its death-empty eyes are two pools that hold the torchlight. Its black lip is pulled back in an immortal grimace of pain. Roscille has never seen a bear before, alive or dead; she has only seen their images decorating house seals and war banners. They have already been hunted to extinction in Breizh, but of course they still roam here. She leans down and examines the bear's curved yellow teeth, each one the length of her finger.

Banquho lights the tapers, casting the room and all its cold stone in a waxy gleam. "The banquet has been set. The Lord is waiting."

Roscille stands up again. Her knees feel limp, like jellied broth. "Yes. Apologies. I will dress now."

She waits, for the span of a breath, to see if Banquho will leave. The Scots have strange beliefs about women. There are whispers that they still practice the jus primae noctis, the droit du seigneur, the right of a lord to share his wife among his men as he does the spoils from his conquests. These whispers have preyed upon her so fiercely that even after she accepted she would be wed, still she did not sleep for days, did not eat for longer, did not even drink until her lips turned white and chapped and Hawise had to force the thinned wine down her throat.

Roscille has heard of a Scottish king, Durstus, who forsook the company of his lawful wife Agasia. This caused her to be forced and abused by his men, in the most villainous and vile manner. Twelve she was when she heard this story, and she knew what it meant.

But Banquho turns without sound and slips through the door. She is alone with Hawise again, and Roscille nearly collapses onto the bear-rug.

There is one small relief, like a slant of light through broken stone. The bed is large enough for her and Hawise to share, but no bigger. Not large enough to accommodate the Lord.

They both disrobe in silence. Nakedness, even among women in private, is still uncommon, uncouth. Bodies are meant to be guarded like gold. The flash of a bare ankle is like dropping a pendant, so that everyone can see it clatter to the ground and know that you hold its richness and likely more. What else are you hiding in your stores, against your breast? How easily might it be stolen? You cannot blame a man for snatching something which has been taunted in front of him like meat before a dog.

As a handmaiden, as a spoil of war, as a girl with no status, Hawise's stores are easy to plunder. Yet her attachment to Roscille has kept her safe, safe from drunken courtiers and their searching hands. She is as virginal as a nun. Soon she will be the only virgin between them.

Hawise has a Norsewoman's build: broad shoulders, small breasts, narrow hips which mean she will struggle to bear children. They are a study in opposites. Roscille's breasts are full enough to need binding under her square-necked gown (why tempt a man with even the suggestion of treasure?). Yet otherwise her body is still girlish, slender, making for an unnatural contrast. Above her waist she has a woman's form, but below she is as lithe as a serpent, something sleek and made for twisting. She wonders what the Lord will think of it.

There is no mirror in the room, only a pail of water, which shows Roscille her bleary, rippling reflection. The veil is as absurd as she imagined it would be. Her limbs are mummified in white linen and lace. Her sleeves are heavy with pearls. Her gown drags after her like a sodden thing. It is difficult to walk.

"Lady Rosalie," Hawise says—in Angevin, for it is the language these Scots are least likely to know. All of a sudden she reaches out and squeezes her hand. "You are the cleverest woman I have ever known, the bravest—"

"You say this as if you are making remarks over my grave," Roscille replies. But she holds on to Hawise's hand.

"I only mean . . . you will survive this, too."

This, too. Hawise does not mention the other thing, the first. She doesn't have to; they both know.

Through the thick door, she hears Banquho's voice. "It is time, Lady Roscilla."

THE FIRST THING SHE NOTICES about the banquet hall is how empty it is. There are six long tables, but none of them are filled to their capacity; in fact, the two farthest from the dais are not occupied at all. Servants skulk about the walls, like brown mice, carrying platters, making no sound. The silence is strange, too. In Naoned, feast days are dense with noise: bards and their songs, courtiers and their gossiping, men bragging of their achievements, women swooning at the attention, draughts tiles rattling, ale mugs clinking. Toasts are made to fruitful harvests and profitable wars. The women wear their brightest gowns and the men comb their beards.

All Roscille hears now is the murmuring of voices, almost as low as the hushing sea. The men at the table press their faces close, so that their words pass only in that tight circle. There is the smell of ale, but certainly no mugs are being raised, no toasts made. The men are dressed in the same square cloaks and kilts, weapons at their sides. Warriors, all of them, who will draw their blades as easily as breathing. There are no bards or draughts tiles, and—Roscille realizes with a shocked inhale—no women.

This is the strangest thing of all. In the Duke's court, it is essential that there be wives for gossiping and bearing children, serving girls for filling plates, kitchen girls for cooking, and even whores for using, though such things must be done with discretion. It was so dark on their journey that Roscille cannot remember the closest town they passed in the carriage; she does not know how far the peasants live who keep their goats and sheep (this rocky land is no good for farming, not green enough for cattle). Where do the men of Glammis find their pleasure, feed their appetites?

She is so shaken by this she does not notice, at first, that Hawise is being led away from her. "Wait—" she chokes out, too loudly—all the men turn to stare. "Please, Hawise is my . . ."

But Banquho does not turn or falter in his course. Roscille watches as Hawise is taken by the elbow and maneuvered past the tables; she cannot keep her eyes on where, because then her lord husband is upon her.

She knows him at once, for his enormity. He blots out half her vision. *Reith,* they call him, Scots for "red," which is either for his hair or for his prowess at spilling blood. His hair is tied back with a thong. The Scots, she remembers, wear their hair long. He is younger than she thought he would be, no silver in his beard.

He is handsome, too, though not in the manner of Brezhon men. She had not expected this, yet it does not make anything easier—his features are brusque, rough. His hands are calloused and his shoulders huge as rocks. The hair on his arms is tufted and scraggly, like hill grass. He looks like he has been born right from the land of Glammis itself, grown out of the earth; his mother the dirt and his father the rain that waters it.

"My lady wife," he says, in his Scotsman's rasp.

"My lord husband," she replies. Her voice is like wind passing through reeds, almost inaudible.

She is wearing her veil, so it is safe for him to look her in the eyes. Even his stare is heavy, and it weighs upon her. Roscille decides it is wise to shrink from him, for now. He will not tolerate anything less than absolute obedience in the presence of his men. She gathers her arms around her middle. She looks down at the floor.

"Your beauty has not been falsely alleged," he murmurs. "Come now. Let us begin."

The next few moments unfold in near silence. They approach the dais, but before she can step upon it, two of the men advance toward her. They wear the same tartan as her Lord, so she suspects they are kin. They seize her under her armpits, and Roscille chokes on her breath, remembering the story of Durstus and Agasia, that unloved, rudely forced wife—but while these two men lift her, another man, beard-less, his flaxen hair rumpled with youth, kneels before her and tears off her stockings and slippers. Before she can speak, a pail of cold water is thrown over her bare feet.

This is a ritual in Breizh, too, the washing of the bride's feet. But there it is performed by older, widowed women, and gently, with warm water and perfumed soap, while handmaid-ens flutter about like birds and give advice about wifely duties. Roscille gasps as the cold climbs her veins. Not a moment is spared for her shock, her upset. She is set down again, bare-footed, on the dais.

Then the priest comes, the Druide, as they are called here. Unlike the religious men in Breizh and France, with their bald heads like little polished rosary beads, the Druide has a long gray beard that touches the floor. It is held in many places with leather thongs, as a maiden's hair is sometimes held with fillets. He does not have a Bible; he knows the words by heart. He speaks first in Latin, while Roscille's teeth are chattering so hard she can barely hear, and makes the sign of the cross over her and then Macbeth.

Her teeth stop chattering long enough that she can listen when he switches to Scots.

"Now is the joining of Lord Macbeth, son of Findlay, Mac-beth macFinlay, Macbethad mac Findlaích, the righteous man, Thane of Glammis, and the Lady Roscilla of Breizh," he says seriously, and his words fill the silent hall.

A length of red rope is procured, and she is yoked to her new husband. His left hand and her right. A Scotsman must keep his right hand to himself, in case he needs to draw a weapon. The hilt of the Lord's blade pushes out from beneath his cloak.

"The Lord and Lady Macbeth," says the Druide.

They are both made to turn toward the audience of men. There are scattered grunts of approval, the rapping of palms against the wooden table. Roscille's feet have gone numb. She cannot find Hawise in the crowd; where has Banquho taken her?

Macbeth sits, tugging Roscille along like a child's horse-on-a-string. His hand looks enormous beside hers, the knuckles split, his calluses yellow and thick. His nails are bitten to the quick. She cannot imagine the Lord chewing on his own fingernails, an anxious habit, betraying an unsettled mind. Nothing else about him suggests such infirmity.

The men raise their cups, and she follows suit, with some clumsiness. She is right-handed and must hold the heavy mug in her left. They mumble a toast in Old Scots, which Roscille cannot understand, but which has the cadence of a song. Then the meal comes steaming before them. Cubes of meat in a dark stew. Mutton, not beef (as it would have been in Naoned). She was right about the goats and sheep.

Before she is allowed to eat, the quaich must be passed. The double-handed silver bowl is filled with amber liquid, that strong drink of the Scots, which is said to scorch your throat like fire. Macbeth takes one handle, Roscille the other, and together they lift the quaich to their lips. The corner of her mouth brushes his beard. It is a quick swipe of her cheek, like the sting of running through bramble. She barely tastes the spirit; there is no flavor, only the burning pain it leaves behind.

The quaich is then passed through the banquet hall: first to the eldest and most proven warriors, then to the youngest, the not-yet-proven. Some of them are even younger than Roscille, boyish still, and they lap hesitantly from the bowl, like puppies. At last, it arrives in the hands of the flaxen-haired boy, whose cheeks flush angrily as he lifts the quaich. It is bad fortune to be the one who has the last sip, the one who finally drains it.

Roscille takes slow bites with her left hand. As she eats, she observes. The men all wear cloaks and kilts of wool, grays and grayed-out greens, occasionally a slash of red in the tartan. Some of their cloaks have furred collars: a fox here, its bushy tail and black eyes intact, an ermine, showing its winter white. She focuses on the brooch pinned to each man's chest. Like Banquho's, they are all made of base metal, iron or something else. No gold or silver, no jeweled inset. In fact, she sees nothing finer in the room than an amber cuff on one of the men, and her own pearls. Even the hilt of Macbeth's sword is no more than tempered bronze.

A hundred years ago, a king, Reutha, sent for craftsmen and artificers from the continent to come to Scotland, to teach the Scots methods of building and smithing and weaving and dyeing. Macbeth is a lord and should not live so sparsely. He is a warrior, too, so where are his spoils?

Slowly, behind her impassive eyes, Roscille's mind begins to turn.

A servant enters suddenly from the dark corridor, and Roscille lifts her gaze. She is hopeful that Hawise is being returned. But the man is only carrying a large iron cage, and inside it, a white bird. She has never seen such a bird in Breizh. It does not have the long beak of a waterfowl, nor the faintly iridescent neck of a dove. It is pure white, like the season's earliest snow, each feather arranged snugly against the next, so that it has a sleek, almost wet look.

"Oh!" she says, in heartfelt surprise. Many of the noble-women in Wrybeard's court keep pretty birds like this, to sing pretty songs. Has her lord husband thought to bring some of Naoned's civility to Glammis? Does he want to please his new wife with a gesture that reminds her of home? "This is a gen-erous gift, my Lord—"

But the servant does not pass her the cage; instead, he flings open the door and the bird flutters out of it, squeal-ing. The men watch it flail around the ceiling, thrashing about the iron chandelier, bouncing from one stone wall to the next, like a bee drunk on pollen. Roscille is too shocked to speak.

Her husband's hand wrenches from hers. He does not untie the knot; he merely pulls hard enough to tear through the rope entirely, leaving her with a rash of red down her wrist and on her palm, which hurts and makes her gasp. Then he has a bow, drawn out from somewhere behind the table, and he is nocking an arrow, and the bird is flapping and then sud-denly it is not.

Its movement ceases instantly, gripped by the sudden ric-tus of death. It falls through the air and lands on the stone floor, hard enough to snap all its fragile bones, but Roscille cannot hear the breaking over the sound of the men cheering and stamping their feet. One of them sweeps up the bird and jerks the arrow from its breast. It has been so immaculately aimed that there is only the smallest spurt of blood, like the pricking of a thorn against the pad of a thumb.

Animal sacrifice is a barbarian practice, sternly abolished by the pope, but Roscille knows it was hard enough for the civilizing Romans to extinguish the tradition of *human* sacrifice here in Bretaigne; before Christianity the Druides practiced strange rites, casking some of their offerings inside a large wicker statue and setting it alight; others still were submerged by force into peat bogs, which mummified their bodies. Sometimes these bodies surface from their hundred-year-old graves, and they look as shriveled as unborn children, yanked untimely from the womb, skin dyed charcoal black.

As the bird is brought toward the dais, Roscille realizes that it is a gift, after all, though not as she initially imagined. This is a show of her husband's strength and skill and virtue, a promise that she will be well protected and well fed and well honored. Not like Agasia.

She reaches down and touches the bird's breast, which is still warm. Its feathers are as smooth as she thought they would be. She thinks of plucking one to keep as a token, but for some reason the idea makes her sad. Macbeth's smile is resplendent. Under her veil, Roscille tries to smile back.

WHEN ALL THE CUPS HAVE been drained, Roscille walks barefooted to her chamber. The hem of her dress is still damp; the linen is so thick it will take hours and hours to dry. Her lord husband walks beside her. He wears leather boots and his steps are heavy like falling stones.

They reach the door, and Macbeth removes an iron key from his belt. Roscille wants to ask how many keys there are, and who has them, and if she will get one (though she knows she will not), and where Hawise is, *please,* and a thousand other things, but she must save up her words and only spend them wisely, because she does not know how many she will be allowed.

He goes into the room first and she follows. The tapers are still lit, though they are mostly burned down now, to stubby white ends that look like a beast's dull teeth. Macbeth glances around, almost as if it is the first time he has seen this room, and then his gaze pins Roscille in place. Her arms are held perfectly straight at her sides, her fingers curled inward.

"Lord Varvek is an honest man," he says. "So far I have been given no reason to think otherwise. You are beautiful, yes, there are none other in the world like you."

Very slowly he is approaching her, until he has her white veil between his finger and thumb, and he is rubbing it like it is an amulet he wishes to polish.

"But is the rest true?" he asks. "Do your eyes, disrobed, cause madness in men?"

"The Duke would not lie to such an esteemed and valuable ally."

Roscille thinks this is the right thing to say. She knows that Macbeth admires Wrybeard, for having defeated the Northmen and banished them from Breizh. In Alba, the Northmen are the most loathsome villains; the Scots have even made peace with Æthelstan, for God's sake, and no one ever believed there could be any love between Scotland and England, much less a joining of the lion and the unicorn.

No, the Norse are the vilest enemy of all. Roscille worries again what has happened to Hawise.

"It would be unwise to do so," Macbeth agrees. "And your father is reputed to be an exceptionally clever man."

Clever indeed, to use his beautiful bastard daughter to secure a valuable alliance. After years of training her to be an ermine, he has pulled a magician's trick and turned her into a pretty bird instead. Yet for months the question has been wheeling like a gyre, ever since the Duke announced her betrothal: Can the canny mind of a weasel exist within a bird's fragile, feathered body?

Macbeth tucks his hand beneath the veil and runs a finger along her bodice. Roscille's words spill out then, not at all as she planned them, but rather in a nasty rush of fear: "I know that there is a custom, in your lands. A wedding-night custom."

His brows arch in surprise. He removes his hand. "What custom is that?"

Her breath squeezes through the narrow siphon of her throat. "It is said that the bride has the right to ask three things of her husband, before they share a bed."

This is her slinking little rodent's plan, cloaked in a girl's shaky nervousness. She worried she would have to feign this nervousness, but right now it feels more real than the wisdom underneath.

There are not many books on Alba in the Duke's library, but there is an abbey nearby, and one of the monks is from Scotland, and he knows its history and its rites. The day her father proclaimed she would be wed, Roscille ran to the abbey. She girded herself in the knowledge of this monk, and began polishing the talisman of her own strategy.

It is something she has clung to in dark hours, like a little girl and her straw doll, when the thoughts of her wedding night come. Part of her did not believe she would speak it out loud, that she would try—perhaps still she will be punished for trying, and it will be worse than it ever would have been before. But she must try, or she will lose her mind, too, the mind she has spent so many years trying to whet like a blade. She must keep something of her own, even if it is no more than the belief that, somehow, she may have stopped the ravishment that is to come.

But Macbeth only replies mildly, "And what would you ask of me, my lady wife?"

Roscille is stunned by his placidness. For a moment she freezes, waiting for a cruel rejoinder, the knife hidden in his sleeve. Yet no blades flash. She swallows.

"A necklace," she says at last. "Gold, with a ruby inset."

This was not part of her initial plan. This she fabricated only hours ago, at dinner, while watching her husband and his men. None of them wore gold or silver or gemstones, and she only has to think back to the whispers she heard in Wrybeard's court to understand why.

There is no precious metal mined in Glammis. It is the remotest, most barren county of Scotland, its only virtues being its enviable position on the water, and the impregnable hills that surround it. All of Alba's gold and jewels are mined in Cawder, and because she has listened for so long, she knows: The Thane of Glammis has many enemies, and the Thane of Cawder is one of them.

Macbeth will not suspect that she knows any of this. A necklace is a very common thing for a wife to ask of her husband, especially when that wife is only seventeen, and especially when she has been raised in a court known for its languid opulence. She will seem frivolous and vain and naïve. Not conniving.

Of course, it is well within her husband's rights to simply laugh at her, or even to strike her for her frivolity and vanity and naïveté. But Roscille thinks of the white bird and she is sure, in that moment, he will not do any of those things. He cares for her honor, if only out of respect for his alliance with the Duke. She is not some spoil of war, like Hawise.

And Roscille's value is in her face. She will be less beautiful with a bruised cheek, and he will be less illustrious in the eyes of his men, for having so rudely damaged this thing that is valuable only for its beauty. It would be like slashing a horse's knees and then shouting, *Well, will it not run?* He would look barbaric. Worse, foolish.

Macbeth steps back for a moment, and his gaze goes elsewhere. He is not thinking of her anymore. He is imagining the campaign he will wage against Cawder for her gold and her rubies. He is thinking of the glory he will win, all the lands he will be ceded, the riches he will be heaped with, the praises that will be sung in his name. And then, perhaps, in the end he will place the necklace around Roscille's throat, and she will be worth even more to him, because now she is the gleaming symbol that proves his might. He is, after all, a warrior at heart.

"A necklace of gold," he repeats, at last. "Set with a ruby." She nods.

He is silent a moment longer. Roscille listens to the sea roaring beneath the floor. Finally, Macbeth meets her eyes, through the swaddling veil, and says, "It will add immensely to your beauty, Lady Roscilla."

And then he turns and is gone. It happens so quickly that it stops Roscille's breath and she collapses to the floor at last, onto the bear-rug, matted down beneath her bridal veil and lace, tucking her cold feet under herself, and pressing her hand to her mouth so no one will hear her sob.

She is not thinking of the necklace either, not anymore. She is imagining her lord husband's throat opening under the Thane of Cawder's blade, and his blood spilling, ruby-hued, before he can even gutter out a noise of shock.

TWO

ROSCILLE WAKES WITH SLEEP STILL WEBBING HER eyes. A second webbing, underneath the first, her bridal veil, which she has not removed. She fell asleep on the bear-rug, and the fur is damp where her face pressed against it. She rubs at the spot and the wetness vanishes, blends with the pelt. Bears have good fur that dries quickly.

She stands up and stumbles. Her bedchamber has no window, but she guesses that it is morning: There are cracks in the stone wall and thin shafts of light come through. She runs her fingers along the crumbling stone, not checking the soundness of her new home, nor testing the toughness of her new prison, but rather judging the age of her new domain. It is all new to her, though to the world it is very old. This castle has seen a hundred men who have called themselves Lord or Thane or Mormaer or Yarl or even King. How many Ladies have preceded her?

Roscille is wondering this when the door opens behind her, and she jumps. Wedged in the threshold is a fair-haired man, not much her senior. It is a moment before she recognizes him. He was the one who splashed water on her feet last night, the one who scowled as he took the last sip from the quaich.

Staring at him more intently now, she realizes he must be Banquho's son. He has the same wide-boned face, though fresher with youth, and he wears the same pattern of tartan.

"Lady Macbeth," he says.

Her skin rises with gooseflesh. The new name is like a ghost that has suddenly inhabited her body. "Yes—good morning—heir of Lochquhaber?"

"Fléance." He frowns. "Am I that much the portrait of my father?"

"The Duke has many bastards," Roscille replies. "Living among them nurtures a talent for matching features and faces."

They are brusque words and—she cannot help it—laced through with venom for her father. This venom nourishes her, in a sick sort of way, like overripe fruit that tastes sweet on the tongue but will turn to bile in your stomach. It is petty cruelty, with no strategy behind it, but she cannot imagine it will offend Fléance. Surely he has no love for the Duke.

Yet Fléance keeps frowning. Perhaps she should not have used the word *talent*. Let them never think of her as boastful of her own abilities. She should brag of nothing that does not enhance her husband's pride.

"It is well past dawn," Banquho's son says. "The Thane likes for his wife to rise when he does. Even if you do not share a chamber." His ear tips turn pink when he says this. She supposes that a court so absent of women would make even a man her own age prudish. "You are wanted in his hall."

"I shall join him there," Roscille says. "Please, will you bring me Hawise? My handmaiden?"

"I cannot. She has been sent away."

Her vision wavers, narrows, then widens again, until she is dizzy. "Why?"

"Handmaidens are not used in Alba," he says. "Women must care for themselves, see to their own needs. It is our custom. We do not use wet nurses, either, as you do in Breizh. To let your child suckle from another's breast—there is something foul about it. When your child comes—"

"I understand," says Roscille. "I will dress and join him."

Fléance nods. His frown recedes tentatively. He has only one scar of battle that Roscille can see: The top of his blushing left ear is an inch shorter than it should be, mangled like something—someone—has taken a bite from it. She would not put such a thing past these Scotsmen.

But the scar does not make him look hardened. He seems in fact more boyish for it: It is not the sort of wound that suggests a brush with death, a sword slipping too close to the throat, an axe landing inches from his head. It is too clumsy for that. It looks like an accident of battle, not a deftly dodged killing blow. She understands his stubborn somberness now. He has not yet proven himself, and cannot afford to look uncertain for a moment, even when he is only speaking to a woman.

"Good," he says. Relief in his pale-gray eyes. "Come out when you are ready."

ROSCILLE TRIES TO BE PRACTICAL. She can dress and mourn Hawise at the same time. Instead of crying, she scrapes the bridal veil off her face and rolls it up until it is small enough to fit in the very corner of her trunk. She tries to wriggle free from the gown but one arm gets tangled around her back and the other gets crushed against her chest. A small sob comes through her teeth, more like a whimper. She cannot remember the last time she has dressed or undressed herself.

She bites down on her tongue so that Fléance cannot hear the confused, mewling sounds that are coming out of her mouth. He said that Hawise has been sent away, but to where? Not back to Hastein and the other Northmen; her father would not take a girl so spoiled by the luxury of Wrybeard's court, so dishonored by her servitude to a delicate little maiden of Breizh (a witch-marked girl, at that). Sent back to Naoned? She would not survive there. It is only her proximity to Roscille that has saved her from the abuses suffered by other servants and handmaidens: pregnancy by some brusque, ugly means, and then kicked hard enough in the stomach to make the inconvenience of an infant go away. Roscille has seen it before, so many times, the same story playing out before her eyes with the relentless rhythm of needlework.

But the Norsemen are so loathed in Alba—and would it not be quicker, easier, sparing the expense of a carriage and a driver and two horses, and then a ship to meet them at the channel—the image flickers across Roscille's vision like a bird scuffling dazedly against a window. One quick, sharp shove, Hawise's mouth widened to a black circle as she goes tumbling limply down the sheer face of the cliff. Her body creates a narrow gash in the water, a single streak of foam, and then it is gone.

Roscille vomits into her hand and then wipes her palm clean on the bear-rug. Enough. Enough. She escapes from the bridal gown and lets out a shuddery breath.

She pretends she has done this a hundred times before. She takes her plainest gray dress from her trunk. It ties in the back, no buttons, easy for her to put on herself. It has short, tight sleeves, and the stitching in the bodice presses so hard against her ribs that it feels like there is no skin in between, just knotty thread grinding at her bones. And then the veil. Always the veil.

In Breizh a married woman is expected to cover her hair, but Roscille will not even attempt to put on the complicated wimple and cornette herself, especially without a mirror, and besides, she does not know the customs of Alba in this respect. If women are meant to see to their own needs, surely they cannot be expected to attire themselves so elaborately. No handmaidens, no wet nurses. No whores, even, as far as Roscille can tell. She leaves the white cloth of wifely chastity and opens the door.

If she has done something wrong in her dressing, she trusts that Fléance will correct her. But he says nothing, only nods and leads her back through the narrow corridors, toward the hall where they feasted the night before. There are windows tucked high into the ceiling, crammed into odd corners of stone, and the sunlight strains through them jaggedly. Now, again, Roscille hears the sea *shush*ing beneath her feet.

All traces of finery from the wedding banquet have been put away, not that there were many to begin with, and the hall is bleak and gray. There are five men huddled around the table on the dais, the same ones she recognizes from last night but cannot name. One is Banquho. Macbeth sits at the head. She did not notice before, but his chair seems too small for him; his cloak drapes over the arms and the wood strains against the bulk of his shoulders.

"The Lady Macbeth," Fléance says. He does not bow, as one would to the Duke. No such stiff rituals here.

"Good," Macbeth says. "Come here, wife."

On numb legs, she obeys. As she passes the men, she makes an archive of each one in her mind. Here is the one who wears the blanched weasel cloak, this one the winter fox, this one the shaggy mountain goat. All different shades of white, some yellowed at the edges with age, others splattered with the rusty hue of dried blood. Weasel-cloak, Winter Fox, Mountain Goat, she calls them in her mind.

Roscille sits beside her husband and folds her hands in her lap. Fléance hovers in the threshold but does not sit. There is no place for him, not even beside his father. Banquho hardly looks up at his own son. This causes a strange churning in Roscille's stomach.

"We are making plans for our assault on Cawder," says Macbeth. His callused fingers spread across the map. His thumb brushes the red flag that marks the seat of the Thane of Cawder. "It will be simple enough; my armies are larger."

He is really going to do it; he will invade Cawder. Many people will die—soldiers, yes, but also peasants whose villages are sacked and burned, even goats and sheep, so that those who survive are left with nothing but ash and gored livestock—all of this because she does not want to lie with her lord husband. All because she will not fulfill the duty that a thousand, thousand women have fulfilled before.

There was a nobleman in Rome who fed his slow or displeasing slaves to a pool of eels: lampreys. It was a death of hours, of needle-thin teeth. This nobleman was rebuked for doing so in the presence of the emperor. One slave threw himself at the emperor's feet and begged for a different death. What a display of barbarity! In disgust, the emperor ordered the lampreys killed and their pool filled. Roscille feels like the nobleman, and the slave, and the lampreys, all at once. All she knows for certain is that she is not the emperor.

Bellona's bridegroom, they call Macbeth; Bellona, a Roman war goddess. He does not know how to sheathe his blade, even when he comes to her bedside. He will damp the sheets with blood the same way he wets the earth in Cawder.

Roscille consoles herself that most of those who will die are men—and how many of them have their own unwilling, unloved wives at home? How many of them have forced servant girls, even their own daughters? But one campaign will not end these abuses; the world will always birth more men, and more women for them to claim. It would take power beyond which any human might possess to rearrange the natural order of the world.

"His castle is ringed with mining villages," Banquho says, pointing. "I have heard that the thane demands exorbitant tithes. They will surrender easily to a more merciful lord."

That depends on whether or not Macbeth can stand to portray himself as merciful. Her husband clenches and unclenches his fist.

"We will have to observe the rite of first blood," he says. "They will not respect my power, otherwise."

Roscille read about this in the monk's books. It is a custom among the clans, when warring, to kill the first man they see, dip their swords in his blood, and then taste it. Roscille considers this: In order to be seen as merciful, one must first be seen as powerful. There is no mercy that a sheep can show a wolf.

"We must think of this, too," Weasel-cloak says. He reaches across the table and prods at the flag that marks the castle of the king. "Duncane."

His words cast the room in silence. All that can be heard is the sea, unremitting, beneath the gray stones.

"Yes," Macbeth replies after a moment. "If I take Cawder, he will wonder whether I plan to take more."

Of course. Appetites cannot be sated by blood; they can only be whetted. Before Roscille even realizes it, she is speaking.

"Then accuse the enemy of that which you may be suspected," she says. "Forge a letter that suggests the Thane of Cawder harbors plans to revolt."

Five men's faces turn toward her. Fléance's, too, from the doorway. Their eyes shift with unease, with shock. Women are not meant to speak at war councils. But perhaps it can be forgiven, since Roscille is so young, a foreign bride, unaccustomed to the ways of the Scots.

"Consider," she goes on in a rush, "you will not only be free of suspicion, but you will look all the more loyal to Duncane, for snuffing out Cawder's rebellion before it starts."

Mountain Goat scoffs, but Macbeth holds up a hand to silence him.

"My wife makes a clever suggestion," he says. "We will do this—*she* will do this. Duncane will recognize my hand, but not hers. The Lady will pen the letter herself."

Mountain Goat slides down in his seat. Winter Fox thins his lips. Weasel-cloak's vision fixes on her, his eyes two deadly points. But Banquho's face is open with interest. He can allow this, because he is more beloved by Macbeth than the rest. He does not have to fear that his Lord's new wife may slip between them. He is his Lord's right hand.

"I will rally my men," Banquho says. "The rest of you, the same."

"Good," says Macbeth. "Go to it. I will speak to my wife alone now."

BUT HE DOES NOT SPEAK to her. He rises in silence and beckons her to follow. Roscille keeps her eyes mainly on the ground, but occasionally she looks up and sneaks glances at him, her husband. There is a scar lacing his throat, white and rigid, like a worm in an apple. It is not a clumsy by-blow. It cannot be anything but death, beaten back.

He takes her down another narrow hallway, in the opposite direction of her chamber, then down a set of crumbling stairs to an even narrower corridor. The sound of the sea rises, and so does the sound of their footsteps, as if the floor is growing thinner. At the end of this hallway is a door. Its iron grate withers with rust.

"A husband and wife should have no secrets from each other," Macbeth says. "And they should keep each other's secrets from the world."

Before Roscille can think of how to reply, he removes a key, tied to a leather thong around his neck. He fits it into the lock. The sea roars up at them, and then is curiously silent. Wood scrapes stone as he pushes the door open.

Behind the door, blackness stretches out in all directions. It is not the barbarian blackness she first witnessed upon arriv-

ing in Glammis, the bleak edge of civilization. This is an unnatural darkness, such that would confound the pope himself.
The air blowing toward them is damp and cold, and although
light slides through the threshold behind them, it halts very
suddenly, the darkness a wall it cannot breach.

Macbeth takes a step forward and there is a splashing
sound. Water, he has stepped into water. Roscille blinks and
blinks, but staring into the unchanging black makes her eyes
gummy, as if with sleep. Is she supposed to follow? The air has
a terrible weight, like the pressure at the deepest chasm of the
ocean.

And then: light. Filmy and indistinct, a single torches flares
in the center of her vision. The reflection of the flame races
along the dark water, in clever beams and quick flashes. The
water has a serpent's iridescent sheen.

Her husband stands in the center of the room, which is
really a cave, rock formations jutting outward from the walls at
strange angles. He is as silent and still as the rock itself.

The current judders around him. Three different currents, all converging, sucking at the hem of his tartan. Three
women stand in the water at a distance, backs hunched with
age, hair scraggly and silver, each holding a sopping garment
in her hands. Each woman slaps the water with her cloth, then
wrings it out, then soaks it again. Submerges, lifts, submerges,
forming her own tight, snarling whirlpool.

Roscille stumbles backward and falls against the mold-
slick wall. She makes a bleating sound of fear, of disbelief,
which her husband does not seem to hear. Then she stands
and crosses herself.

But the act feels like mockery: She invokes the Holy Trinity, the Father the Son the Holy Spirit, as the three women advance toward her, their faces white as lightning. They are so thin under their own wet garments that each notch of their spines can be clearly seen. Their hair is so long that the ratty ends brush the water.

"*Buidseach,*" Macbeth breathes. The world is cold smoke in the air. Witch.

It is only then that Roscille sees the shackles around their bony wrists, and the long length of rusty chain that ties them all together. As they move, it drags against the cave floor. If they come any closer, they will strain their binds, and the metal will cut into their soggy flesh, which looks as though it would fall easily off their bones, like rot from a log.

"Macbeth," one of them says. Hisses.

The other two echo her: "Macbeth." "Macbeth."

Roscille read this among the monk's tomes: Duncane has written a treatise on witchcraft in Scotland. Witches exist; he has proven it. They kill swine and perform spells with their entrails. They send storms to chase sailors to their watery graves. They turn men into mice, and women into serpents who swallow them. They can hide in the skin of any woman, but they may be identified by their sharp teeth. Or by their silver hair.

In Breizh, there is no such canonical accounting. The Duke would not waste his efforts on the creatures of hell, just as he does not waste it on the matters of heaven: Only rarely can he be persuaded to attend Mass. In Alba, the punishment for witchcraft is death. What is the punishment for keeping witches as prisoners?

Macbeth casts his torch across the water. "I come to hear your prophecy. Tell me my fate."

Their eyes are milky white, with mortal blindness. Their noses are just notches in their faces. When the light catches them, their skin seems to sizzle, like oil in heat.

"All hail Macbeth," the first one rasps, "Thane of Glammis!"

The other two clap in approval, chains jangling. Their damp, soft flesh slaps together.

"All hail Macbeth," cries the second, "Thane of Cawder!"

And then, together: "All hail Macbeth! All hail Macbeth! All hail Macbeth!" They shout and shout, until their voices pile on top of one another, like heavy gouts of rain into the river, water upon black water. They shout until the words blur, their thin-lipped mouths open in bacchanalian glee, as if they are expecting wine to pour from the very air and down their throats.

Perhaps Roscille should drink from it as well. Her plan, once merely callous, now made blasphemous, vulgar, truly evil, sanctified by these unholiest of creatures.

Macbeth turns to her, his face gleaming in the torchlight.

"You see," he says. "My lust for blood will be rewarded. We leave for Cawder at dawn."

THREE

DAWN, IN GLAMMIS: A GRAY SKY WITH THE THIN-nest line of watery light at the horizon. The men are girded and braced, their horses saddled, their battle tartans donned. Swords are sheathed at hips and spears are chucked, clattering, into the back of a mule-drawn cart. There are no bows: That is a coward's weapon. Only birds and stags may suffer the ignominy of being slain by arrows.

Her husband is fixing his saddle, checking its tightness. Wrybeard would never saddle his own horse; that is what squires are for. It is a part she might have expected Fléance to play, only she cannot find his face among the crowd.

Roscille holds her breath and casts her gaze around the court-yard, noting each of the men that make up the war party, won-dering which one of them killed Hawise. She will never know. It does not matter. Any of them would and would again. Even if she found the body—what then? The dead cannot speak.

Mountain Goat and Winter Fox and Weasel-cloak are of course among them, each flanked by six of their best men. They mutter; they grow silent and glance at Roscille and then mutter some more. Even though Macbeth did not tell them that her want of a trinket engendered this war, she sat at the council table, she spoke with assurance. That alone is enough to tarnish the glory of this fight.

She turns, and at last she spies him. Fléance. He is not saddling his horse or loading his spears; he stands at the edge of the courtyard, his face dark. From such a distance she cannot read his expression, but she watches Banquho approach his son and whisper something roughly in his ear. Fléance's shoulders rise and his hand grips the pommel of his sheathed sword.

Then Banquho, alone, walks away and sits astride his horse. He looks quite determinedly away from his son. This small, foul interaction can mean only one thing: Fléance is being left behind. Roscille cannot help but wonder how this decision might have been reached, and whether it was Macbeth who ordered it. She can imagine the low tones, the gritted teeth. Dishonor encrusting Fléance like pond scum. She watches Fléance for a moment too long, and is surprised by the slippery feeling of deprival that sneaks beneath her skin.

When all the horses have been mounted, her husband comes to her. He cups her face and toys with the edge of her veil. His hand on her cheek is like rough fabric, scraped dry against river rocks. Thinking of laundry makes her think of the basement, the witches. Roscille flinches.

"You will have your rubies," he says. "And I will have what is mine."

The witches' words echo from the deep recesses of her mind.

Macbeth, Thane of Glammis.

Macbeth, Thane of Cawder.

And then, the voice of the Druide asserts itself.

Lord Macbeth, son of Findlay, Macbeth macFinlay, Macbethad mac Findlaích, the righteous man.

He does not kiss her, but their lips are close. Even though she does not close her eyes, she is not looking at him, she is outside of herself: a bird scuffling against a windowless wall, a boar with a spear in its side, a hart dogged through the woods. She is nothing but a panicked beating heart.

Then he lets go, paces back toward his horse, and mounts in one fluid motion. His huge body seems to dwarf even the horse. There is an obscenity to it, his largeness. It makes something as ordinary as riding a horse seem brutish. How much weight will the poor animal be forced to bear?

The wind funnels into the courtyard and then flattens, like water filling a trough. Her skirts blow back as the barbican grinds open and the party trots through it. It is a long train and it takes a long time for the last rider to vanish into the mist. The barbican shuts again.

Roscille wonders how many women have stood precisely where she is standing, watching their husbands disappear. Roscille wonders how many of them have imagined the sword-thrust that will make them widows. She wonders how many smiled at the thought.

Without noticing, Fléance has come to her side.

"Inside," he says. His voice is brusque. "Now."

THE CASTLE IS EMPTY OF all but servants; there is not another sheathed blade or spear in sight. Fléance's footsteps ahead of her are rough and hurried.

Fléance's anger does not scare her. It is the first time, Roscille realizes, since arriving in Glammis, that she has not been afraid. In fact, his anger nourishes her, in a strange way. It is that same sweet-tasting poison, the last overripe fruit plucked from the otherwise empty vine, which will keep her alive but also kill her slowly. She stops walking.

Fléance turns. "What, Lady?"

"How long has this castle stood?"

This question is too innocent to provoke any alarm. He will not see the long strings that connect her words to the room in the basement, to Duncane's treatise, to sharp teeth and silver hair. She is a young girl from a foreign country, naturally curious about anything that is new (or old). Fléance's brows come down over his pale eyes.

"Since before the Northmen were raiding. And before the Romans came with their roads. Do they say, in Breizh, that Flatnose built all of the isles?"

Flatnose is a Norse king of many centuries past. He stuck his flag all over the rockiest, bitterest soils of Scotland, grim and savage Glammis among them. In Breizh, it is said that the Scots could build nothing with their two hands except the oak barrels for spirits. It is said that they lapped water straight from the river like dogs. But Roscille shakes her head.

"Your Druides," she ventures. "They are older than the Northmen and the Romans, too."

"Of course."

"So they have seen the native evils of the land."

Fléance's gaze flickers. He will not hurt her, Macbeth

would kill him for it, but he will tell his father of the Lady's strange questions and then his father, the Lord's right hand, will tell the Lord.

Or will he? Roscille remembers the coldness of Banquho's face in the courtyard. She has seen enough displeased fathers and displeasing children to know when the ice is starting to show its black-veined cracks.

"Yes," Fléance says slowly. "Every old soil has its evils. But they do not live in Glammis. The clan of Macbeth is powerful and pious enough to expunge them."

He does not know. Why would he? The basement is Macbeth's secret, guarded like a hoard of gold. It is safe for her to step farther. The ground will not yet give way.

"But your king, Duncane," she says, her voice soft and guileless, "has written a treatise on witchcraft in Alba."

At this, Fléance's brow darkens. He will not hurt her— but perhaps Roscille has misjudged her position. She is still a foreign bride, her edges singed with the smoke of witchcraft, robed in the ghostly tales of her unnatural eyes, her unpropitious birth. Ill omens are writ on her skin like runes.

"The Lord does not believe the rumors that come from Francia," Fléance says. "He may be the king's vassal, but they are not always of like mind."

Roscille almost laughs in relief. He thinks she worries only for her own stature, her own esteem.

"That is good," she says. "But others—they might believe such rumors."

"Perhaps. But they will never speak their suspicions aloud to the Lord."

"True, men are honest only in whispers."

Fléance's mouth twists in a peculiar expression, as if he wants to laugh at her wit but is perplexed by the urge. "You will be safe here," he says at last. "In Glammis."

"I know I will be safe with you."

It is crude flattery, but it works. Fléance's face opens.

"Yet King Duncane says witchcraft is alive and well in Alba," she presses on carefully. "Do you know of such acts? Have you seen them?"

In Breizh, they are called les Lavandières. They stand in the shallows and wash the clothes of dead souls. They have webbed feet and webbed fingers. Seeing them is a portent of doom. If you step between them and the water, you will die. If they ask you for help in their washing and you refuse, they will drown you.

"There are stories," Fléance says. "Witches are women, but malformed. Likely they have some traits of animals—perhaps a naked tail, or scales on their bellies. Perhaps they cannot speak, but only yowl like a hound or squawk like a crow. A fish's unblinking eyes, set on the sides of their faces, or wings that unfold from their backs. A feline's sharp teeth. To cross one is death, or a curse upon your blood. Your grandson's grandsons will know well a witch's wickedness."

He does not mention silver hair. Perhaps she is safer with him than she imagined.

"A curse," Roscille repeats. "What sort of curse makes the king quiver under his crown?"

Torchlight spasms across the wall. The corridor they are in has no windows. Fléance's eyes narrow to slivers.

"There is one story known across Alba," he says. "Once, a nobleman offended such a virulent creature. The witch cast a curse, not upon the nobleman, but upon his infant son. Every night, when the boy slept, he would grow fur and fangs and become a vicious, killing thing. His blood ran with hunger in the moonlight. He ravened under the black sky. Only the rising sun restored him to his natural form."

Roscille wants to ask why, but she already knows. *A witch does not need a reason, only an opportunity.*

Instead, she asks, "And what did the nobleman do to his blighted boy?"

She thinks she knows the answer to this, too.

"He put a blade through its black-furred chest," Fléance says. "But the sword rusted and fell away, and the wound resolved itself. The boy could not be slain by mortal means. So he tied his son to his bed each night and closed his ears to the sound of the beast slavering and yowling and twisting under his binds."

The world is rheumy from beneath the veil. Roscille blinks her death-touched eyes.

"So he was not dressed in bridal lace and married to a lord," she says.

"No," Fléance says.

"King Duncane must chafe at this union." Macbeth may have the authority to silence his men's voices, but he does not have the power to shape their thoughts; no man has such power. The rumors of her silver hair and maddening gaze will drift silently through these halls, like cold mist. The words may never be spoken aloud. Yet the mind itself can make the sea into a desert and a frozen waste into the greenest meadow.

"Macbeth is the king's distant cousin," says Fléance. "Duncane trusts him to keep his wife in check, even if such rumors abound."

Of course. Roscille is chained, too, in her marriage bed.

And this is when she realizes, with the slick, sudden heat of a fever, that she has made a mistake. She is Macbeth's wife now, his property, and if he dies in his fight, she will be part of the spoils claimed by his enemies. Macbeth values his alliance with the Duke, yet such vows are worth nothing to the Thane of Cawder. Macbeth may keep his witches in chains, but if the Thane of Cawder is anything like Duncane, he will put his blade through their hearts. She has not saved herself. She has only given herself a different death.

In this state of fever, her mind returns her to Naoned. She is deposited at the feet of her father, kneeling like a supplicant. When she looks up, she can see only the wily black twists of his beard.

"I am more than a draughts tile," she says, her voice trembling. "I am the blood of the ermine, I am—"

"You are whatever creature I make you," Wrybeard says. "All things in Naoned serve me."

"But—" Her voice shrivels in her throat. She stares down, pitifully, at the floor. "Do you not love me?"

A stupid question. The Duke will not even deign to answer it. She might as well have asked if he loves his own hand or his own mouth.

Naoned fades, and the winding corridor of Glammis flowers up again before her. Here she is, believing herself a canny animal, believing she could cheat the fate her father so coldly imposed upon her, when in truth she has done nothing other than promise the spilling of a great ordeal of blood—between her legs and from the throats of so many nameless, faceless men. Roscille of the Veiled Eyes, Roscille of the Witless Plans, Roscille the Great Fool.

Roscille is fiercely glad that Fléance is too afraid to meet her gaze, so that he has not seen the water gathering along her lashes.

She cannot undo what she has done; her husband and his war party are already miles gone. Yet—she is not completely bereft. If Macbeth falls beneath Cawder's blade, if Cawder's men pound at Glammis's gates, perhaps she may still survive, if she has but one friend inside these walls, one sword that might rise to defend her.

Roscille gulps down the castle's stale air. Two quick inhales, and her nickering heartbeat begins to calm. She can still save herself, maybe. She can bind herself to Fléance with a secret. With a debt. And already she has seen his desires gleam out from him, those hard, sharp, angry pieces, whetted by bitterness, polished by his father's cold rebuffs.

Very slowly, she lifts her gaze.

"I have to write a letter," she says. "Will you help me?"

IN THE CASTLE'S LARGEST CHAMBER, which is both the banquet hall and the war room, Fléance brings her a quill and parchment. He tells her the Thane of Cawder's name, shows her his sigil. Roscille's quill tip hovers above the page, hesitant. She has never forged a letter before; she has never tried writing in any hand beside her own.

"Will Duncane know it is a woman's script?" Roscille wonders aloud.

"He will not suspect it," says Fléance. "Most women in Alba do not write."

She should have known. The women in Naoned read only

the Bible. Hawise could not read or write until Roscille began to teach her. Thinking of Hawise makes her throat tighten. With some difficulty, Roscille says, "Who are Cawder's allies?"

Fléance names several lords. Roscille chooses the one whose name will be easiest to spell. Since she does not know how to write in Scots, Fléance leans over her shoulder and places his hand on her hand, guiding the quill. She feels him flinch as he touches her skin. The blue marbling of her veins looks particularly garish against his ruddy flesh, cold where he is warm, lifeless where he is vital. As soon as the words are done, Fléance steps briskly away, red coloring his cheeks.

Even if he has, by some chance, touched a woman before, he has never touched a creature like Roscille—bloodless, as they say, like a trout—and he has certainly never touched the wife of a lord. Roscille wonders if he recognizes the danger in this. He has already seen how easily her fingers can spin lies; can her lips not also fashion falsehoods?

To copy the signature she must carefully layer one parchment over another, and trace the Thane of Cawder's name. Fléance watches her at a distance, his mouth a thin line. She notices the mangled tip of his ear again, the accidental and inglorious scar.

"The Lord has placed my life in your hands," she says.

Fléance's gray eyes flash. When he speaks, his voice cannot hide his anger. "It was my father's choice, too. He says there will be other wars. Other occasions to wet my sword."

"The battlefield is not the only place where one may wet their sword."

"Lady—" His brow furrows.

"Roscilla," she says. "Please, call me Roscilla."

"Lady Roscilla," he says, after a moment. His expression is uneasy, but not uncurious. "What do you suggest?"

"My husband has done you a disservice, I recognize this," she says. "He is a great warrior, though his judgment was too hasty on this occasion."

She must be as light-footed as a fawn on frozen water. She must appear hesitant, even if she is not. She must not dishonor her husband with a word or a look.

Fléance's gaze is still hesitant, but there is a lidded desire in his eyes. She has nearly coaxed it out into the light—the lamprey within him, waiting for flesh to suck.

"And your father," she goes on, voice lowering, "has been uncivil in this matter as well. To not help grow his own son's valor, to not wish for him to win acclaim on the field of battle, to enhance his pride . . . it is a boorish slight."

His eyes' desire gleams brighter. The lamprey slinks ever forward.

"But you can mend their mistakes," Roscille says. "You can illuminate their errors, and show your own strengths."

Silence seeps between them, cool and clear, like the air at evening's last hour.

"How," Fléance says slowly, "do you mean to prove such a thing?"

IT IS THE FIRST TIME she has been outside the castle in Glammis when it is light. Dawn has come, and gone, and the sun has settled at its highest point, swaddled in fleecy clouds. The wind has the same obliterating rhythm of the ocean, pressing the green-gold grasses flat, making her veil cling tightly to her face, like a caul.

A near-forgotten panic stirs in her. She felt this panic the first time Hawise placed the veil over her eyes. The way it obscured the world, dulled her most important sense, made her feel like an animal, bucking under its yoke. Prey animals have their eyes on the sides of their heads, a blind spot in what should be the center of their vision. It took a long time for Roscille to adjust to the world this way, darkened and mud-dled, to its dangerous blurry spaces. Glammis makes this old fear feel new again.

But she prods her horse along, so that it follows Fléance's mount down the hillside. These horses are accustomed to the terrain. Their hoof-steps are sure, no pebbles caught in their shoes, no tripping over the sun-warmed rocks that jut up dan-gerously from beneath overgrown tufts of grass.

From this distance, with the castle at her back, Roscille can finally see Macbeth's advantage, the reason Wrybeard thought it worth sending a daughter all this way. Every cluster of trees, every thatched-roof hut, every spire of chimney smoke: all set out before her like trays on a banquet table. Miles and miles and miles. No enemy can so much as flash his sword without giving her husband an hour's warning, at least. The castle has held Roscille in a stricture of fear, a newt writhing in a cupped hand, but by this measure, Glammis is the safest place she has ever been.

"These villages," she says, sweeping her arm toward the specks of houses below, "they all pay tribute to Macbeth?"

She has to raise her voice to be heard over the wind. Flé-ance nods.

"Yes, they are all Findlaích, if not by blood then by allegiance. The clan," he adds, as though Roscille does not remember her own husband's status. *She* is a part of clan Findlaích now.

"Surely," Roscille says, "there is some discontent among them."

Every strong man has his enemies. Even if it is just the kitchen boy whipped for spilling soup. Even if it is a farmer forced to foster soldiers who ate all his food and then took his wife to bed. Perhaps it is a nephew or a cousin, passed over when honors were given. An ally left without his apportioned spoils. A beggared miller chafing under the Lord's exorbitant tithe. Someone. Anyone.

Fléance narrows his eyes in thought. "There is a man—"

"Good," she says. "That is enough."

Most men do not need a reason, either. Only an opportunity.

Fléance leads her to a copse of trees, warped by the wind, scraggly and strange. Yet there is a small hidden place among them, where the grass is soft, as if the weather-beaten trees have protected it. A pool—curiously bright and clear, though fed from no source that Roscille can see.

She catches her reflection in the water, a quicksilver flash. Long, loose pale hair, more white than gold. A sharp chin whittling down an otherwise round face. Her eyes are as black as a swan's, wide-set, pupil and iris barely distinct from each other. Unsettling eyes, she cannot deny it. Superstitions have been built on less. She looks away.

"Tell the Lord I begged you to show me my new home," Roscille says, sliding down from her horse. "But we were not even out of sight of the castle when the masked men came."

"How many?" Fléance dismounts his own horse with a heavy thud.

Roscille thinks. "Three," she says at last. Three is not so many that it taxes belief, but it is enough that Fléance's courage and skill will be commended. Three is also a propitious number, a Christian fetish, whatever that is worth here in Glammis.

The memory of les Lavandières leaps up at her, the white shock of their emaciated bodies in the dark. Roscille's stomach clenches.

"Will the Lord not ask to see their corpses? Proof of blood?"

"No, you need not have killed them," Roscille says slowly. This is the trickiest part of her plan. "We will say you sent them running—if we have our own blood to prove the labor of battle. The nearness of death."

Fléance's brow furrows as he begins to understand. "I will have to strike my own near-death blow."

Roscille thinks of Macbeth's wound, the long, ropy band of scar tissue that adorns his throat. She does not know how he survived it. To another man it would be certain death.

She thinks of les Lavandières again. *My lust for blood will be rewarded.* They anointed this mission to Cawder, armored him in favorable prophecy. Could they have done the same before? Is their magic more than mere augury—is it protection in battle? An aegis that covers these lands like new-fallen snow? Are these unholy creatures what keeps Death at bay in Glammis?

"Yes," Roscille says at last. "Or—I will do it for you."

Fléance says nothing, and Roscille's chest tightens, fearing he will refuse. He does not. He only asks, "Why? Why will you aid me in this?"

"I am the Lady of Glammis," Roscille says. "Is it not for my benefit that the strength of its men is recognized, and allocated and awarded?"

Her face is hot, but her cheeks—bloodless—will not show it. Fléance looks at her for a long time without blinking. Then, wordlessly, with only the hushing sound of metal against hide, he removes his sword from its sheath.

He will want to have a scar that shows proudly. Nothing as stark as her husband's—he cannot outdo his own Lord, of course—and nothing that will truly risk death. Nothing that will not heal in time, or that will leave him less able on the battlefield. Roscille is pondering where, and how, when Fléance puts the sword in her hands.

And then he tugs down his jerkin, straining the fabric to expose his collarbone. Roscille sees the small hollow, just below his throat, where she is meant to aim. The skin is pulled taut, thin over muscle, with little fat to slow the progression of the blade. It will hurt. Badly.

"Here," Fléance says.

Roscille feels the blood turn to ice in her body.

"You will have to press harder than you think."

Her gorge rises. She does not want to do this. Always she has prized herself on her strategy, the coldly removed arranging of tiles on a draughts board, never a butcher. But she needs this secret, the alliance it will spin. The lampreys are writhing, hungry. She will not deny them their feast.

"Wait," she says suddenly. "My— I must show proof of this skirmish as well."

Fléance frowns. "How do you mean?"

There is a spear in one of his horse's saddlebags. She takes it. It is light, the wood smooth as a rosary bead. The tip flashes silver in the muted light. But she does not hand it to him tip-first. Instead, she offers Fléance the shaft.

She points at her own temple, right at the corner of her eyebrow. One thrust of the spear-shaft and it will show a perfect circle, a single bruise that proves Fléance's courage and Roscille's worth (for what else do men value if not the things other men wish to take from them?) and the silent union which will, however fragilely, protect her. Perhaps Fléance is not the lamprey at all. Perhaps he is the nobleman, puffing with pride in his little power, only to be degraded by the emperor's preeminent scorn.

"Together," Roscille says.

Fléance hesitates. She does not. She sees the blood spray, speckling her gown with red. It comes in such quick spurts that it slicks the grass under her feet, but Roscille does not have to witness the horror long, for Fléance gives a furious growl, the base anger of being wounded so suddenly and remorselessly, and then he drives the spear-shaft hard against her temple.

Her vision turns white. Heat spikes through her skull, following a straight path from one temple to the other, as if the pain is an arrow, cleanly slicing the muscle and meat of her. And then there is only the fuzzy, star-pricked darkness.

DUSK, IN GLAMMIS: PURPLE LIGHT spread through the irregular pattern of clouds. A grayish, bruised miasma, like smoke from a cauldron. Roscille stands against the wind, so that her own veil does not choke and blind her.

Fléance is at her side, hand resting on his sword's pommel. The barbican grinds open, and the war party floods the courtyard, all these loutish, scraggly men boasting their victory, tartans torn, blood still in their beards. It is the blood of many: some soldiers, some not, anyone unfortunate enough to be found in the path of Macbeth's army. All blood spilled at Roscille's orchestration. She looks down at her hands, as if she might see them stained, too. But they are white, cold as they have always been, which is almost more sickening, somehow. She looks up again, and searches for her husband among the returning men.

He cleaves through the crowd, nearly twice as big as the next-biggest man. His hair is matted with dried blood, but the first thing she notices is that he bears no new scars. It announces clearly that the Thane of Cawder is dead, and that he did not protest his end too much. Macbeth did not even have to imagine his own death, his own absence from the world. As if this is a thing most men are capable of imagining.

He dismounts with a thud that seems to crack the earth. His legs are bare between the cuff of his boots and the hem of his tartan, and Roscille sees that his knees are bloody, too— a dense, dark blood, which has come from deep inside the body. She knows the difference between the thin, bright-red blood that surfaces easily, which can be drawn from any prick of a blade, and the blood that flows black and thick near the heart.

Macbeth's smile is all teeth. He approaches her, something gleaming between his large fingers.

And then—the smile is gone. The gleeful light in his eyes goes dark. The languid, preening victory of his gait turns stiff, muscles tensing. He grasps her face roughly in his hand, turning it to the side, so that he can look at the bruise on her temple. Even beneath the veil, it pulses a fresh and garish violet.

"Who has done this?" Of course he recognizes immediately that the bruise has been made by the thrust of a spearshaft. He has delivered the same wounds to countless women before her, the ones who spat at him as he burned their huts and snatched the meat from their larders. Still holding her face, he whirls toward Fléance.

"My Lord—" Fléance begins.

But Macbeth sees his scar, too. Roscille struck cleverly and struck true: The mark cannot be fully hidden beneath the collar of his jerkin. It snakes upward, along the side of his throat, still gruesome with old blood and the sloppy dark stitches that Roscille sewed herself, trembling as the needle worked its way through gristle and fat.

"There is treachery in Glammis," he snarls. "I have known it—now there is proof. Tell me, now. Who has made this despicable assault on my wife?"

Fléance starts to speak, to explain, and Macbeth listens, though all the while he is opening his other hand and showing the necklace with its thick, heavy chain. He unwinds it, slow and deliberate. Roscille says nothing, her cheekbone burning from the unremitting press of his thumb.

A ruby gleams at the necklace's center. When he clasps it around her throat, the metal is hot, from being held so long in his hand. Macbeth lets go at last and steps back, appraising her. But the pride he should feel at robing his beautiful wife in beautiful things is sullied by that ugly bruise on her face. He makes a wordless noise of disgust.

"Tell me," he says again. "Who has done this? I will kill him. I will kill his sons. His line will end at the point of my sword."

"The men were masked," Fléance says. "I could not see—"

Macbeth draws himself up to his full, obscene, horrifying height. "Did they not strike you a near-death blow?"

"They did," Fléance says hesitantly.

Roscille notices Banquho peering over his Lord's shoulder. His gaze skims across his son, eyes fixing on the throat-wound that Fléance wears openly. Pride flickers in his eyes. Brisk, but unmistakable.

"Perhaps the traitors will not speak," Macbeth says. "It is no matter. There are rites which can be performed. Your blood will speak for them."

ACT II

THANE OF CAWDER

Four

THE CHANCELLOR IS THE HIGHEST AND HOLIEST OF THE Druides, and he comes all the way from Moray, where the king keeps his court. Such grave matters and such gruesome rituals cannot be left to the discretion of just any priest.

Roscille is not presented to him, not introduced, but she sees him from the parapet as he enters the courtyard. He is on horseback, flanked by three soldiers in Duncane's colors. He wears robes finer than her bridal linens, and his gray beard is braided with fillets of gold. This is when Roscille begins to feel the floor slip out from under her. She feels as if she is plunging down the sheer face of the cliff, down to where Hawise's body likely lies, where the eels are sucking dead flesh from her bones.

The chancellor is imbued with Duncane's royal authority and the pope's holy authority and the celestial authority of God himself, and any of them alone would be enough to divine her secret treachery, but all three together will not only discover but also punish her, such that even her flimsy alliance with Fléance will not save her. Fléance will face judgment, too.

Banquho and Macbeth are greeting the chancellor, but their words cannot be heard from such a distance. Roscille is trying to listen anyway, so she leaps in surprise when, suddenly, Fléance is at her side.

"You must not go near the hall when the Druide is here," he says. Close to her ear, his voice is a rasp. "Whatever you must do to stay away, do it."

"I know," Roscille whispers. Her fingers are trembling.

"He is here to perform cruentation."

"I know."

To perform cruentation, a priest must stand over a dead body and speak some sacred, secret rites. Then, in the presence of the murderer, the body's death wound will begin to bleed anew, to bubble over in hot, dark gouts. In Wrybeard's court, this is the stuff of primitive superstition, such that he would not tolerate. A fortnight ago she would not have feared it. But Roscille has been in Glammis long enough to know that the rules of nature are different here. Witches rattle chains in a prison under her feet. The world is so much wilder than she has known. Fléance's wound stands out against his throat, as black as a burned tree.

Roscille feels as though she is choking on her own veil. She wants to tear it off, to gulp in the cold, unobstructed air. But she cannot, when Fléance is here. Instead she breathes in short, painful gasps.

"I did not know cruentation could be performed on the

living," Roscille says at last—only for something to say, because Fléance is looking at her with a furrow of concern between his brows.

"Yes," he replies. His voice is tight. "And if the chancellor speaks the words in your presence, my wound will reveal us. So you must stay away. At any cost."

Roscille nods. Her heartbeat is a feral thing, furious in its pounding. Her eyes trace the line of Fléance's scar again.

"And your father," she asks, through the thickness in her throat, "was he pleased?"

"He was," Fléance replied. "He did not apologize for leaving me behind, but next time—he swears it—I will be on the battlefield beside him."

The corner of Fléance's mouth twitches, as if he wants to smile. He looks boyish to her again, almost more now because of the scar, how its gruesomeness contrasts so sharply with his unlined, plump-cheeked face. She wonders if this is the way she looked to her father, as she knelt before him and begged to be given a different fate. A sensation of disgust winds its way through her belly, like a lamprey in its pool.

IT IS EASIER THAN SHE expected, to stay away. When Banquho comes to her and explains what will happen—the chancellor's mystic words, the ghastly spilling of blood—Roscille makes her face a mask of terror and feigns swooning. *Oh, please,* she says, *I could not bear to witness it.*

Banquho frowns as he catches her, his hard fingers holding tight to her slippery form. He is thinking: Here is a seventeen-year-old bride, new to these lands, doted upon by her father, raised in luxury; the most horror she has ever witnessed is the pricking of a needle. None of this is true, aside from her age and her greenness in Glammis, but she is a good liar, and Banquho is a willing audience. He does not want her there, either, his Lord's unfirm foreign wife, exuding witchcraft.

So Roscille does not meet the chancellor, but she sees the train of villagers as they are brought into the hall. Broken-toothed farmers with black gums, shepherds with stooped shoulders leaning heavily on their crooks, millers old enough to be missing most of their hair. They are all accompanied by sons, grandsons, with smaller, younger versions of their faces. The faces are weather-burned, like ancient leather. Their eyes are squinted and damp and filled with fear.

Roscille sits with her back against the wall outside the chamber, the stone leaching the heat from her body. She can hear muffled, indistinct words from the other side. Angry words, from her husband's mouth. And then the high-pitched, panicked pleading of the peasants. All of a sudden Roscille's legs cannot support her weight. She slides down, crumpling to the floor, knees pulled up to her chest.

Her mind writhes with possibilities, like maggots in rotten meat. Perhaps, when the chancellor speaks his words before one of the peasants—say this hunched, decrepit shepherd—Fléance's blood begins to run, not because of any divine power, but because Roscille's stitches were sloppy, because Fléance used his muscles too much before they were healed enough, for no reason, for any reason. Macbeth has said that he will kill the man and his sons and his grandsons. He will end their bloodline, cut it brusquely and bitterly, like the bodice of a protesting woman.

Here is another story: In the ancient world there was a war

between the Greeks and their exotic Eastern enemies. The exotic prince killed the lover of one Greek soldier. The Greek soldier took his vengeance upon the prince. Then another Easterner killed the Greek soldier. Then the son of the Greek solder killed this Easterner. But he did not only kill the man: He killed his six sons, too. He dashed the head of the infant child against the castle walls, cracking its skull and pulverizing the yet-unformed brain beneath. This was so the Easterner's sons could never grow up and take revenge upon him.

Vengeance is not a wooden cup that empties. It is a jeweled chalice which endlessly spills over. Roscille puts her head between her knees. She fears she will be sick all over the floor. In her efforts to escape her husband's violence, she has only diverted it, flooded it to fill another vessel.

Strangely, here in the empty hall, her father's words return to her. *You are whatever creature I make you.* He sent her to Glammis as a bride, a limp body inside a white gown. But perhaps, disguised beneath the veil, he smuggled in an ermine after all. A clever creature—maybe. Or merely one with pitiless sharp teeth.

Hesitantly, Roscille lifts her veil and, with it, removes the real world. The gray stone of this windowless corridor shudders away. She slips into the memory easily, like a fish in a current.

It goes like this: Roscille is thirteen. The stories about her are only whispers, pale smoke at the edges of her vision. Other than that, she is beautiful; the Duke has high hopes that she will make a propitious match, forge a valuable alliance. She sometimes imagines herself being wed to a handsome Angevin prince, but such imaginings are distant, hazy. Now she thinks only of a certain stable hand, who has eyes like blue cut-glass and a furtive smile for her. She begins to linger around the stables, hoping to see his smile flash. The muscles of his back are strong, and where his sweat-damp tunic sticks to him, it shows every virile ridge.

Stable boys, of course, do not wed noble ladies, and noble ladies, unlike noblemen, cannot enjoy breezy couplings in haylofts with their servants. By then, Roscille has been taught not to make eye contact with a man, to keep her head down, just in case. The whispers have not yet solidified into truth. The rules are not rigid. There is no white veil to enforce them.

So one day, Roscille goes to the stables and takes the stable boy's hand. She lifts her head. She meets his eyes.

It is said that some memories are too appalling for the human mind to bear and are thus pitted with black holes, so that the miserable parts do not cut over and over again, like bits of shattered pottery, sharp on all sides. Roscille wishes she could remember this only in bearable flashes. But she remembers it all. The stable boy's eyes darkening. His grip on her hands tightening, pulling her body against his. Their lips, a whisper away from meeting.

And then a voice that comes from neither of them: the protest. The stable boy's hands unlatching from hers. He is hauled backward, and struck across the face by the stable master, and she hears the crack as his fine-boned nose breaks, skewing sideways, spraying blood.

Roscille screams.

He is brought to Wrybeard in chains. The Duke listens to the story, rubbing his long, twisted beard with ring-adorned fingers. Roscille shrinks into the corner of the hall, staring at the floor. Her terrible eyes prick with tears.

Her father's order is too low for Roscille to hear. There

is only the choked gasp, and the splatter of something wet against the stone. By the time she looks up, all of it is cleared away: the boy's body removed, the stable master returned to the stables, her father's dagger back in its sheath.

The Duke approaches her. Maids are already scrubbing the red-dyed floor.

"I'm sorry," she whispers. Too afraid, now, to meet his gaze.

Her father extends his hand to her. It is the only time she can remember seeing it stained with blood. He does not ever dirty his hands over trivial things. Grim, quotidian violence can always be deferred to someone lower and weaker. Her father taught her this: Violence is like coin. If you spend it easily, people will think you imprudent and reckless. If you save it and spend it only in the most vital moments, people will think you canny as an ermine. For this, Roscille thinks her father the cleverest man in the world.

"Apologize for nothing," the Duke says. "The boy is dead. And you have taught yourself a better lesson than I ever could. Sometimes no words are as eloquent as the spilling of blood."

Roscille takes her father's hand and stands. Her knees are trembling. Her gaze does not leave the ground.

Soon after, there is the visit from le Tricheur and the fitting of the veil. After that, she is given Hawise as a handmaiden: a shield against the ravening appetites of men, if a fragile one. But this story is not a secret. This story is known to her father, and to the stable master, and to Hawise, and secondhand to most members of Wrybeard's court. The story is a good lesson, a good warning.

The secret is this: Roscille wanted the stable boy's hands on her hands and his lips on her lips. It was lust that overtook him, not madness. It was her desire, fed into his blood like poison from a barb. She wanted him and she made him want her back. That is the danger of her eyes. That they may compel men to do as she wishes.

If the truth were known, it would not be a veil and a bridal gown and a marriage to a faraway lord. It would be a noose or a blade or a pyre. To cause lustful madness is one thing—any beautiful woman has that power, if she wishes to exercise it, and even if she doesn't, even if such a thing can be called power—to mold a man to her will is another. Wrybeard could not save her, if the truth were known. Nothing could. And so she has been sent here, to the bleakest, grimmest brink of humanity, so that the world may be kept safe from her.

Roscille reassumes her veil. It flutters with the long breath she exhales. Then she rises and walks far away from the chamber, so she cannot hear her husband's anger, and so she cannot hear the peasants, begging for their lives.

SHE IS LYING CURLED ON her side in the bed, staring at nothing. Well—she is staring at the blank stone wall. It is impossible to stare at nothing. But behind her eyes, her death-touched eyes, the same scenes are playing out over and over again. The stable boy's lips, so near to touching. Her father's blood-slicked hand. The shepherd hobbling into the chamber, his son and grandson at his side. Her husband, roughly grasping her face, turning it over like a bauble he wants to buy.

The door opens and Roscille shoots up. Macbeth enters. There is no blood on him she can see, and no coppery rust-smell blooms outward from his body. But his eyes are angry slits.

He strides toward her, and Roscille cannot help but flinch.

Perhaps it is better that she does. All men like it when women cower.

"Did you find them?" she asks in a small, tremulous voice, as her husband towers over her. He is so enormous it is almost farcical, a droll god's study in extremes.

One of her first thoughts was that her husband is handsomer than she expected, for a man near twice her age, but rough, his edges craggy, like the cliffs of Glammis. It looks as if he grew right out of the rocks. Now Roscille thinks this again. There may as well be a stone pillar between her and the door.

"Fléance's wound did not bleed," he says. "Nor did he recognize any of the men that were brought before him."

Roscille swallows. "It is difficult," she says. "They were masked. And it all happened quickly."

"Of course." Macbeth does not speak for a long time. His gaze runs over her. He does not fear staring right into her eyes, through the veil. Then he says, "Your prize would suit you better if the chain were tighter."

Roscille's hand jumps to her throat, to the necklace. Before she can protest, Macbeth moves behind her, pushing aside her hair, unclasping the necklace and then clasping it again. He has made it so tight that it chafes with every movement, even just the drawing of a breath. Now she will never forget that she is wearing it.

"Thank you," she says hoarsely, as he steps away again. "I am blessed to have a husband who honors me in such a manner."

"Yes, I honor you, and I honor the ancient customs of Glammis."

Ancient. Roscille thinks of the three washerwomen. It occurs to her that perhaps he *must* honor these old traditions, that he is bound up to les Lavandières the same way they are chained in his basement. Perhaps if he does not abide the ancient ways of the land, their power will weaken. They will no longer be able to protect him or speak his prophecies.

This thought makes her braver. "You have fulfilled the first of my three wishes, and so swiftly."

The room is suddenly blanketed in silence. And then, to her shock, Macbeth sits down on the bed beside her.

Roscille's heart stutters with panic. But he merely lays a hand on the edge of her dress, as if to gently pin her in place, and his gaze looks past her, thoughtful.

"Lady Roscilla," he says, "do you know what it means to be a righteous man?"

That is what *Macbeth* means. Righteous one. It is not a patronym, as she initially thought. It is not his father's name, passed to him through birth and blood. It is one he has earned by his own actions.

In Breizh, to be righteous means to be pious, to accede to the directives of the pope, to take a priest into your rooms for counsel. Lord Varvek is not a righteous man, nor has he ever pretended to be one. He prefers to be the ermine, not the lion. He luxuriates in stories of his wily nature.

Macbeth is not a righteous man. He keeps witches for counsel. He is wed to a foreign hagseed. But perhaps in Glammis, *righteous* means something more.

"I am just a woman," Roscille says. "My mind is not disposed to wonder about such things."

Macbeth does not make a noise of agreement, but he does not dispute her, either.

"In Alba," he says, "to be a righteous man means to honor your oaths to your clan. I am Thane of Glammis, the head of clan Findlaích. It is my duty to protect my people and to always seek their advancement. But what am I to do when my clan does not honor me in return?"

Roscille blinks at him. Is he asking her for counsel? No, it cannot possibly be so. He is merely speaking to the air, and she is an incidental audience. At least, this is what she thinks, until Macbeth turns to look at her, his gaze serious.

"You must seek out those who *truly* honor you," she says, uncertainly. "And keep them close."

"Yes," Macbeth says. His fingers curl into the fabric of her dress. "I should hold you close, then—my clever wife, my loyal wife, who keeps my secrets and honors her vows."

It sounds like a compliment but it is a threat. She will only continue to be his wife if she continues to do these things, to be clever, to be loyal, to keep his secrets, to bow to him always. And if she is not his wife she will be Hawise, rotting at the bottom of the ocean.

Roscille nods.

"Good," Macbeth says. When he rises, his head nearly brushes the ceiling. "The chancellor's efforts at cruentation have failed, for now, and Fléance's memory fails him, too. I shall seek counsel elsewhere. I have no other choice. I must know where the treachery grows, and tear it out by its roots."

Roscille stays silent, perched on the edge of the bed.

"Come," says Macbeth.

And then she rises, too.

ROSCILLE KNOWS THE PATH TO the basement well, even after only one visit. She could feel her way down these narrow, twisting corridors in the dark. She needs only to listen to the nearing sound of the ocean, louder with every step, as if brushing against the floor that separates her from the sea, like the thin membrane between life and death, the earth and the underworld, as the Romans believed.

In Breizh, there is a story about a drowned city, Ys, which will rise again someday from the waves. Whoever first sees its church's spire or hears its bells will become king. And then Paris will be swallowed by the water and Ys will surge up to take its place. This story exists beyond the purview of the pope and has outlasted all of Christianity's civilizing efforts.

Of all the ancient tales, this is the one Roscille has heard the most, for it speaks to man's basest desire: that his enemies will be destroyed and that he may be the ruler of the world's new order. It is a very equalizing story, beloved by peasants and nobles both. Any man with the faculty of eyesight has a chance at becoming king.

As she walks, Roscille runs her hand along the wall, feeling the stone. She wonders if it is as old as Fléance claims. Her dress drags on the ground, making a second hushing sound, slightly out of rhythm with the waves beneath the floor. Macbeth walks without looking back. And, with every movement, the necklace rubs a red rash upon her throat.

Macbeth turns the last corner to the wood-rotted door and slips the key into the lock. Before he turns it, Roscille risks a question.

"Do they always speak prophecy to you?"

Macbeth turns, surprised but not displeased. "Sometimes it is prophecy. Sometimes it is counsel. But all counsel is prophecy, I suppose. A warning of what will happen if you do or do not act."

Perhaps her husband is wiser than the brute she has considered him to be. "Did they speak such to your father, as well?"

Then Macbeth's face shutters. She has ventured too far.

"You are not given to know this much, Lady Roscilla," he says. "This power is for the Thane of Glammis alone."

Yet he has answered her question anyway. The Thane of Glammis was his father, too, and his grandfather—this she learned back in Naoned, before they wed. Such a thing is rare in Alba, and even in Breizh. Titles are slippery things. Sometimes they fall out of a father's hands before they can be passed to his son. A birthright is never guaranteed. There have been whole generations extinguished in a single battle. Crowns and castles smuggled away, melted in the forge, burned to ash.

There is power in having held the same title for the span of three men's lives. But there is also danger. Time does not strengthen. It withers.

Macbeth opens the door and the cold salt air blows back her skirts. Her veil pushes itself into her mouth. She coughs and steps through the threshold into the cave's imperfect, distorted darkness. The torch in the center is still lit, and it casts strange patterns on the ceiling—no, not patterns, nothing that could ever be constellated or mapped or made reasonable. It is obscure. This is all she has been given to know.

The chains sing their inconsonant song, rattling like bells. They emerge from the darkness, pale and sudden as bolts of lightning. In the sallow glow, their white skin turns a nauseous, iridescent color, slick and sickly. The silvering that comes when meat has begun to rot. This time Roscille does not cross herself, even though the instinct rises.

Macbeth wades into the water. In the witches' hands, the

fabric is so wet that it is translucent, showing the knobs of their finger bones. Over and over again, slapping the clothes in the water, lifting them, wringing them out. Letting them fall again. They do not appear to even notice Macbeth until he reaches the torch, and then they look up with their milky, unseeing eyes.

"Macbeth," the one in the center says. The teeth in her mouth are broken, but sharp.

"Macbeth."

"Macbeth."

He acknowledges each one. "*Buidseach. Buidseach. Buidseach.* The prophecy has been fulfilled. The Thane of Cawder is dead. I wear his mantle now."

"Then the Thane of Cawder lives," says the leftmost one. Her rasping voice has a wry amusement in it, as if she is delighting herself in the jest. It is the first time Roscille has thought of them as even remotely human. Serving their own purposes rather than merely acting as an extension of her husband's will.

"Yes," says Macbeth. The word curls from his mouth, a cold spiral. "But there is treason in Glammis. Someone in my own clan works against me."

The torchlight glimmers in the witches' eyes, like silver fish darting through murky water, showing themselves only in quick, bright bursts.

"Seek out treason," murmurs one.

"I do," says Macbeth. "But so far I have failed in finding it. What counsel will you give me?"

The witches murmur unintelligibly among themselves. Roscille wonders if they even know she is here. They have never given any evidence of it. Is her presence nothing, not even a shift in the currents of stale air?

"No counsel," the center one says at last. "Prophecy, again. Would you like to hear it?"

Macbeth's face is damp, icy condensation gathering on his beard. "Always."

"All hail Macbeth," the leftmost one says. "Thane of Glammis."

"All hail Macbeth," the rightmost one says. "Thane of Cawder."

There is a pause. Water drips somewhere in the silence.

"All hail Macbeth," the center one says. She raises her head to the ceiling, to the jutting rocks that pierce the air like daggers, to the water that falls like sand through the siphon of an hourglass. "King Hereafter."

And then they are slapping the water and shouting, in their unrestrained, freakish joy, as a stone hardens in Roscille's throat and drops down into her stomach, as Macbeth turns to her, a look of disbelief on his face, which soon molds to pleasure.

"All hail Macbeth!"

"All hail Macbeth!"

"All hail Macbeth!"

"You have heard it," Macbeth says, in breathy awe. "*King Hereafter. Once told, the prophecy cannot be undone."

He returns to her, trudging through the water. The witches scream behind him, so loud that Roscille cannot believe it is not heard beyond these rooms, that it does not echo through the halls, their sound and fury signifying what carnage is to come.

Macbeth nearly slips on the steps, and thrusts his arm out to catch himself. Roscille does not know what possesses her to do this, but she reaches for him in turn, catching his arm, steadying him. The smile on her husband's face is almost innocent. But this innocence looks deranged in the darkness, with the witches howling, with their words turning the air smog-choked and filthy.

"Do you understand?" Macbeth asks, when he has righted himself. He holds both of her wrists in one hand, dragging her until their faces are close.

Roscille's heart flutters. "I am only a woman—"

"No," he says. His grasp on her is tight enough to bruise. "You are Lady Macbeth. Queen Hereafter."

FIVE

ROSCILLE SLIDES HER HAND THROUGH THE BARS of the kennel and the dogs all press toward her, yipping and sniffing, rasping their rough tongues across her palm. A dozen mouths are snapping and sinewy with spittle. Pink tongues loll over curved yellow teeth.

She has always liked animals. They do not cringe from her, unlike men. Also, they are uncomplicated. Amoral. They are concerned with merely their own survival and the idlest of pleasures. Even if it means bringing misery—a rabbit's neck snapped in those powerful jaws, a rival male turned on his belly and made to whimper.

Roscille consoles herself that she is doing the same thing, surviving. Her fingers grow damp with the dogs' licking. They must be tasting the oil of the morning's meal on her skin. Yet the more she tells herself she is not terrible, the less she believes it. A dog is always terrible to the stag it has cornered or the fox it has treed. She removes her hand.

At least the steady flow of peasants to the castle has ceased. The prophecy has overtaken her husband's mind, made his fear of treason small by comparison. But what blood has been stemmed for now will be compensated soon; Roscille knows that.

King Hereafter. The dogs whine, pushing their muzzles against the bars.

As if her thoughts have summoned him, Macbeth enters the kennel. The wooden doors are barely parted, just wide enough for Roscille to slip through slantways, and he does not pause to push them open farther with his hands; he lets his large, puffed-out chest split them apart. Light falls in a single beam, striping the dirt.

She has been crouched and now rises to her feet. "My Lord."

He does not ask why his wife has been kneeling among the dogs. "Lady," he says. "Fléance tells me you have the letter."

A cold feeling spreads in her stomach. "Yes," she says. "Here."

Roscille reaches into the folds of her skirt and removes the sealed parchment. She has kept it on her person since the moment she first stamped the wax. She gives it to Macbeth and says, "Fléance helped me to compose it." Another thread tying them together.

Macbeth's fingers crumple the parchment. "You should learn to write in Scots; it is your tongue now. I will have one of the Druides come to teach you."

"Thank you, my Lord."

"It is nothing to thank me for. It is your duty."

Queen Hereafter. Roscille's throat swells, chafing beneath the gold chain. Her gaze follows the letter as it is placed in the pocket of her husband's cloak, as it vanishes. She had thought she had created a talisman of protection, something to hold back the spilling of blood on the battlefield or in the sheets of her marriage bed. But she has only created an instrument of violence.

Yet she could not have known that. The world was different, before the witches spoke their prophecy. Now every glance that passes between Macbeth and the king will be singed with smoke, touched with poison.

The lampreys circle and circle their small pool.

"I—I have not yet made my second request," Roscille stammers out.

Macbeth's brows arch. For a moment she is afraid she has misjudged her position; perhaps Macbeth is not bound to this ancient custom, as she thought. Or perhaps the prophecy has imbued him with such arrogance that he no longer cares for his shackles.

But he merely replies, "Then make it now."

This, still, is arrogance. He thinks there is nothing on earth he cannot have. Whatever Roscille says next will be no hurdle; it will only be a way for him to enhance his own status, prove his own strength. But she is not ignorant of these things. She has had many hours to deliberate, to choose her words. Her request is an apple, and the first sweet bite will not reveal its rotted core.

"You have beautiful, exotic creatures in Alba," she says. "Ones that I have never seen before. It would delight me to have a cloak, stitched from the furs of six different white animals."

The second request is a natural successor to the first. On the surface it still shows her seventeen-year-old innocence, the enduring indulgences of Wrybeard's court. Yet it also shows a change in her she thinks will please him. She wants a cloak born from the soil of Scotland. She wants to robe her body in the natural beauties of her new home. If she were a lady of Breizh before, one foot still in the Loire's ice-white waters, now she has begun to cross over, to set her other foot firmly in the rocky lands of Glammis.

And, too, it will show this: that she is not so eager to keep her husband from her bed. This request will seem simpler than the first, her girlish resistance eroded. Six white hides is a single hunting trip, one blustery foray in the woods and fields, spear-tips flashing, cheeks high in color. This can be accomplished in an afternoon.

Or so Macbeth will think. He smiles, pleased by all the things Roscille has arranged to please him.

"Very well," he says. "A white fur cloak. It will complement your color beautifully."

He raises a hand to her cheek. He is wearing gloves today, and the leather is soft as petals. A calf must have been slaughtered, to make leather so soft.

"Thank you," Roscille says.

Macbeth's hand slides from her face. Then he says, "Your father told me you had a certain fondness for animals."

Her skin pulses with heat, a pressure that might grow into panic. Why would the Duke pass along this petty piece of knowledge? Why would he imagine Macbeth might care to hear it? She can only think of that day in the stable. The blood gleaming on her father's hand; the boy's invisible death. Has he told this story to Macbeth? How much has her husband been given to learn?

Roscille's silence lasts long enough that Macbeth narrows his eyes. "Was Wrybeard wrong in his accounting?"

"No," she manages. "He was not wrong."

In Macbeth's presence the dogs have gone quiet, whimpering in the corner of the kennels. They must remember the feeling of his boot against their bellies, his lashes on their haunches. Roscille feels sorry for them.

"Well," Macbeth says, rolling back his shoulders. "Dress in your finest. The king is coming."

THE KING IS COMING, AND the castle is bracing itself for his arrival as a warrior girds his body for battle. The king is coming, and Roscille can do nothing but put on her loveliest gown and softest slippers. She spends a long time deciding whether or not to cover her hair. It is not the tradition, in Glammis, as these last days have taught her. But Duncane is very pious. He is what the Brezhon would consider a righteous man. He keeps the chancellor in gold-limned habits and invites him into his strategy room for counsel, to ensure that each war he fights is a holy one. It would please him to know that Roscille is observing a married woman's proper Christian modesty, though she fears it will anger her husband if she chooses the king's preference over his.

Queen Hereafter. Roscille opens the trunk at the foot of

her bed and retrieves her gray-blue gown. It is in the style of Wrybeard's court, but there has not been time to sew her any dresses adhering to the customs of Glammis. Roscille does not even know what such a gown would look like. There are no other ladies here.

Dressing without Hawise is still difficult. In the end, she chooses to leave her hair loose and uncovered, but to reassume the heavier bridal veil. Duncane will surely want another layer of protection against her death-touched stare. He knows the stories. He tracks witchcraft like a hound.

She is still unnerved by Macbeth's question at the kennel. All this time she has thought no one in Glammis clever; she has thought herself a lonely ermine among grunting boars. Now she is beginning to think her husband has his own wiles, masked by a brutish exterior. And there is nothing more dangerous than a creature who pretends to be one thing and is in truth another.

This time the bridal veil is a reassuring weight. She does not want to see these men, any of them. Roscille feels she can no longer trust her own eyes. There is another world, spreading cold beneath the one she has always known. Dark water and darker words. Bloody auguries. The stones of civilization have been built upon raw, perverse madness.

ROSCILLE DOES NOT GREET THE king in the courtyard; she stands in the castle's main chamber, with Fléance, as Duncane and his party are led through the twisting halls. Fléance's scar is turning blue-white, but it is still raised and ugly enough that anyone who looks at him will marvel at how his life was nearly stolen. A falsehood, of course, but what does it matter? Most of the things men care about are their own inventions—titles, honors, crowns—imposed upon the world.

"The chancellor will perform no more cruentation," Fléance murmurs. "We are safe."

Roscille opens her mouth to reply, but then the archway to the main hall clusters with bodies. Her husband is first and largest by far. Banquho is at his side, his right hand. Then comes a smattering of soldiers, dressed curiously unlike the Scotsmen that they are, bereft of tartan, their hair and beards short.

Then comes Duncane. He is so small and hunched that she nearly misses him among his men. Stoop-shouldered, he looks old enough to be grandfather or great-grandfather. His short beard is patchy and leaden gray. When he comes into the torchlight, Roscille can see the pockmarks on his cheeks, the red blisters on his nose, the rheumy brightness of his wind-scalded eyes. He stops a moment to cough. Two of his men help him up onto the dais, where he sinks immediately into Macbeth's chair.

An t-llgarach, he is nicknamed in Scots. The wasting. There is no name for his affliction, and no cause. It is said he had the vigor of a man half his age until one day he was struck down, as if with a plague from God. But this cannot be divine punishment. It must be merely a cruel accident of nature. Duncane is God's loyal servant and powerful soldier. Yet Roscille cannot imagine the man before her penning the vicious treatise she has read.

The fearfull aboundinge at this time in this countrie, of the Wytches, or enchaunters, hath moved me to dispatch this following treatise of mine. My intention in this labour is to prove only two things: The one, that such devilish arts have been and are. The other, what exact trial and severe punishment they merite.

It is still a wonder to Roscille how Macbeth could be convinced to marry such a creature as her, and how he has the recklessness to show her openly to a king who abhors witches with every sickly drop of blood in his body.

Macbeth knows better than to grimace at seeing the king sit in his chair. He says, "My wife, the Lady Roscilla."

Duncane lifts his bleary gaze to her. When he speaks, it is with a clarity that is belied by his weak state and by the dead skin gathered in the corners of his mouth.

"I do not know why you are moved always to marry such troublesome women," he says. "But I trust you to keep your new wife as biddable as the first."

New? Roscille's mind stumbles through his words. She is Macbeth's second wife? No one has told her this. Was her father even told? And what has happened—she must know, she *must*—to the first Lady of Glammis, the other Lady Macbeth?

"Roscille is docile as a lamb," her husband says.

Her heart is beating fast at this revelation. There must be a reason such vital information was kept from her. Perhaps the first Lady Macbeth died of illness; perhaps her husband mourns too much to speak of her.

But Roscille cannot make herself trust such banal thinking. Not when her husband keeps a whole second world hidden beneath his castle, witches in chains, forced to parrot out his prophecies. He is slippery like the cold side of a cliff. And layered, like striated bands of erosion, green and white and rust-colored lash-marks of the sea. Each time she thinks she knows him, the water level lowers, and another shade is revealed.

Roscille is panicking silently, privately, when two more men enter the hall.

They arc as different as the seasons of winter and summer. There is one shorter, stockier, with a copper-colored beard and hair. His face is pleasantly ruddy, as if his journey here was a vigorous one on horseback rather than sheltered inside a carriage. His gait is robust and eager. He clops to the dais and sits beside the king, cracking his proud jaw open with a yawn. He cannot be anything other than a prince.

"My Lord," he says, nodding to Macbeth. "And Lady. Thank you for receiving us."

"My son," Duncane says, "Evander."

Evander, the Latin variant of a common Scottish name. Iomhar, Ivor, he could choose to go by either. Yet the king chooses Latin. This is not insignificant.

The second man is a prince, too. The king has two sons. But this man does not walk in the assiduous manner of a prince, and he does not sit beside his father. Instead, he stands at the edge of the dais, dark where his brother is light, sallow where is brother is sun-reddened.

"My elder son," the king says. "Lisander, prince of Cumberland."

Lisander, too, is a strange name for a Scot. His mother (dead now, felled on the birthing bed), some half cousin of Æthelstan, was very pious. Æthelstan is now calling himself *rex Anglorum,* king of the English, and he has the dispensation of the pope to do it. Perhaps these names are to appease his dead mother's people. In Angevin he would be Landevale, in Norse, Launfale. In Brezhoneg, Lanval.

He is very handsome. Tall, but not bulky. When he does move there is a stunning grace to his limbs that makes Roscille think of the capal-uisce, the water horse that takes the form of a man and seduces maidens to follow him into the drowning drink. (If the serpent-woman Melusina had a mate, it would be such a creature, she thinks.) The prince's hair is black and shines like the sea under moonlight. His features are fine—almost delicate, in a way men usually are not.

It is a beauty that would be well appreciated in Breizh, or Anjou, or even Paris, a beauty that would make kitchen girls go weak in the knees, that would make them trip and stumble just to put themselves in the path of his gaze. But here in Alba, Roscille knows it must be the subject of disparagement and suspicion, even greed. *What sort of man is twenty and bears no marks of battle?* One whose crown has been given to him like a child is given a toy. One whose crown might be taken from him just as easily.

It is true, the prince has no scars Roscille can see. It is strange to look at skin so immaculate after spending weeks observing only her husband and his men, all of them scraggly and loutish with old wounds. The prince's face is beardless, pale, and unmarred save for the deep, dark circles under his eyes. He looks very, very tired.

"My Lord." Lisander nods to Macbeth. And then he turns to her. "Lady Roscille. What they say is true. You are so beautiful the moon itself is shamed from rising."

Roscille. Her Brezhoneg name. Its familiar syllables have not caressed her ears in so long. If the Duke's courtiers could see her now, they would know that she can indeed blush.

"I had not heard the prince of Cumberland was a poet," she says, face warm.

"I am barely a prince, and even less a poet."

The room falls into a discomfiting silence. Duncane's succession is a matter still left unsettled, though it is a mystery as to why. Lisander is the elder; by the laws of any kingdom his head should be next to wear the crown. Yet Duncane has not proclaimed this.

Is he sickly? Roscille wonders. Like his father? But no, he cannot be. Duncane would swiftly have passed over an ailing son and onto the next. Even a bastard might be named, if the first legitimate child were so enfeebled—the Scots would understand; there is no pity spared for a crippled horse or a hen that cannot lay. Evander would have been named and all questions put to rest. But he has not been, and so despite his sallow, tired face, it cannot be that the prince of Cumberland is in ill health.

Banquho clears his throat, ending the unnerving silence. "My lords. I hope your journey was not too rough."

"Not so rough, no," Evander says. "We stopped over and took rest at the keep of Macduff. A day's ride away."

Roscille does not miss the way Macbeth stiffens at this name. She wonders if there is some private discord between him and this other lord, or if he merely bristles at any man who keeps close company with the king.

"Your chambers have been prepared," Banquho says. "I hope tonight will prove restful as well."

Evander then begins to thank his hosts, to speak of stag hunts and suppers, and of course ceremonies, to officially name her husband Thane of Cawder. Lisander is quiet and still. The gulf between the brothers seems vaster now than ever. It should be the elder son making such arrangements, dealing in pleasantries. What strange circumstances have occurred, to reverse their roles in a manner so extreme?

From beneath her veil, Roscille watches Lisander. She thinks she is being furtive, but evidently she is not—his gaze darts to her, as though he can feel her stare. His eyes are as green as a serpent's tail and, set within his ashen face, curiously gemstone-bright.

It is then that her husband reaches into the pocket of his cloak and retrieves the letter. Her letter. Roscille's blood grows cold. He passes the parchment to the king, whose hand rises, trembling, fingers carbuncled with gold rings. It is a long time before those thin fingers finally manage to grasp the letter. He stares down at it, blinking, straining to clear the moisture from his eyes but cannot.

"Father," Lisander says. He steps forward, and without another word the king gives him the letter. The necklace seems to tighten around Roscille's throat. Lisander breaks the seal and unfurls the paper.

"This was discovered among the Thane of Cawder's things," Macbeth says. "For a long time treachery has grown like rot in Cawder. I believe this to be proof."

Lisander's eyes skim the page. Roscille's cheeks are warm. He might as well be staring at her with equal scrutiny; she feels the heat of his gaze as if it were running over her instead of the paper. Fléance directed her, but perhaps there is still something about her penmanship that gives away the ruse. Perhaps there is something irrepressibly womanlike about her hand. Or perhaps it is merely that Lisander's senses are not dulled like his father's. No sickness of the body leaves the mind untouched.

Duncane has been living this posthumous existence for years, since at least the births of his sons. There is the mark of a trephine on his forehead: the place where a Druide sliced into his skull to let the evil spirits seep out. It has not worked, and now he will wear this mortifying blemish forever, until his dragging, miserable death. There is no honor in dying of disease.

At last Lisander looks up. "The writer professes displeasure at your rule," he says. "But only in the vaguest terms—there is no firm plan to unseat the House of Dunkeld."

Roscille blushes more furiously. She wrote the letter in vagaries on purpose—she feared the minutiae might be her ruin—but now Macbeth's gaze has snapped to her, just for a moment. The same fear from her wedding night fills her body, cold and familiar, like water flooding its accustomed tributaries.

Duncane stares into the middle distance—stares at nothing, stares at the dust-choked air. He says, "Better to kill the serpent while it is still in its shell."

A slow, pleased smile overtakes Macbeth's face.

"I knew I carried out your will," he says. "If any snakes remain in Cawder, I will snap their spines and break their teeth."

The king nods. It is a painful gesture to observe, his head bobbing precariously on his scrawny neck.

"That is my will indeed," he rasps.

SUPPERS, CEREMONIES. NO STAG HUNTS—YET. Roscille cannot help but wonder when Macbeth will set out to fulfill her second request. She reassures herself that it will not be at least until Duncane is gone. He is otherwise too occupied.

They are sitting in the main hall, which has been recon-
figured to accommodate the presence of the king. There is a
longer table on the dais, with enough room for Duncane and
his sons, and Macbeth, and Roscille, and then Banquho at the
very end. Duncane is at the center, but not really. There is an
even number of occupants, so there is no true middle—well.
The true middle would be somewhere between Macbeth and
Duncane. Right now, the center is a blank space, empty of all
but breath and air.

Roscille takes decorous bites of her stew, which is difficult
from under the thick mesh of the veil. She has not removed it,
scarcely even lifted it; she is afraid to, in Duncane's presence.
Yet it allows her to look where she pleases, without drawing
another's notice. She looks down the table at Lisander, who
leaves his food mostly untouched. He watched her before—
she knows she did not imagine it—but his eyes do not find
her now.

She wonders about the dark bruises under those eyes.
What keeps the prince of Cumberland awake at night? Is he
bookish, pious like his name suggests, hours at some phil-
osophical toil until the candles burn down to their ends?
Perhaps. Does he amuse himself, as so many men do, with
women—serving girls and pleasure slaves? This is harder to
imagine. It would certainly displease his father, Duncane, the
righteous man. And for some reason the thought displeases
her, too. It winds a strange, deep-green, serpentine feeling
through her belly.

He is half English—is he Æthelstan's lion, noble and preeminent? Perhaps the unicorn of his father's blood, mystic
and pure? The bold stag of Ireland, or the scaled dragon of

Wales? All these free, wild creatures, stamped with the virtues of men. From the way his gaze cuts through the room
so cleanly, she wonders if he is the ermine of Breizh, canny,
a master of disguise. There is something glimmering behind
his eyes that she cannot flush out. She watches him until his
gaze lands upon her, *finally,* and then she turns away, her skin
prickling.

The endowment of Macbeth's new title amounts to
this: Her husband kneels before the king. The king makes
the sign of the cross with his trembling, jewel-thick fingers. His crown, a plain iron circlet, barely disguises the
mark of trepanation on his forehead. The contrast between
this simple crown and the thick, gleaming rings is poignant,
even from a distance. Roscille will later learn these rings are
more function than decoration, that they keep the king's
trembling fingers from slipping out of their joints. Weakness, dressing up as strength.

"Thane of Cawder," he says. "Rise."

And Macbeth does, his largeness dwarfing the king. It
casts a sheen of absurdity upon the ritual, making it perverse.
A wolf kneeling to a sheep. He takes his seat, and the meal
goes on, mostly in silence. Roscille turns to Lisander again.
The prince of Cumberland who dared to speak to her in
Brezhoneg.

There is no reason for him to know her language, and yet
he does. She imagines Lisander speaking it again: not only
what he would say, but the shape his mouth would make
when saying it, the flicker of his tongue across his lips, the
quick white flash of his teeth. She wants to bathe herself in the
clear blue waters of Brezhoneg diphthongs and vowel sounds,

cleaning off the grime of Scotland. To do it she would have to strip off all her clothes, the veil, the ruby choker, and reveal her flesh to the air. Thinking of these things while looking at the prince of Cumberland makes her face grow hot. She has to avert her eyes.

WHEN THE BANQUET IS DONE and the servants are carrying away the trays, Evander speaks with Banquho, arranging for tomorrow's hunt (much wine has been imbibed between them and their voices are loud, syllables scraping the ceiling). The king is helped down from the dais by his two chamberlains, who all this time have kept their swords sheathed at their sides. The king himself is not armed. No one will indulge the fantasy that he is strong enough to wield a blade.

"Are your accommodations satisfactory?" Macbeth asks.

Duncane blinks. "My chambers, yes. But for my son, a room without a window."

He indicates Lisander, who says nothing to confirm or deny this. A room without a window? Both Roscille and her husband are silenced by such a bizarre request. All of the explanations that her mind supplies are hollow and trivial: that he cannot sleep with the sound of the wind so close, that the salt air makes him sick, that he has a fear of heights and does not want to be reminded of how steep the cliffs are upon which the castle of Glammis sits. Lisander's expression gives nothing away.

After a moment, Macbeth says, "A room courtyard-side, then. I will have my servants show the way."

They depart: the king, his chamberlains, Lisander, Evander, Fléance, and Banquho. The room empties of all other occupants, even the scuttling servants. Roscille and her husband are alone. The air is greasy with the smells of the feast, thick with odors of wine and men's sweat. She adjusts the necklace at her throat; the rash is growing beneath the gold.

When the footsteps of the other men have faded, Macbeth turns to her.

"You nearly dishonored me," he says. "With that letter."

His voice is rough and low. Anger shows in the lines of his face, the lines that remind her that he is twice her age, that he had a wife before her (*how, who?*). Roscille's heart stutters.

"I am sorry, my Lord," she says. "I did not know—I did not mean—"

"The prince of Cumberland is too clever," Macbeth cuts in. "There is a chance he has seen through the ruse. And all because your hand faltered. It was on your advice that I accused Cawder of treachery."

She is shocked to hear him admit it, that he acted upon her directive. That this was arranged by her hand. Roscille draws a breath, trying to steady herself.

"I am sorry to have failed you," she says softly. "Please, my Lord, tell me what I can do to make it right."

She has barely finished speaking before Macbeth grabs her by the arm. He drags her toward him. Roscille closes her eyes and ducks her head, biting her lip on a whimper.

She will be struck: She has seen it done a hundred times to women, by their husbands or fathers or brothers, by their lovers or their masters. One of the Duke's courtiers showed Hawise the back of his hand and for a week a violet bruise pulsed on her cheek, and every time Roscille looked at it she was filled with a sick, fettered anger. Roscille has never been struck, having been a noble lady, a dutiful daughter and heretofore wife. She was foolish enough to believe that the Duke would never allow such a grievous assault upon her person. But the father she thought she knew has shriveled and vanished from this earth. He is, at most, a ghost—nothing solid enough to put between Macbeth's hand and her cheek.

But her husband does not strike her. Instead, he tears the veil from her face. She is so shocked she cannot help crying out, a short, bitten-off sound. Before she can move or truly speak, Macbeth's broad, hard-callused hand claps over her eyes. Blinding her completely. The world is black, swimming with bleary stars.

His other arm holds her around the middle and pins her back to his chest. His mouth is close to her ear. His voice dampens the nape of her neck.

"I know what you are," he rasps. "Witch-marked, they call you, hagseed, but no. You are more than just an unlucky maiden, cursed with supernatural beauty. Your wiles are beyond those of a duke's bastard daughter. I know witchery. I can smell the power on you like smoke from a pyre. That flesh-burning scent. You do not enchant by accident. You compel."

"Please." A rising sob chokes the word. "I have no power."

"You will not lie to me," he snarls. "You are my lady wife."

Her mind falls through the cracks in the floor. It flounders in deep waters. "I would never harm you, my Lord, I swear it. Please. I am no spy, no traitor—"

A sudden laugh, spittle against her cheek. "Harm me? I

do not think you spy or traitor—if you were, Wrybeard would better disguise you."

"He would not . . ." Tears sting her eyes. "My father would never betray an ally or broker a false peace."

But she does not know that. Her father has become obscure to her. *You are whatever creature I make you.* Yet blinded like this, she cannot see her own hands, whether they are sullied with blood. She feels the points of her teeth—are they sharp or dull? Perhaps all of this is occurring at her father's design, a plan deeper and more devious than she can fathom—or perhaps she wants to believe there is a strategy behind it, because that is more bearable than the thought that her father has merely thrust her down the cliff to drown.

Macbeth's hand is so large that it covers her nose, too. She can only breathe through her mouth, and she gulps as a fish starved for water.

"Think no more of your father," he says. "You are not a lady of Breizh anymore. You are a lady of Alba, of Glammis, of Cawder. Lady Macbeth. And if you choose it, you can be more."

She cannot see, but her other senses rally to her like men-at-arms, and hold up the workings of her mind like a spoil of war: blood. She tastes it on her tongue. She smells it in the air. She feels it gather on her palms and hears it drip down onto the floor.

"More?" she manages.

Macbeth retracts the arm that has been holding her middle. Slowly, almost tenderly, he reaches up to stroke the hair back from her face.

"You are my wife," he says again. Lower, now, almost a whisper. "Your purpose is yoked to my own. And I am not infirm of purpose. I am sanctioned by prophecy. There is not a man who would squander what is his right."

Roscille swallows. The ruby presses against her throat. "*King Hereafter.*"

"Yes." Macbeth breathes the word. "And now you are the dagger in my hand."

Six

THE VEIL IS TORN AND IT CANNOT BE REPAIRED. MAC-
beth leaves her, and Roscille stumbles through the
dark halls, keeping her eyes on the ground. Beneath
her feet, the water rises, meets the floor, and dissipates again,
into tongues of foam that she can hear, for the way they sim-
mer like grease.

She remembers how the king's hands shook as he struggled to lift his goblet to his mouth, how the wine spilled from
the open corners of his lips, droplets that stained his jerkin.
King Duncane (a righteous man) would not suffer a witch
to live. That he tolerates the presence of Roscille (hagseed)
is a miracle. Now Macbeth is asking her to steal the merciful
breath from his lungs.

She will not do this. She cannot. She may be witch-
marked, she may be cleverer than her sex allows, but she is
not a murderer. Her single enchantment was a mistake, a folly

of youth, one that colored her father's hands, not hers. But perhaps even this is absolution she does not deserve. Not once did she raise her voice to stop her father's dagger. Not once did she consider how she might have damned him, this inconsequential stable boy, by inviting his peasant lips to soil her noble face.

Perhaps it is not cleverness that seeps through the generations but cruelty. One cold creature weaning another.

Roscille's staggering footsteps take her to the parapet, where she breathes in dense, frigid night air. She can smell the salt that dries in white blisters on the black rock. She can hear the roiling tide. The wind on her cheeks is surprisingly painful; they have been turned raw with tears and, for the first time since arriving in Glammis, her face is bare, unprotected, unleashed. She presses her hands to her burning cheeks. Her palms are like two stones.

She looks down the sheer face of the cliff. She imagines Hawise's body tripping down it, and then she replaces Hawise with herself, her torn veil floating like a jellyfish, her hair spreading like seafoam. The water swallows this imagined Roscille in half the length of a heartbeat. It is fast and bleak and final.

It is difficult to hoist herself onto the balustrade, because the stone is cool and slippery and her hands are cool and slippery and her arms are river weeds, trembling. Her ripped veil blows around her face, snatched by the wind.

Now she imagines her body joining Hawise's on the seafloor, their bones curling together like mollusks. Her deathful eyes will be eaten out of her skull by the fish, her flesh sucked by the eels. Her heart rocks as though on a pendulum, swaying between comfort and terror.

A voice, behind her, as sudden as a clap of thunder. "Lady Roscille?"

Brezhoneg. Hearing her native tongue turns her blood to wine, florid and sweet. The shock of it unbalances her, feet slipping against the stone. Her fingers grasp for purchase and find only air. The black water surges up at her. But before she can fall forward, down the cliff and into the sea, a pair of strong arms lock around her waist.

"Close your eyes," comes that same low voice.

She does. Lisander lifts her gently down from the parapet, as if she is weightless, gripping her under her knees and her shoulders—it is what in Breizh they call the bridal carry, which would seem befitting to an outsider, with her tattered veil now draped loosely over them both, if they did not know she was not only not a bride, but another man's wife.

Lisander sets her on her feet again. Her knees are still weak beneath her.

"Whatever he has done," Lisander says, "it is not worth this."

Her eyes are still shut, but of course he can see *her*, the torn veil, the tears on her cheeks. In that moment she is any woman whose husband has handled her too roughly. Lisander need not know what words passed between them. He has no reason to think they spoke of magic, of murder. Of treason against his father. Perhaps she should make showier tears. Let him believe her no more than a misused wife.

"Please," she whispers. "Don't tell my husband."

"I won't." A pause. "Yet it would please my father to know he treats his second wife as brutishly as his first."

Roscille thinks of King Duncane's treatise on witches. *My intention in this labour is to prove only two things: The one, that such devilish arts have been and are. The other, what exact trial and severe punishment they merite.* Perhaps she has misjudged the degree of his mercy. Perhaps he gladdens to see a witch-marked woman wed to a man who might as well be her jailer; perhaps this is the *severe punishment* of which he wrote.

Second wife. When Roscille speaks, her voice is far more tremulous than she wants it to be. "And was his first wife a hagseed, too?"

Silence. Roscille wishes she could see his face. His serpent-green eyes, and the tired bruises under them.

"Some men like to see all women treated brutishly, no matter their nearness to witchcraft," he says at last. "But your husband does make a habit of choosing wives with their own . . . mythologies. It vexes my father, yes."

King Duncane, who robes his Druides in gold.

"Does it vex you?" she asks.

He exhales, sounding almost amused. "My father is heartier than he looks. You need not worry about what I think."

"I only meant the opinion of today's prince," she says. "Not tomorrow's king. Today's barely-prince," she adds.

Her angling is not subtle at all, and she does not really expect Lisander to give her the answer she seeks.

"You wonder whose head will wear the crown," he says. "The younger son, who has the nobility of a lion and the golden graces of a storybook knight, whose only defect was being born second, or the elder, whose grim presence makes men shrink from him, whose only asset is the order of his birth."

Roscille draws a breath. She had not thought he would state it so baldly.

"I know what it is," she says, "to see men shrink from you."

She feels the air shift, the coldness evaporating. Warmth seeps between their bodies, but it is a strange warmth, less like the blaze of an open flame and more like living flesh, heated by the blood pulsing below.

"I imagine so," he says softly. "Just as I imagine you are well aware—Glammis is not a safe place for women like you."

Her heart skips. "Tell me of her. The wife who came before."

But before Lisander can speak, there is some commotion in the hall. Footsteps and distant voices, voices she doesn't recognize—perhaps the guards in Duncane's retinue. With one hand on her shoulder, Lisander maneuvers her from the center of the corridor to the wall, pressing them both to the cool stone.

"Time escapes us," he says. "But—Lady Roscille. If your lord husband puts his hands on you, whisper to me the ugly deeds he does in the dark, and I will stop him."

Unexpectedly, his words land like an arrow, lodged painfully between her ribs. It is not the purview of a prince, the way a noble lord treats his wife. Surely it would be taken as a great offense. Surely Duncane would not allow it—allow his son, even the less preferred one, to disgrace himself by coming to the defense of a witch. He is prince, not king, not emperor. What right does he have to rescue the slave from his death by the eel's teeth?

"Why?" she manages. "Why dishonor yourself for my sake? Why risk your birthright?"

A stretch of silence, the night warping and shifting around them.

"Because," Lisander says at last, "I do not wish to see you

live without shelter." He pauses. "And because the crown is not mine to lose."

THEY DEPART, EACH FOR THEIR own windowless room. She opens her eyes at last, and they ache. It feels as if her lashes have turned inward, stabbing at the soft whites. She unclenches her fingers and the tattered veil falls to the ground. She watches it drift down, lace draping itself over stone.

Three things she has learned, from this exchange.

The first: Her husband has a proclivity for witch-women.

The second: He will not hesitate to replace one witch-wife with another.

Roscille imagines the fate of the First Wife, imagines her like Hawise, smothered by the black waves. She cannot be sure, of course, that the First Wife drowned. But it is the easiest death, in Glammis, where the sea is always here, always churning, and always hungry. If Roscille does not please Macbeth, she will share this fate. It is the dagger in her hand, or it is death by her husband's orchestration. *Glammis is not a safe place for women like you.* Macbeth is like Wrybeard, in this respect. All things in this castle must serve him.

The third: Lisander wishes to protect her. Yet this is a flimsy piece of knowledge; mostly, the prince of Cumberland is still a mystery to her. She should have been below his attention, just another lord's misused wife. He must have seen hundreds of them by now, girls cringing in their white cornettes, thighs freshly bloodied, or old matrons whose mouths have shrunken into their faces. His own mother was likely one of them. If ever he has a daughter, she will be the same.

She does not know why he stepped between her and death. And at the heart of things, she cannot be certain that he will again. He told her he had no inheritance to lose—but without the promise of a crown, what power does he have, truly, to save her?

Roscille leans over and rests her forehead against the castle's stone wall. In the theater behind her eyelids, she watches the eels circle in their pool. She hears the cut-off scream of the stable hand as he dies. And she thinks, perhaps, the poison has already seeped through, turning her heart black.

ROSCILLE HAS NEVER BEEN IN her husband's chamber before. It is half again as big as hers, with a large window, gridded in iron. Right now, it is morning, and she slept only in choking stops and starts, and the rheumy gray light that leaks through the windows makes her vision ripple. She has replaced her torn veil with another one, and she is grateful for the screen it provides between her stinging eyes and the world.

Behind her there is a bear-rug, identical to the one in her room. The same immortal snarl, the same yellow teeth. Perhaps they were a pair, mates, slain by twin spears.

The bed is behind Macbeth, and it, too, is half again as big as hers. Large enough, easily, to hold both of them at once. Seeing it makes Roscille's stomach roil and churn. She reminds herself of her husband's vow, this ancient rite he must observe. She still has two requests left. Two impossible tasks separating her from blood-slicked sheets.

Where the light streams through the window grate, it makes a thatched pattern on the floor. There are a mere two squares of light between her and Macbeth. When he exhales, her veil ripples.

"Tell me," he says. "Tell me how you will do it."

It has all been laid out for her, like a map unfurled across the council table. His plan, his words, snuck into her brain. Roscille draws a breath.

"I will go to the king's chamber in the dead of night." Her voice is a whisper. "I will ensorcell his chamberlains. I will kill him."

"And tell me why I cannot do this myself."

"Because," she says softly, "when the king is found dead, the chancellor will perform the rite of cruentation. And when the words are spoken over Duncane's body, the death wound will start bleeding in your presence."

He lifts a hand, cups her cheek. "Exactly. And I will be sure to keep you far from the chamber. No one will suspect a woman capable of such violence."

When spoken aloud, it sounds so easy. Oversimple. But this plan is porous with black spaces, all of which Roscille may fall through. What if she cannot ensorcell the chamberlains? She has done it only once before, that day in the stable, and never since. She does not know the margins and contours of her power. What if she cannot kill the king before he cries out and alerts someone? What if she cannot bring herself to deliver the death blow?

And then there is Lisander, his words curling in the shell of her ear. *I do not wish to see you live without shelter.* Not even a promise, merely a desire—and if no vow was spoken, can she truly betray him?—yet a knife twists between her ribs when she thinks of him.

All she can manage to say is, "I am afraid of failing you, my Lord."

His thumb brushes her cheekbone, a fraction of an inch below her eye. "You will not fail. Do you remember? Your purpose is sanctified. The witches have spoken their prophecy. I did not fail in Cawder, did I?"

She shakes her head.

"Then your hand will not falter, either."

Roscille cannot bring herself to look at him. She merely nods, gaze on the ground. "Yes, my Lord."

His hand leaves her face, travels down her throat, until he grips the chain of the necklace. The ruby catches between his finger and his thumb.

"I drove my sword true," he rasps. "Cawder's blood was so thick and hot as it covered me that I thought I might never be clean again, my jerkin and my tartan, all soaked. My hands, red enough to shame a saint. And yet I did not hesitate; I do not regret. It is the way of the world, violence."

Men are all keen to say this, *Yes, it is my will that is right, my desire that is natural, all things arranged to my pleasure.* Even the Duke, who is more miserly with his violence, is no different. She envisions her father's hand again, slick to the touch with blood.

"I brought back this title for myself and this necklace for you," Macbeth goes on, quietly. "Two hungers sated with one act. And this will be the same. Queen, hereafter."

She wants to close her ears to his voice. She does not want to think that she has started this, set it all in motion with one request, for the ruby that now chafes painfully against her throat. Her fear, transfigured by her husband's appetites, made swollen and monstrous with his greed. All because she could not bear to submit herself to him like all the world's women have before. This is the cruelty that her father's seed engendered. The wickedness, growing long green tendrils through her veins.

When she looks down at her hands, for a moment she sees red. Red and red and red. Her heart gives a horrified jolt. But when she blinks, they are pale again, unblemished and saintly white. They will not remain this way. She tucks her hands back into the trumpet sleeves of her gown, so that they vanish from her sight.

"Yes," she whispers back at last. "It will be so."

FIRST SHE MUST SURVIVE ANOTHER supper with the king. This one is for Macbeth and his treasured guests only. There is Banquho, of course. And Fléance. Her actions have ensured him a place at the table beside his father, proudly wearing his garish new honor-wound.

Yet—it is now Roscille who sits at her husband's side. Not the man who has been his right hand. She can feel Banquho's gaze on her all evening, his anger scorching her skin. He has been displaced, the order of his world made unfavorable and bizarre.

King Duncane sits at the table's head, and he is having trouble eating, dribbling wine on his jerkin, the food falling before he can put it into his mouth. It is horrible to watch, his helplessness, his infirmity. Roscille stares down at her plate. Macbeth leans away, as if the king's shame is catching. Or perhaps it is only the knowledge that this is the last time he will see Duncane alive.

Yet whatever guilt he feels now will not buffet him from his course.

"We will hunt tomorrow," Evander—Iomhar—says. "Banquho says the sun will be high. A rare thing, in Glammis!" He laughs loudly, and the huge empty room throws the sound back at them. Roscille flinches.

"Good weather portends a fruitful hunt," Banquho says.

There will be no hunt. Tomorrow there will only be a cold body and grieving sons and a kingdom breaking apart like the ground over a tree's new roots.

Lisander sits at the other end of the table, in a good position for her to watch him. As before, he eats very little, and does not say much, but his quick-darting gaze shows that he listens intently to the words passing around him. And every so often, he does glance toward Roscille. Her skin heats when he does, blood drawing close to the surface.

Can she risk confessing? Can she speak of her husband's intent and let the king clap him in chains? Lisander said he would protect her—but that does not mean he will believe her, or that his protection would be enough, in this court of men. Macbeth is Duncane's cousin, and he has only just proven himself loyal with the killing of Cawder. They would sooner kill her for treason against her lord husband, or perhaps they would merely laugh, at this woman with her addled mind. *Is she one of those prostrating martyrs who claims she can talk to God? Does she believe the wind speaks to her in auguries? Better keep a tight grasp on this tricky wife. Even better: Cut out her tongue. Stitch her lips shut.*

No one notices that she, too, cannot eat. Evander lords over the chamber with his boisterous words, until her husband cuts in.

"Have your accommodations been comfortable?" Macbeth asks.

The king's cloudy eyes prick with interest. "Oh. Yes. Lisander?"

Lisander lifts his stare. For a moment Roscille half fears, half hopes, that he will look at her. But he merely meets Macbeth's gaze steadily and replies, "Comfortable enough."

"Good," says Macbeth. "I am pleased."

Roscille is sure that no one except her pays attention to his fingers, clenched tight around the edge of the table. His bitten-off, yellowed nails dig into the wood. Time passes sluggishly, like a river still choked with ice, and then supper is over, and the servants come to take the platters and uneaten food away.

The king's chamberlains help him up from his seat. There is a streak of dried wine on his chin. Lisander rises when his father does, and unexpectedly reaches over the table, using a cloth to wipe the king's chin clean. The tenderness of it shocks her, as it does the rest of the hall. They cannot decide if he is a good son, for attending to his father so vigilantly, or if he is a bad son, for calling attention to his shame. Duncane reaches up, tremulously, and grips Lisander's hand. With dry, chapped lips, he kisses his son's fingers and closes his eyes. The moment seems to halt the progression of time, and when Duncane at last releases his hand and Lisander steps away, the minutes begin to pass again, though strangely, like a ship rocking in unruly waters.

More pleasantries: Good night, good night, good night. Hunt tomorrow, high temperatures, honors done.

Duncane limps out of the room, his chamberlains girding him and his sons following behind. Macbeth's eyes cut to Roscille, and he gives the most imperceptible of nods.

THE CORRIDORS ARE EMPTY OF all servants; Macbeth has made it so. Roscille walks slowly, slippers hushing against the stone. The impossible has happened already: She has begun not to hear the ocean at all. She must pause and listen for it, reacquaint herself with its rhythm, to be sure that her senses are not dulled. Most of the torches on the wall are extinguished, but she follows the ones that are lit (perhaps this is Macbeth's doing as well) and they lead her to King Duncane's chamber.

His two chamberlains are at the door. They are whispering to each other in low, rough voices, amusing themselves as they pass the long hours at their post. These are not good guards. If they were Wrybeard's men, they would not be talking or laughing. They would be as still and silent as his draughts tiles, arms folded behind their backs. Roscille approaches them.

They stop their snickering, but their faces still show proof of their laxity; their cheeks are red. Roscille would not be surprised if they had snuck some wine from the kitchens. The left one straightens, clears his throat, and says, "Lady Macbeth. What are you doing here at so late an hour?"

Naturally, she has considered what she will say. But the words turn to ash on her tongue. The men's swords are sheathed at their sides and, unlike the weapons of her husband's men, they are hilted in gold. Roscille tries to see them for what they are: servants, and displeasing ones at that. Their blades are irrelevant to her aims. They will not raise them in a lady's presence.

Instead of speaking, she reaches up and carefully folds back her veil. The men startle, choking on their protests. Before they can raise their voices, she meets the gaze of one, then the other, and says, "Quiet."

Their mouths snap shut. Their eyes fix on her, unblinking. The change has come over them so suddenly, the metamorphosis almost invisible, no panicked writhing like a nymph turned to a tree or a mortal into a flower or fish. Roscille's throat tightens.

This is power. With a single word, a single look, she has arranged the world to her liking. This is how kings must feel, every moment of the day, how her father must feel as all of Breizh bends and warps to his will.

The men are still silent and staring at her. They rock slightly back and forth but their gazes never falter. Roscille inhales.

"Open the door," she says. "Let me into the chamber."

Their bodies move as naturally as breathing.

THE KING SLEEPS ON HIS back, hands clasped across his chest. His wheezing snores fill the room.

Roscille approaches the bed. Duncane does not stir. She is able to take in his features as she could not before, from a distance: his bushy brows, threaded with silver. The deep lines that bracket his mouth, suggesting that once upon a time he smiled often and easily. Despite his age, his hair is thick and full, and in places Roscille can still see patches of its original color—copper, like Evander's. His chest rises and falls gently with his breaths.

This is a man with a beating heart and pulsing lungs and hot-running blood and Roscille cannot do it. She claps a hand over her mouth so the king will not wake to her choked-out whimper. When Macbeth told her how he killed the Thane of Cawder, he made it sound like the simplest, headiest of pleasures. How can it be so?

She has the dagger in the bodice of her gown—Macbeth's dagger, the one he wielded against Cawder. Anointed, she supposes, with the prophecy of les Lavandières. But as she begins to draw it out, something occurs to her, something that passed beneath her husband's attention. He was certain he could keep her from the Druide as he performed cruentation, but what if he cannot? And what if—Roscille does not know the shape of her power, how long it will stretch, whether she can plant a thought in these chamberlains' minds that will not wither away when she is gone from their sight. What if, when she vanishes down the hall and they blink to themselves, as if woken from slumber, they remember the Lady who slipped into the chamber and slipped out with blood coating her hands?

Panic crests like a wave, then dissolves into sickly foam that turns her stomach. At least the king does not stir. Even in sleep he wears those thick, jeweled rings. Very slowly, Roscille turns around and faces the two chamberlains.

Their stares have not averted; they have not even blinked. All the rough amusement, the jesting in their eyes, the wine-flush on their cheeks—gone. Her belly is slippery with nausea. Will power always feel so precarious? Will it ever be so natural that when it is taken from her, it will be like someone has slashed open her throat?

"Come," she says hoarsely. "Draw your swords, and—"

The men move like bronze statues roused to life, excited only by her will. They come to the king's bedside and unsheathe their blades, and the whisper of metal against hide makes Duncane twitch at last, eyelids fluttering. The only light is from the hearth, a steady but distant orange glow, and he is half blind even in the best of circumstances, so now he cannot see; he can only hear the presence of others, and—

Fearfully, he spasms, crying out, "Lisander! Lisander!"

Roscille's heart briefly stops. Here is a man withered, ancient, sick, hardly lucid, still half dreaming, and yet he keens for his son like a mother over her infant's cold crib. In that moment she thinks she would rather slash open her own throat than harm him. But his cries grow louder, and someone will come soon, so she presses her hand across his mouth (across the same lips that kissed Lisander's fingers) until his words are garbled, and only his rheumy eyes dart with blind, animal terror.

"Kill him," Roscille chokes out. "Please, make it quick, please—"

She sounds like a child herself. And then—she will never know if it was true or not, her fear. Because that is when her mind unlatches from her body, as if someone has taken a trephine to her skull, cracked it, and released the black mist of bad spirits. She watches, outside herself, as two blades vanish inside the king's slack belly. The hilts twist and twist. Duncane coughs, blood running down his chin. But they have stolen the breath from him, and thus stolen his screams.

The blades reveal themselves, gleaming and slickly red. The wounds they have made are mostly hidden beneath the sheets and the king's sleeping tunic, but the blood pours forth anyway, sluicing through the fabric, splattering the floor. Every second stretches to the length of a lifetime. Roscille, still outside her body, hears herself gasp.

The chamberlains' arms fall to their sides. Their blade-points drip. How long until her power is used up, wrung out? This is the thought that presses her mind back; she inhabits her body again like a spectral possession. She cannot keep the men under her charm forever. Their eyes will clear. Their limbs will move again of their own accord. And then their mouths will open, their lips will move, and they will say, *It was the witch-woman, that foreign bride, that Lady Macbeth.*

Roscille meets the eyes of each one. It is easier, this time. They are already inhuman, no more than expedients to her, swords without arms attached, tools, draughts tiles. It is not pleasure, exactly, but it is still something that fills her up. She is satiated, gorged, even, though the food she has consumed has no particular taste.

"You will take your swords," she says, and now her voice does not shake, "and put them to each other's hearts. You will need to press harder than you think."

The blood on their swords has not even had time to dry. It is still gleaming, ruby-hued, holding the firelight. And this time, there are no blankets to stop Roscille from seeing: The blades are driven forward, slicing through the sinew and gristle of their chests, shearing bone. Two mirrored wounds. The blood sprays as the swords are wrenched out again. It splatters Roscille's face, the front of her dress, hot as licks of flame.

Roscille has already stolen their humanity, so the men do not cry out as they die. Their bodies topple wordlessly, like felled trees. Their eyes do not even close. They crumple where they stood, limbs folding at odd and gruesome angles, cheeks against the cold stone.

The blood pools. It laps at the hem of her gown. Her slippers soak quickly, sticking her to the floor. It is what every man says, when he first kills another: *I did not know there would be so much.* Roscille hates herself for thinking this dull, common thought.

THERE IS A BUCKET OF water in her room, which she uses to clean her hands and face. The dress cannot be saved. She strips it off as the blood dries on the linen, turning it stiff, the color of rust. She lights a fire in the hearth and tosses the dress inside. Sparks erupt.

This part, at least, is passionless, function only. Roscille kneels naked on the bear-rug and scrubs her skin until it is stinging and raw. The ends of her hair, beneath her fingernails. The blood clings in clever, curious places: behind her ear. In the cleft of her chin. She scrubs until the veins show blue through her skin, standing out as clear as cracks in ice.

Near the end, she catches her reflection in the murky water. Once she would have seen a girl, beautiful, yes, but a bit strange, especially in the eyes. Once she would have opened her mouth to see if she had suddenly grown an ermine's sharp teeth. She had so badly craved that little power, whatever would make her more than a limp body inside a bridal gown.

Now she sees her cheeks, reddened at last, by the blood of King Duncane. Has she been transformed? Or merely revealed? All she knows is that she is not Roscille of Breizh, not Rosele, Rosalie, not even Roscilla. She is now only Lady Macbeth.

ACT III

KING
HEREAFTER

SEVEN

S HE WAKES. IN THE SAME SPOT WHERE SHE FELL ASLEEP, naked on the bear-rug, still-damp hair clinging to her like a caul. She sits up, unfolds her limbs. The strange thing is that she does not cry. Does not even want to. She digs through the linens in her trunk until she finds a gown and gets dressed. She puts on her most gossamer veil.

Should she appear frozen with shock, expressionless, only cold bewilderment in her eyes? Should she weep like a confused, panicked child? Should she keep her gaze to the ground, as if deaf and mute? Roscille of Breizh would choose this last option. Do not give them anything which they may in the future use against you. That reasoning feels overly simple now. It is better to be one thing on the surface, and another beneath it. Perhaps she should mourn openly. Perhaps it would not be the falsest thing. When she brushes her hands together, she swears she can still feel the faint stickiness of the king's blood.

What will Lady Macbeth do? She does not have time to decide. From down the twisting corridors, someone is shouting.

SHE ARRIVES LAST AT THE scene: Every man who matters is already here. Her husband, standing with his arms crossed, his face unreadable. He has chosen murk and depths. Banquho beside him is flint-eyed, but his chest is puffed out, secretly luxuriating in being so close to his Lord again, no wife to slip between them. Fléance presses close to his father, unable to hide his face: horror and nausea, a greenish tint to his skin.

Roscille pushes farther into the room. She is still below the men's attention, every man but Macbeth. He sees her and beckons her toward him.

Blood reaches all corners of the room. The chamber is a living thing now, with a spreading nexus of veins, flowing outward from its heart, the three piled bodies. Roscille cannot bear more than a glance. She sees the inside of one man's wrist, a marbled white, somehow unspoiled by the carnage around it. That tenderness, curiously protected, in the center of this slaughter, restores her memory. This is a man. *Was* a man. A mother once held him at her breast. A lover once clung to him in sweat-damp sheets.

Evander has dragged the king's body out of his bed, and now he holds his father's limbs to his chest. Tears wet his lashes and he sobs openly, guttural sounds of fury, of sorrow. This is one of the only occasions when a man can weep without being shamed for it—when his crying is threaded with the promise of vengeance.

Lisander kneels in silence. It might be taken as a posture

of penitence, with the chancellor standing over him, but there is no expression on his face. She is glad for his impassiveness, because this is the one thing that might break her, to see his grief.

He reaches forward, into the mess of bodies and blood, and touches the throat of one of the chamberlains. Two fingers pressed, as if searching for a pulse.

"The bodies are hours old," he says, rising. "All the blood is dry, and the rictus has set in."

The chancellor's voice is grave. "We will perform the cruentation at once."

"They will pay," Evander rasps. Still clutching his father's body to his chest, he looks up, with his fierce, damp eyes. "Whatever traitor has done this—I will string him up and tear out his bowels; I will gorge them with milk and honey and let the insects feast on their fattened flesh. I will—"

"The traitors are already dead," Lisander says.

Evander shucks his anger for surprise, redness painting his cheeks. "What? How?"

"Our father has two wounds," he says. "And the swords of his men are soiled with his blood. He is dead by his chamberlains' hands."

Roscille, at last, reaches her husband's side. She watches as understanding slowly overtakes his expression. There is a certain gentleness she has never seen on him before, one that seems to soften his edges. Without warning, he grasps her by the shoulders and pulls her into his chest.

It shocks her so much she is glad her face is hidden against his jerkin, so that no one can hear her quick inhale. Macbeth holds on to her tightly, one arm braced across her back, the other hand pressing her head to his front, large fingers spanning the entire breadth of her skull. He holds on to her as if *she* were the buoy, and he the drowning man. This gesture of affection between husband and wife—there is nothing he could have done to surprise her more.

From between Macbeth's fingers, she sees Lisander's gaze cut to her. It is not angry, exactly, but it is probing. He seeks the secret pain on her face, the evidence of her husband's abuse. She wishes he would not. She fears he will see her poisonous betrayal instead.

"No," Evander says. "These men were loyal and served our clan for years. There is nothing that would provoke them to betrayal. To *this.*" His voice grows strangled. "Our father was loved by all his attendants. I do not believe it."

"The rite of cruentation will reveal all," the chancellor says. "And then, my Lord, you will have your vengeance."

It is time for Macbeth to speak.

"There is treachery in Glammis," he says. "My own wife was attacked not long ago, by masked men. These same men may be your murderers. I will do everything in my power to discover them. And then I will have the vengeance that is owed to me, too."

Clever. He and the prince are now joined in their purpose. Roscille steals a glance at Fléance, to see if he is solid enough to have no reaction to Macbeth's words. The greenish hue has faded from his cheeks; he now looks as pale as the corpses. But this is merely residual horror, she thinks, not genuine fear that they will be discovered. She thinks.

Evander nods slowly, and inhales in a very tremulous way that makes him sound far younger than his years. Grief turning him into a child again. Lisander reaches over and lays a hand on his brother's shoulder, squeezing once. It is this gesture of tenderness that nearly undoes her. How easy these metamorphoses are: men crawling backward to their boyhoods, cold masks slipping to reveal the stricken faces beneath. Roscille knows the secret of how gentle Lisander's hands can be.

So many secrets, she thinks, so many lies, reaching out in all directions, tying her to one man or another. She once feared she would have no allies in Glammis, no confidence. Now she is a creature in a conch shell, everything spiraling out from around her.

IF THIS WERE NAONED, there would be a seamstress kneeling at Roscille's feet and fitting her for a black dress and a black mourning veil. But this is Glammis, so Roscille—who is now accustomed to it—clothes herself. Because she has burned the pewter dress, she has no choice but to wear one that is pearly blue, its neckline far too low to intimate mourning. She does not think the men will take any special note of it, though. The promise of vengeance enacted, blood spilled, and, of course, a crown claimed, obliterates all else.

She empties a bucket into the hearth, where the flames sizzle and die. Bits of gray fabric are caught amid the charred wood. But the room only smells of ash now. There is no rust-tinged treachery in the air. In that moment, Roscille slips out of herself and, like a specter, Lady Macbeth slips in.

THE HOUSEHOLD STAFF IS GATHERED in the main hall; it is the first time Roscille has seen them all together. Messengers, attendants, servants, soldiers. Cooks cringing in their dirty aprons. Stable hands in mud-caked boots, staring at the ground. The guards look most contrite of all. Especially because Evander rages at them for what seems like nearly an hour, face red with lascivious rage.

What is the use of you, if not to keep the king from an enemy's blade?

Are you deaf and cannot hear screams in the night?

I should take your swords and twist them into your own bellies; then you will know the same pain as my father.

I will execute you all for the crime of incompetence. It is just as great a sin as treachery.

Macbeth allows this. Evander is a prince and, even more important, the matter of succession has not been settled. Duncane is no longer alive to execute his will (whatever it might have been). When a crown falls, many arms reach out to catch it. There will be strife between brothers; there always is. And there will be the vultures like her husband, circling overhead.

The firstborn son watches his brother rage in silence. When it seems he will never exhaust himself, Lisander lays a hand on Evander's arm and says, "Enough. You have done your job. They are afraid."

It is true—the messengers and attendants and servants and soldiers, the cooks and stable hands, are all shaking. Evander's chest rises and falls with great, heavy breaths.

"It will never be enough," he says.

He is Roscille's age, or not much older. Seventeen, eighteen. He would be a boy in Glammis, as green as Fléance, without even a near-death wound to display proudly.

"You are muddling your own intention," Lisander says. "With every moment that passes our father's body grows colder."

This pacifies him at last. Evander takes a seat on the dais, head bowed. Roscille thinks she can see him wipe away a tear. With his head bent over like that, he whispers, "Chancellor."

It is an embarrassing display. Roscille knows her husband is thinking it, too. He has not shown strength but rather ungoverned emotion. *How will he rule Alba if he cannot even rule himself?* It is what all Evander's detractors will be coached to say. If there were a tally under each brother's name, this would be a hard mark against him.

The king's body has been laid flat on the dais, his hands clasped across his chest. Because Roscille has seen him sleep, it looks almost as though he is sleeping still. Someone has even brushed his eyelids shut. The chancellor, wielding a jewel-encrusted crucifix, kneels before the body.

The dead chamberlains have been brought forward without ceremony, their bodies heaped at the edge of the dais. The chancellor runs his hand over the king's blood-soaked tunic, murmuring to himself.

"I must be alone for this, with the corpses only," he says. "If you would like me to find out whether these chamberlains were the ones to make the king's death wounds."

"We will test this first," Lisander says. With his unnatural grace, he steps down from the dais. He wears mourning-black, and his leather coat fits tightly over his gamy muscles. The dark circles under his eyes are more pronounced than ever, but his gaze gleams sharp and green above them. An almost inhuman green, like moss the morning after a storm. A color Roscille has not seen since leaving Breizh for barren, wind-blanched Glammis.

Lisander does meet her eyes, then. Unflinching, unafraid, even defiant. Her stomach clutches with fear. *He does not know. He cannot know.* All he knows is that two nights ago she stood at the edge of the cliff and contemplated throwing herself off it. He knows that she has the singe of witchery. He knows that her husband treats her meanly (though this is hardly a revelation). He knows the weight of her body in his arms.

He cannot know the way her throat closes when she sees him or the way tension gathers in her lower belly like a taut metal coil, heated on the forge. Roscille's cheeks burn. She looks away before he does.

Macbeth takes her by the shoulder and leads her from the chamber. His grip is gentler than she expected. Lisander and Evander heave the wooden doors shut.

THE CHANCELLOR WORKS SO QUICKLY there is hardly even time for Roscille to worry. She knows little of cruentation, but apparently it is an easy rite to perform. In minutes, the chancellor is calling out for them, and Evander bursts through the doors.

"What news?" he demands, striding through the hall, overturning a wooden bench in his wake. The scrape of wood against stone makes Roscille flinch.

Yet they need only approach the dais to know. Both of the king's death wounds are leaking. The old blood is sluggish, more black than red, like mud forced from its banks by the melting of spring. But he is bleeding indeed.

Evander gives a choked cry and drops to his knees. He shields his face, though that cannot disguise the sounds of his weeping. Lisander puts a hand on his brother's shoulder again. There is even more significance to this gesture now; it speaks so many words while saying none aloud. Roscille has no siblings and cannot understand the special affection which grows between them. But she does understand the message that Lisander means to send. He loves his brother. It will not come to war between them, over their father's crown. At least not easily.

"These were not men who would turn on the king for nothing," Lisander says, "and give their own lives for it. There is greater conspiracy at work here. In Glammis."

He turns to Macbeth and, by extension, Roscille. They have stood together this whole time, husband and wife. The hand and the dagger. Lord and Lady Macbeth.

"As I have told you, there is treachery here," Macbeth says. "Sowed discontent among my clan. Fléance—come. Tell the prince what you know."

His voice roughens on that word, *prince*. Hesitantly, Fléance steps forward. The wound Roscille bore him stands out even in this half-light, still healing, still a bit gruesome. His honor will not be doubted.

"I took the Lady for a ride about the lands," Fléance says. "She was eager to see more of her new home. There was no reason to think— The Lord is a respected man. He does well for his clan."

He pauses. Roscille closes her eyes. Let them think she grieves at remembering this fearful moment. Let them think nothing more.

"A man without enemies is a man without power," Macbeth says. "Go on."

Fléance swallows, his throat bobbing, distorting the wound.

"There were masked men, three of them. They struck the Lady to unconsciousness. I fought them off, but I could not give chase without risking the life of Lady Roscilla."

Lisander's gaze flickers to her. "Lady Roscilla—is this true?"

Roscille used to think there was no state more powerless than one of forced silence. Of words that mean nothing, touch no one. But now she is a dog, commanded: *Speak.* Lie for your life. This is a castle of consequences. Every word has its echo.

"Yes," she says, meeting his eyes. "It was— I do not wish to recount it."

Lisander holds her stare for a long moment. She remembers Macbeth's words. *The prince of Cumberland is too clever.*

At last, Lisander says, "Understandable." And then he blinks and looks away.

Roscille exhales.

Words pass among the princes and the chancellor and Banquho and Macbeth. One clan is named, then another. All men who may be killed falsely, whose lines will be ended for her lies.

"I will ride and seek out these traitors," Evander declares. "They will know the sting of the blade, and I will taste the tang of their blood."

"Our Druide has already performed cruentation on all the men of the nearby villages," Macbeth says. "But there are still more, in farther towns. I swear to you, I will not rest until we both have our vengeance. In King Duncane's name."

Evander nods. "Then let us go."

"Forgive me," the chancellor says, "but I cannot allow this matter to go undiscussed. Soon the world will know that Alba is without a king. And a country without a king is a meal for vultures."

This is the man who has sat in the king's war councils. He is right: The peace with England is Duncane's peace, his dead wife's peace, the peace buoyed by the Saxon blood running through the veins of his sons. Æthelstan has no love for Scotland otherwise. And the Irish and the Northmen and the Welsh are sharpening their own claws in the meantime. A king's death is a wound: It cannot be left untreated for long. Blood will fill it.

The room thrums with silence.

"Brother," Evander says. "You know our father's will. It must be you."

Lisander's face hardens. He does not speak. Roscille is as puzzled as the others in the silent hall—any man would leap to claim this easy power, presented to him like wine for gulping.

At last, he replies, "And you know our father's mind was muddled by sentiment."

Fiercely, Evander shakes his head. "No. It is the duty of the living to respect the wishes of the dead. Our father's body may have been impaired, but his reasoning was not. You are the elder. You are—"

"Not fit," Lisander cuts in.

He speaks in Saxon. There is a rumbling among the men gathered in the hall. Not all of them know Saxon and many will not understand. Even the ones who do will be perplexed. Lisander is a discomfiting presence, dark and silent where his brother is ebullient and bright, but this alone is not enough to warrant him being passed over. Far more ill-fit men have ruled kingdoms before.

"You refuse what any other man would slay a thousand

for," Evander responds, in his own angry Saxon. "You think yourself not a man—it is your mind that is muddled by sentiment in this matter, brother."

The air in the hall is growing dense and hot, as if filled with smoke. For a long moment neither prince speaks. Then, blinking and clearing his throat, the chancellor steps forward.

"We may put off the coronation until we return to Moray," he says—in Scottish, to quell tempers. "But Alba's enemies are many and they are hungry. We must not show an infirmity."

It is almost funny, to hear him say this—Scotland has been ruled for decades by infirmity; its king diseased, wasting. Moray is the chosen seat of Duncane's clan. It is a week's ride from Glammis, at least. Enough time for news to spread like the light from signal fires; enough time for distant lords to gather their armies and distant kings to consult their war councils and seek the blessings of their priests.

"We will go to Moray, then," says Lisander. "And if there is talk, we can say the king died of illness. It would come as no surprise."

"And leave our father's murder unavenged?" Evander demands. "No. I will not go to Moray until I have found the traitors and slain them. Any further rule will be tainted, until this is done. Already clan Dunkeld is—"

He stops himself abruptly. Yes, there are rumors about Duncane's clan; with such a mysterious and terrible and enduring affliction, how could there not be suspicions that it is divine punishment? It is said often that this is why Duncane wed a pious woman, why he dresses his Druides in gold and seats them at his council table. All of it silent penance for a secret crime. Of course, these are stories only, true in the minds of some, and ash in the mouths of others.

"Let us ride out now," Macbeth says to Evander. "I will bring you to every village in a day's distance—Fléance, you will come as well. I will bring my own Druide. And I will find these traitors, on pain of death."

Evander's ordinarily bright, ruddy face is uncommonly pale, yet even now he and Lisander barely look like brothers. His chest swells.

"Fine," he says. "I will go on with you and the boy. Lisander, you and the chancellor must prepare to depart for Moray."

Lisander is quick to reply, "We should not be apart from each other in this moment; it will show weakness. Let us go to Moray together, now. We can return to Glammis again with the force of an army."

Macbeth looks as if he will say something, but Evander's response is immediate.

"I will not leave Glammis without wetting my blade," he snaps. "We owe our father this much."

The two brothers wage a silent war. Separate and stay, or unite and leave? But Evander is the sun and his heat and rage cannot be tempered by Lisander's cool, remote reasoning. Eventually, Lisander averts his gaze.

Roscille has known her husband long enough now to read his expression, even when his eyes try to hide their burning. Now it is the twitch of his lip which gives him away. Though it does not quite dare to be a smile, he is pleased.

To Fléance, Macbeth says, "Saddle the horses."

Fléance, still chafing at being called *boy,* dips his head and takes slightly mutinous steps out of the chamber.

"Shall I come as well, my Lord?" Banquho asks.

"Yes, you might as well," says Macbeth—and now it is Banquho who fumes: He has become an afterthought.

Macbeth then turns to Lisander. And then to Roscille.

"I wish you safe travels," he says. "My wife will see that you are sent off with supplies and goodwill."

MACBETH AND HIS PARTY EXIT the castle and Roscille cannot breathe. It is the necklace, curling around her throat like a seizing serpent. It is Lisander's stare, his singular presence, the fact that they are alone for the first time since the night he rescued her, promised his protection, the offer that she spurned so horrifically, instead dampening her hands with his father's blood. It is the way her husband looked at her before he left, the way he said *my wife,* the two syllables falling like stones. When his gaze cut between her and Lisander, it was with the sharpness of a blade. There were two second, secret syllables hidden in that look.

Kill him.

She cannot. It is too much; he cannot expect her to do this. She has only just cleaned her hands. She has given three different men their deaths. Is this what it means, truly, to be Lady Macbeth? Sorceress, murderer, the dagger in her husband's hand? Or perhaps she has always been this. All of Wrybeard's courtiers, le Tricheur—they were right to fear her. Glammis has peeled off the dressings of innocence and uncovered the inhumanity beneath.

Lisander has been watching her in silence. Even in this mostly dark hall, his black hair catches the light and gleams. He brushes it back from his face, a swift, common gesture that makes her throat tighten even further. His hand moves with such deftness, the tendons on the inside of his wrist flexing.

In a quiet voice, she says, "I will have the kitchens prepare rations for your journey. Let me give them the order. Wait—wait here . . ."

Lisander nods. His lips part, and Roscille is momentarily fascinated by this simple action, too—the delicate opening, the skillful flick of his tongue.

"I will be in my chamber," he says. And then, before Roscille can say another word, he exits the hall.

THE KITCHENS. ROSCILLE HAS NEVER been before, but at least here there is little difference between Macbeth's castle and the Duke's. There are the blood-soaked butcher blocks, the baskets of apples and root vegetables, the hanging braids of garlic, the fire-grease-rust scent in the air. The cooks stammer out their greetings, as surprised to see the Lady here as she is surprised to be here. She waves them off. They scatter.

She still has Macbeth's dagger in her chamber, but she will not use it. If she must do it, she cannot kill him with the same blade her husband used to kill Cawder; she cannot give him the brusque, ugly death of a stranger to a stranger. A kitchen knife is the closest thing there could be to a *woman's weapon*—perhaps it will make Lisander's death wound suspicious, but that hardly matters now. By the time the sun sets, Duncane's line will be ended.

King Hereafter.

There is a place where wooden pegs have been driven into the wall, and instruments hung upon them. Blade after blade, some of them serrated, others smooth, some meant for dicing and chopping, others for sawing and rending. Roscille's hand hovers in front of her eyes. It looks as white as the rotten hands of the washerwomen. It is shaking.

She takes the smallest knife, the one whose absence will attract the least attention, the one that will slip most easily into her bodice. The metal is cool against her skin. Her flesh does not warm it. She is bloodless, a serpent-woman. When she leaves the kitchens, she does not even hear her footsteps on the floor, only the tide that rushes up from the darkness below, as if straining toward the light.

Lisander's chamber is easy to find—courtyard-side, without a window.

Roscille does not knock, just steps inside. The room is not unlike her own: equally as small, though without the resplendent bear-rug. Lisander is kneeling in front of the trunk, his lithe hands working to pack things away. Clothes, a bedroll. She tries to see if there are any blades glinting among the cloth, but she cannot find any. If Lisander has weapons, they are well disguised.

It will not matter, she tells herself. *Once I lift my veil, nothing will matter at all.*

Lisander looks up at her. "Lady Roscille."

He knows. She does not know how, or how she can perceive this knowing from him, but Roscille's veins suddenly run with ice. It is something in his eyes, those impossibly, surpassingly green eyes. Her heart stutters. His hand curls around the edge of the trunk.

Roscille takes a step forward, feeling the knife against her ribs. Lisander starts to rise. But as soon as he is on his feet, she raises her hand, and does not merely lift her veil but removes it completely, tearing it off, letting it drift to the floor.

Unguarded, her eyes meet his.

She has only ever known this feeling once, with the stable boy, but years have passed since then, and as her body has grown, her passions have grown with it. Bloomed red and hot, as quick as marigolds. Roscille takes another step, and then falls, and Lisander catches her arms with his arms and her mouth with his mouth.

Once he has hold, he presses her to him. Her hand finds the nape of his neck, and his skin there is as soft as she imagined it would be, like the velvety petals of a rose. Her lips part for his tongue, and he moves into her without contrition, as if his body is made for this purpose alone. One arm lowers to circle her waist, and the other tangles itself in her hair, tugging her head back so that his lips can brush along her jawline, down her throat.

Roscille whines, a keening, puppyish sound she never knew she could make. That coiling heat in the bottom of her belly moves lower, deeper, until it is a pulse between her thighs. And then, as if it is pulsing outward, this desire, Lisander grasps her firmly by the waist, lifts her easily, dexterously, and lays her on the bed beneath him.

He looks down at her, straight into her eyes. No mortal man has done this and lived. Her hair spills out silver against the sheets.

"You are beautiful," he whispers.

She does not know what compels her to whisper back, "Strange. Unnatural."

"No," he says. "You have been made to fit a shape that confines you. That does not serve you."

Roscille cannot figure out where her compulsion ends and he begins. Whether these are her words that have merely snuck into his mouth. She considers it for a moment, with a twist of guilt, of grief—and then finds she does not care. The air is heavy, thick and sweet. Whatever this fire is, it consumes them both.

His lips are against her throat, and another sound rises up in her, unbidden. She feels shameful in her need, so she presses her face to his shoulder, muffling her moan against his jacket—the leather, too, impossibly smooth. His mouth will leave marks; she has seen them on a hundred serving girls before, a cluster of bruises, purple with red pricking through them as blood rises to the surface but does not spill.

Roscille almost protests, for this is certainly beyond what her husband will allow, even within his order (*Kill him*). Before she can, Lisander unclasps her necklace. He slips it off her, and it is lost in the sheets.

"I have hated seeing you wear this," he murmurs.

Roscille unhides her face. "Why?"

"Spoils from his conquest of Cawder, yes? Your husband's garish pride, stamped upon you."

She feels bold enough to capture his face in her hands, tilting his chin toward her. "What if I told you it was not only his pride, but my protection? It is like a shield."

The corner of his mouth lifts. "Then I will allow you your armor again when we are through."

Lisander slides between her thighs. His hips, cleaving her apart. He kisses her mouth once more, and her fingers fumble at the laces of his jacket, but he is not there long enough for her to get it loose: His lips touch the hollow of her collarbone, and then he follows the line of her bodice with his mouth— *the knife, the knife,* she panics briefly, but the fear is washed away in waves of pleasure—until his head is ducked between her knees.

He kisses her up her thighs, grasping at her flesh, which is white and soft with the ease of a noble lady's life, until he reaches that place where she has hardly dared to touch herself—first because it is a sin, for a woman to find pleasure on her own terms, absent of a man, and second because she does not want to be weak in her wanting, slave to the lusts of her body. She has always believed her form cannot be trusted, that it will betray her calculating mind.

Now she cares nothing for these convictions. She fists the sheets as Lisander moves between her thighs, his mouth hot and sweet, and there is something cresting in her, like blood trying to break the skin. She arches her hips off the bed, and puts a hand over her mouth to muffle the mortifying and too-human sound. She has never felt so horribly, wonderfully embodied before.

Suddenly he stops. Lisander lifts his head and leans over her, no longer gentle as he grasps the knife through her bodice.

Roscille's heart crashes to a halt, but she cannot speak. When he meets her gaze, there is no more languid tenderness there. It is sharp, like green cut-glass.

"Wait—" she chokes out.

She tries to push him off, to rise from the bed. But then his hand is around her throat.

EIGHT

IS HAND DOES NOT EXERT ENOUGH PRESSURE TO hurt, not really—not unless she strains against him, and then it is more panic than pain, the feeling of breath slowly leaving her. Roscille makes a wordless noise of protest as Lisander's other hand reaches beneath her bodice and retrieves the knife. He examines it for a moment, with a low exhale that is almost amused, and then tosses it aside. It clatters against the stone, far out of reach.

"Macbeth must be an impoverished warrior, if he sends his wife to do such ugly work for him."

"Please," she says. "Let me go."

"So you may try and ensorcell me again?"

"I was not— I am not—"

"You *are*," says Lisander. "You are what they say, Roscille of Breizh. *Witch*."

He uses the Brezhoneg word, not the Scots. Roscille

grasps at his wrist with both of her hands, trying to pry herself loose, but her efforts are fruitless; he is too strong. Tears come to the corners of her vision. She squeezes her eyes shut and says, "I am nothing but the dagger in my husband's hand."

The words are empty; they have no echo. Lisander lets out another half-amused breath.

"You may succeed in convincing others of this, others who luxuriate in the idea that women have no power except that which men grant them." With his free hand, he reaches down and smooths her skirts back over her thighs: an absurd gesture, almost chivalrous, as if to help her regain her lost modesty. "You may not have driven the blade yourself, but I know those men died at your orchestration."

Roscille is now aware she will not win by playing at innocence, so she tries anger, which only ends up sounding petulant. "And how do you know that? The chancellor performed the cruentation himself."

"The chancellor has no wisdom, only dry ritual."

"It is bold of you to dishonor your father's favorite adviser."

"Not so bold as murdering my father in his bed."

Roscille has no response to this. She presses her lips shut.

Unexpectedly, Lisander loosens his grip, just enough for Roscille to shove his hands away and push herself to a sitting position. Her eyes are hot. She tries to spy, over his shoulder, the knife glinting on the floor, but she cannot find it. And Lisander and his lithe, strong body are between her and the door.

"Do not try to run," he says.

"I was not planning to."

A series of incredulous events unfold: Lisander reties the

laces of his jacket, where Roscille wrested them open. He fishes for the ruby necklace among the sheets and holds it out to her. It is coiled in his palm like a cold snake. She snatches it back, face burning.

"Thank you," she bites out.

Lisander nods.

Roscille is suddenly overcome by a novel humiliation. The last moments play over in her mind: her falling wantonly into his arms, him pressing her into the bed and kissing her breathless, all while she believed he was under her lustful spell. He had not truly been ensorcelled, and those passionate words that had so enflamed her were spoken under false pretense. He had been concerned only with the knife in her bodice and how to take it from her.

"Did you mean none of it, then?" The words come out before she can stop them. The question of a vain, frivolous little girl.

"Should I not ask you the same?" Lisander's sharp gaze meets hers. "All your desire feigned, the means to an end— a way to maneuver the dagger to my throat?"

She feels almost numb with embarrassment. "Witch, you name me. Such creatures have no sentiments."

"I do not believe that."

He says it without hesitation, and with such conviction that it surprises her. She regards him, skin still prickling with heat. His hair is mussed from their exertions, but still it shines, like the ocean under moonlight. His narrow nose, carved as if by a sculptor's chisel; his cheekbones high ledges below the dark, sleepless shadows. A purple bruise blooms on his throat. Roscille feels an odd, debauched sense of satisfaction, know- ing she has marked him, too.

"What will you do with me?" she asks at last. "Slit my throat in your bed?"

Lisander's gaze darts to the corner, where finally Roscille spots the knife, its blade glinting in the hearth's soft firelight. It will take him two strides to reach it. Another two strides, the thrust of his sword-arm, to pare away her flesh with it. She can do nothing to beat back her death. Her eyes do not ensorcell him; she has no more protection than the flimsy necklace. She feels even more humiliated now, to have called this stupid bauble *armor.*

"No," he says.

Here, though, he does hesitate. Can she truly blame him? She came to his chamber with a knife; she orchestrated his father's death. And she gave him a witch's death, at that, the swords only reaching King Duncane's heart thanks to her powers of compulsion. There could not be any greater disgrace upon his father's name.

Further still, she has thrown all of Alba into chaos. Made him reach for a crown he does not even want. As much as she tries, she cannot think of a reason why he would spare her, now.

Roscille tilts up her chin. "Why not?"

"You are of no use to me dead," Lisander says. "If I am to bargain with your husband, it would not do to start negotiations by presenting his wife's corpse." He pauses. "But I suppose it is perhaps too hopeful of me, to believe he may allow words to pass between us before he reaches for his sword."

Roscille thinks of Macbeth, his horrifying largeness. It has become ordinary to her, and therefore less horrifying, but whenever Roscille is outside of herself, mind untethered from her body, he is a mountain again, a great rock creature, fed and formed by the soil of Glammis. Lisander is strong, and sleek like a water spirit, but she cannot imagine he could match her husband, Bellona's bridegroom.

She should not grieve this. It should relieve her. Moments ago, she thought she would die with Lisander's fingers around her neck. Suddenly her own hand leaps up to her throat, where the bruises made by his mouth are pulsing. Fear pools in her stomach.

As if he can read this fear, Lisander says, "The necklace will cover them."

A fast, red flush again. "You will not reveal me?"

"Revealing you would damn us both, Lady Roscille. Does Macbeth really need another cause for killing me?" He shakes his head and is silent a moment. Then, lowly, he says, "I promised you protection from him. I will not relinquish that vow."

"I did not think you the sort of man who holds to vows merely because he made them, even when they no longer serve him."

Lisander does not reply; he merely looks down at her, gaze strangely soft. His stillness and silence force Roscille to contemplate her position, which even now is quite compromising. Though he has allowed her to sit, he keeps one arm braced around her thigh, holding her in the bed.

Then, abruptly, the corner of his mouth lifts. "A clever way to say you think me dishonorable."

Roscille tries to keep her expression serene, remote. "What other reason would you have for refusing the crown? Spurning your dead father's wish?"

Finally Lisander's face shutters. He stands up, withdrawing his arm from around her leg, and Roscille cannot help but feel bereft at the loss of his touch.

"I do not relish this," he says. "But you have given me no choice. Stand."

She does. Her legs feel limp; between her thighs, she is still slick.

Lisander reaches for the sheet. He tears a strip free easily, muscles scarcely flexing; she is surprised by this subtle, graceful strength, which seems almost inhuman. He guides her arms around her back and binds her wrists together. The fabric is not coarse, but it is still tight enough to chafe.

Then he leaves her standing there and walks across the room to retrieve her fallen veil. When he bends over, Roscille sees the way his spine presses through the leather of his jacket; she can count every notch of bone, protruding sharply like fins.

As he approaches her, he keeps his gaze on the ground, but when he reaches her, and they are standing close again, he looks up, directly into her eyes, pinning her in place with his stare.

Roscille stares back, chin trembling with defiance.

Without his gaze ever shifting, Lisander sets her veil back in place. His ministrations are precise, and gentler than she deserves. When the fabric falls again over her eyes, he stares for just a moment more, and then averts his gaze at last.

From his trunk, he retrieves a sheathed sword. His movement is again too deft: The sword is lifted and then strapped to his belt in the time it takes her to blink.

"Come," he says, beckoning her toward the door. His voice is hard and cold.

Roscille has no choice but to obey.

Her thoughts have been so scattered that she has not had time to ruminate upon this. Now, without other occupation, as Lisander prods her through the threshold and into the corridor, the realization forces itself into her mind. No mortal man has ever looked into her eyes and lived, yet Lisander did and still he moves and breathes and runs with blood. He was not compelled, not ensorcelled. Roscille looks back over her shoulder at the windowless room, and her eyes follow the strange marks slashed along the stone wall, no pattern to them, nothing her senses can constellate, and knows, with the certainty of a lightning strike, that Lisander is no mortal man.

AS SHE IS MANEUVERED THROUGH the long, twisting hallways, Roscille crafts excuses, for when Macbeth will inevitably command her to speak.

He was too strong, my Lord, he knew I was coming. I am sorry. He is too clever, as you have said.

I will do better. I will not displease you. I will not disgrace you.

And then, for the bruises at her throat: *It is the necklace, my Lord. Your honor leaves its mark on me.* It all sounds whinging and witless, even in her own mind. She has lost her innocence, well and truly. It is a trick that is now forbidden to her, a mask she may no longer wear. Roscille of Breizh was timid; Lady Macbeth is not.

Lisander forces her at a pace, and by the time they reach the courtyard, she is breathless. The chancellor has found his way here as well, red-cheeked with exertion that must be unusual to him, after years spent luxuriating at King Duncane's side. He leans over, hands on his knees, looking very old.

There is another man hidden inside the chancellor: a

farmer, a fisherman, a shepherd. The monk he must have been once, shaved head as bald as a baby's, before he was plucked from his quiet abbey to attend the king. Roscille sees these men layered over one another, like the rings of a tree, more ancient closer to the center. She is surprised that she can still manage to glimpse this, cold creature she has become. But when she blinks, the vision dissipates.

The barbican grinds open. Three horses skid into the courtyard, kicking up dust. Spooked horses, their eyes rolled to the whites, snorting and salivating. One rider is Banquho, another Fléance. The last, Macbeth.

Tartans are ripped and brows are sweat-dewed, but Roscille can see no injuries. While there are no open wounds, blood is in the air. Macbeth breathes hard as he dismounts his horse, fury rolling off him in waves.

"You false, shrinking coward," Macbeth snarls. "Unhand my wife."

"Coward?" Lisander echoes. "It is you who sends your wife to do your rough work."

Lisander's sword-point is pressed against the small of her back. If there is any sudden, graceless movement by either of them, she will be stuck through with its blade like a pig on a spit.

"Cowardice runs in the blood of Duncane." Macbeth begins to circle them, his own blade flashing. "Your brother fled at the sight of our swords, like a frightened deer. He will first seek refuge at the keep of that witless Macduff, and then he will make his way to Æthelstan's court—too craven to fight his battles alone."

"Most would think it more craven to come at a man with

three swords against one." Lisander nods toward Banquho and
Fléance, still astride their horses. "Your right hand is clumsy,
Thane of Glammis. Hardly more able than his sulking son. All
three of you, outridden by a man barely out of boyhood."

With a furious growl, Banquho drops down from his saddle. Fléance follows him, chest heaving, and from this vantage
point even the near-death wound seems faint, pale, drained of
its honor.

Macbeth does not speak to defend them. Instead, he smiles
thinly.

"Clearly you understand the arithmetic of your position,
Prince of Cumberland," he says. "One sword will never triumph against three, and unlike your brother, you have nowhere to run."

The wind blows in a great, sweeping gust through the
courtyard, grasping at Roscille's veil. She hopes this will account for the way her eyes are watering, that her husband
will not see her crying—or if he does, he will think it out of
fear for her own life, not out of grief for what she imagines
will come. The sword-thrust that will strike Lisander from the
earth.

But if Lisander feels such fear, he does not show it on his
face. His green gaze is steady.

"I would suggest you think on your position, too, Thane
of Glammis," he says. "My brother will reach Æthelstan's court
within the week, and once he arrives, all of England will be
moved to his cause. Name yourself King if you choose, but
Alba is a country in pieces. How many thanes will join you
when they know it means standing against Æthelstan's army?
I am your only hope for gaining allies in Scotland, and your

only hope for peace with England. Evander will bargain for my life, but he will make no concessions for a corpse. And you know well that the lion always devours the unicorn."

Macbeth grows still where he stands. The wind brushes through his hair and beard, braiding it with cold. Roscille's blood is frozen in her veins. Lisander does not blink, does not falter.

Her husband may be an artificer of violence, but he is not completely without reason. Roscille knows by now he is more than a dull brute. These long moments pass like water, rising, falling, drenching the shore, retreating, rising, and falling again, smothering the sand with streaks of foam.

Finally, Macbeth's words come through gritted teeth.

"Drop your sword," he says to Lisander. And then, over his shoulder, he calls out to Banquho and Fléance: "Clap him in chains and put him in a cell."

The pressure in her back is relieved as Lisander's sword falls to the earth. She exhales, but there is no true alleviation of tension, of terror, as Macbeth strides toward her and grasps her around the shoulders, pulling her small body against his colossal chest.

"I'm sorry—" she begins.

"No," he says, quiet but firm. "Not now."

She cannot bring herself to watch as Banquho and Fléance descend upon Lisander, grasping each of his arms, dragging him out of the courtyard. Yet she cannot bear to look away, either. She meets Lisander's eyes, which are still cold and unreadable, and too appallingly, exquisitely green.

"Traitor!" cries a sudden, warbling voice. "You, Macbeth—turncoat, apostate! You slew the king in his bed!"

Slowly, Macbeth turns. It is the chancellor who shouts from across the courtyard, trembling in his fine robes, clutching the jeweled crucifix in thin, gnarled fingers.

"Silence," Banquho bites out.

Macbeth holds up a hand.

"Think on your position, Chancellor," he says. "Your old master is dead and cannot protect you. You are trapped now, in the castle of his killer. You have two choices: You may bow to me, or you may follow Duncane to his grave."

The chancellor quivers, like a reed blown through with wind. His mouth opens, then shuts. Because she's still pressed to Macbeth's chest, Roscille's vision grows blurry and hot and she cannot breathe.

After several moments of silence, the chancellor lowers himself to his knees. He sets his crucifix down in the dirt and raises his arms above his head. He tips forward, face to the dusty ground, palms flat and open against the earth. Pure supplication. Complete surrender. Macbeth will savor this image like the headiest of spirits.

Macbeth approaches. His footsteps are as loud as stones dropped from a great height. When he reaches the prostrating chancellor, he tips his head to the side, considering the lowly form of this man. Shame stirs up from him, like clouds of dust.

The blade drives swift and true through the chancellor's wattled neck. Macbeth has killed so many men that he knows precisely where to strike, how to deliver the exact wound he desires. He crafts each kill with the cleverest touch. Sometimes there will be a showy bleeding, a gasping for breath, a long, drawn-out dying, if this serves his purpose. But now it is brutal and brief. The chancellor has no last words. His already-slumped body hardly moves from its position. There is a single spasm, like the flopping of a fish. And then only a growing red circle in the dirt.

"I have no use for another driveling priest," says Macbeth.

He removes his sword with a subtle twist, which creates the sound of splintering bone. He lifts the blade in the air and licks its tip, tasting the chancellor's carefully crafted death. And, too, he has crafted this message, shown to all who can see the redness wet his lips: He is observing the rite of *first* blood, which means there will be more blood soon to follow.

MACBETH DOES NOT GO TO his hall, to quench his thirst with wine or to spread maps across his war table. He goes instead to his chamber. Roscille has been ordered, with only a sharp jerk of his head, to follow. She trails after him in silence, and when they reach the room he ushers her in, then shuts the door behind her. All this time he has not even looked at her, not into her eyes, through the veil.

A servant comes with a bucket of water. Roscille stands on the bear-rug with her hands clasped in front of her, gaze fixed on the dead animal's face, praying she can appear contrite enough to please him, praying that his eyes do not linger too long on her throat.

She raises her head only when she hears her husband drop his sword unceremoniously onto the floor; it clatters on the stone, blade still flashing red. Then he unlaces his jerkin and yanks his shirt over his head.

Her mouth turns dry with fear. No, she thinks, no, there

are still two of her requests left to fulfill, still two trials before bloodied sheets and bloodied thighs and the terror of a child growing inside her—but perhaps her failure, his anger, will have moved Macbeth beyond care of the old custom. Bile rises in her throat.

But her husband still does not face her as he says, "Bring the water and cloth."

With slow, creaking movements, Roscille kneels beside the bucket. She soaks the rag in the water, then draws it up and wrings it out, until it is damp but not dripping. Then she rises again. Macbeth turns to her at last, naked from waist to head, and looks expectant.

Roscille has never seen this much of her husband, or of any man, before. His chest is a craggy landscape, broad hills and narrow valleys, long divots like dried-up streambeds, bones fitted together in an intricate puzzle under his skin. The skin, cratered with scars. One broad and short along his left shoulder; another, long and sinewy, across his abdomen. It is transformed by the swelling of his muscles, made all the more gruesome and bizarre. The way it is raised, the wound must have been terrible. Deep.

Hands trembling, Roscille approaches him. A thin film of sweat and grime covers his skin. She lifts the rag and dabs it on the hollow of his throat. This seems the least frightening place to start. She has, after all, seen this part of him before, the first near-death scar. Macbeth's pulse throbs under her hand.

Roscille is a noble lady and has never cleaned anything in her life; only now that Hawise has been taken from her has she learned to wash herself. She scrubs hesitantly at the line of his collarbone.

Macbeth grunts. "Am not made of glass."

Her own neck prickles. "I'm sorry, my Lord."

She scrubs harder, at first with the rag held between her thumb and forefinger, and then, when she reaches the broader planes of his chest, she spreads the rag beneath her open palm. Macbeth's heart beats in steady thumps. She feels it humming up through his skin.

When Roscille kneels to rinse the rag and soak it with new water, Macbeth says, "You did not kill him."

Her fingers curl around the cloth. It drips and drips and drips onto the stone floor, the only sound in the room. The water is cold and now so is her hand.

"No," she says slowly. "I did not."

The water forms a small pool on the floor. Her husband watches her, through the veil. Can he know? Will he see the way her lips are swollen, just slightly, tender to the touch? Will the necklace slip down to reveal the red marks made by another man's mouth? Can he smell the adultery on her, like blood alerting the senses of a hound? Roscille draws a breath that sucks the veil inward.

If she chose, she could reveal Lisander for what he is—or rather, what he is not: He is not a mortal man. But what will this achieve? A secret only has value until it is spent. Then it is dust. She cannot see how it will advantage her, to spend this secret now.

And Lisander is the only man alive—so long as he remains alive—who may see her truly, her unguarded eyes. When she is gone from the world, she realizes, a piece of her soul will go with him—the clandestine, mystic knowledge that Roscille is almost too afraid to discover. *What do you see, inside me? Speak truth. Tell me what mortal men cannot.*

"It is good," Macbeth says. "He is of greater use to us alive."

The knot in her stomach loosens slightly. "As hostage?"

"As a hostage, yes—who knows how much Æthelstan will cede for his safe return? In the meantime, he will provide good knowledge of our enemies. Their plots, their powers. How many Scotsmen will rally to his brother's side—and how great an army Æthelstan can raise in England. He will not disclose this information for nothing, of course. But there are ways to make men speak."

Roscille feels her throat closing. She is no stranger to this, of course; she was raised in the court of Alan Varvek. The Duke is miserly with his violence, but when he does spend it, he spends it lavishly. His torture chambers are as opulent as his feasting halls. His racks are always well oiled, so the metal does not scream when the victim does. His saws are sharpened weekly. Breizh's finest blacksmiths crafted the spikes on his chair. His breaking wheel has never once broken.

She has to swallow hard before she can ask, "Will this not affect his value as hostage? Evander may pay less for a damaged good."

Macbeth huffs. "No man comes out of war intact and clean. Even the cosseted boy-prince knows this." He looks down at the rag dripping in her hand. "Go on."

Roscille raises her hand and scrubs again at his chest. He is solid, impenetrable. Nothing gives way beneath her touch. She hopes he cannot feel the way her fingers tremble. If she closes her eyes for the briefest moment, if she even blinks, she can see the darkness of a dungeon, pricked with the light of glinting silver blades. If she were alone, she would retch.

If Macbeth does notice her quaking, he does not remark upon it. Instead, he says, "I will entrust this to you."

A shock along her spine, as if she's been prodded. "What?"

"I leave for Moray tomorrow, with the joined armies of Glammis and Cawder. Once I take Duncane's throne, the rest of Alba will fall to its knees before me. And while I am away, you are the Lady of Glammis. The prince's questioning will be your purview, the whole castle under your keep."

Roscille stops scrubbing. "You will leave me here alone?"

Macbeth mistakes this for attachment. Affection. He smiles.

"I will not be gone too long," he says. "And when I return, Glammis will be the new seat of power in Alba. I will be King, and you will be Queen, hereafter."

Her mind returns to a dark place. Not an imagined dungeon this time, but the basement, with its damp, filthy air. With its churning waters and rattling chains. Les Lavandières gleam in the blackness, showing streaks of curdled skin. Their blind eyes are too cloudy to hold the torchlight. Their augury rises from the water like fog, syllables of prophecy scraping the jagged ceiling.

All hail Macbeth, Thane of Glammis.

All hail Macbeth, Thane of Cawder.

All hail Macbeth, King Hereafter.

"I do not know how to keep a castle," Roscille says at last, weakly.

"You will have help. I am leaving Banquho and Fléance behind."

Bewilderment shadows her thoughts. Fléance has proven himself, however falsely, an able soldier. Banquho promised him time on the battlefield, swore that he would not be forsaken again. And Banquho himself?

"But my Lord," she says, true puzzlement in her voice, "Banquho is your right hand."

Macbeth's gaze rests upon her for a long moment. She cannot read the emotions behind his eyes. Lisander's words return to her. *Your right hand is clumsy.* Perhaps these words, spoken merely to rile and taunt, are truer than she imagined.

"A great warrior can fight just as well with his left," Macbeth answers finally. "They let the prince escape. I cannot worry that they may falter again." He pauses. "And I have not forgotten the treachery among my clan. I will not risk you to more of these masked cowards. Banquho and his son will serve and protect you, in my absence."

Is *this* attachment? Affection? Surely it is intended mostly as a punishment for Banquho and Fléance, for the extremities that failed him, but it would be punishment enough to be left behind without suffering the ignominy of serving a woman in the place of their Lord. He disgraces his own most loyal men to feed the honor of his wife. Roscille tries harder to read the look on Macbeth's face.

She tries to see herself, from his eyes. Here is the foreign bride who is learning to speak Scots like a native. Here is the girl asking for a cloak made from the creatures of her new homeland. Here is the Lady who has killed for him three times over, and then washed the blood from her hands and pretended to shrink and simper under her veil. Here is a witch who wears her manacles like bracelets, who calls her shackles *armor.* Here is the wife who has served him in every manner a wife is meant to serve her husband. Except for one.

She has arranged herself into a shape that pleases him. She

sits comfortably in the order of Macbeth's world. And for this she has earned *his* prophecy. *Queen Hereafter.*

A vision spreads out in front of her, a waking dream. The pool of lampreys, bordered neatly by stones, the eels swimming in their unending circles. Their lithe bodies twist in and out of the water, silver spines braiding the blackness. Light and dark and dark and light. Her reflection ripples in the pool's center.

The lampreys converge on her, blind mouths feeling for flesh. Within moments, Roscille of Breizh has been consumed. Lady Macbeth stands above the water, and the eels resume their circling, waiting for the next creature that will be pushed before their teeth.

"Your faith honors me, my Lord," Roscille whispers.

He does not know that she once prayed for his death. Tried to push him before the blades of his enemies. He does not know that she needfully opened her legs for another man.

"You have proven yourself worth honoring," says Macbeth. He takes the rag from her hand, drops it into the bucket. "I know that Glammis will be well kept in your care. And I will expect a messenger soon, bearing the confessions of the prince."

Roscille swallows.

Macbeth suddenly clasps her by the shoulders and pulls her toward him, crushing her body against his bare chest. His skin is cold, damp. Hard and ridged, practically stone. Roscille feels his stillness spreading to her, like lichen blooming white on deadwood.

Then he leans down and presses one brusque kiss to her forehead, through the fabric of the veil. His lips are rough. The kiss reminds her of a dog's tongue, rasping her palm. He holds her more tightly after that, for just a moment, and she is seized with terror, wondering if she is meant to return this gesture, somehow.

But then Macbeth lets her go and strides across the room. He approaches the large wardrobe, carved in oak wood. He opens one of the doors, ancient hinges mewling. His hands seek something inside of it.

After several moments pass, he turns to her again. One hand is a closed fist, the other an open palm. Resting on his palm is a rusted key.

"This is under your purview now, too," Macbeth says. "Should you choose to seek counsel in my absence."

The rusted key fits a rusted lock. The rusted lock is inside a rusted door. Behind the rusted door is that imperfect darkness, cut through with scythes of light. A single torch, pulsing, making the water crease and pucker.

There is the primal magic upon which Macbeth's power has grown, swelled like roots in the rain. Roscille remembers another story from antiquity, the story of a nobleman who cut down the trees in a sacred grove. Nestled inside one of these trees was a wood nymph. His axe sliced cleanly through her delicate skin, her slender divinity parting under his blade. When the goddess to whom the grove was dedicated saw her death, she bade the spirit of Famine curse this nobleman, so that he hungered endlessly and would never be sated. He ate up everything within the reach of his hands, and then he ate himself.

This nobleman was a fool. He should have kept the nymph in chains and bound the goddess to his bidding. Roscille takes the key and slips it into her bodice. The cold metal slides neatly against her cold flesh.

THE COURTYARD AGAIN, AT DUSK. Every soldier girded and braced. Horses snorting and kicking up dust. Everything is washed in a dim gray light, wrung through the clouds that stretch over Glammis like wet cloth. Men are jostling one another to fit in this small space, and still there are more soldiers spilling out past the open barbican, trailing down the great hill. Roscille can count half a dozen different war banners rising above the mass of bearded heads. Each one bearing a clan's sigil, and the clansmen gathered in their matching tartans beneath it.

Winter Fox and Mountain Goat and Weasel-cloak are among them, shouting over all this disjointed noise. Macbeth struts his horse in front of the crowd, back and forth, to swelling cheers.

"All hail Macbeth!" the men cry out. "King of Scotland!" Their swords jab the air.

There are only two men without armor or horses. Banquho and Fléance stand on either side of Roscille, swords at their sides, arms folded across their chests. Neither hides his face: Storm clouds bloom and burst on their brows, and their eyes burn red like embers. Fléance's scar looks not nearly as garish as he had hoped. In this light, it shrinks into his skin.

Weasel-cloak trots over to Macbeth and presses the flanks of their horses together. He is in his position at Macbeth's right. This is where Banquho should be.

The wind picks up, blowing Roscille's veil against her face. Once she would have shivered, but now the cold of Glammis is in her marrow, and she feels nothing at all.

"Let us go inside," she says.

She turns, and with barely checked fury, Banquho and Fléance follow her. The men are still chanting, yet as she walks farther into the belly of the castle, their words are swallowed up by the wind, and lost with distance.

NINE

ALL ROSCILLE KNOWS OF RUNNING A CASTLE IS WHAT she learned through observation in Wrybeard's court. The Duke's wife by law is Adelaide, who is not her mother but is still the reason Roscille exists.

Adelaide is not beautiful, though this alone is no excuse to spurn a marriage vow, not with how many priests Wrybeard is required to keep in his company, or else risk recriminations from the House of Capet and the pope himself. It is an unfortunate consequence of her breeding. Her native House of Blois are a rough-skinned, damp-eyed, long-nosed lot, the result of of too many cousins marrying cousins, and not even an infusion of Angevin blood could correct this—Adelaide is cousin to le Tricheur, whom Roscille nearly spooked out of his mind.

No, the problem with Adelaide is not her beauty—or rather her lack of it—but that Adelaide is simple, like a stable hand kicked in the head by a horse or a baby left to lie too long on its side in the crib. Her humors are perpetually out of balance. She is suffused with a calamitous mixture of black bile and white pus, resulting in a diseased mind. In an effort to rebalance these humors, Adelaide has undergone trepanation not once, not twice, but three times. It has left one half of her mouth in a permanent rictus, and she must carry a handkerchief with her always, to wipe away the spittle which gathers in the corner of her lips. When she speaks, it is with a throaty moan, like a bullfrog.

Even this unbalance is not entirely unforgivable, not cause enough to shun a wife from such an ancient and noble—if uncomely—house. But these humors have given Adelaide a temperament both phlegmatic and melancholic, which means she must be kept away from sharp things. She must have a cadre of ladies at her side, to keep her from open windows and long falls, from hastily tied nooses and weighted dresses. In the night, she can sometimes be heard burning herself with hot wax, and moaning as if in ecstasy. Her wrists are deformed with circular scar tissue, the lesions running over one another, like ripples in a pool.

Suicide is, of course, a sin by the pope's reckoning, and Roscille was in the room when Wrybeard proclaimed to the priests, "If it is my wife's desire to shirk her earthly duties, then I should be no longer bound to my own earth-made vows." There is logic in this that makes the priests' brows wrinkle and their heads bob on their skinny necks. They take this logic back to the House of Capet, who take it to the pope. The pope says that he will not annul the marriage, for this, too, is a sin, but he will unofficially release Alan Varvek, Duke of Breizh, from his matrimonial bonds.

So there is her father, openly and unashamedly bedding the second or third daughters of the lords of his fiefs. He will not stoop to ushering serving girls into his chamber, because they tend to get ideas above their station, when they believe they have been divinely chosen to carry the child of a duke. Noble girls know better than to expect some elevation of status just because the Duke finds them attractive enough to breed.

Roscille's mother was one of these second or third daughters, but her name is lost to time, her life released from her on the birthing bed. But any lesson a mother might impart her daughter Roscille has learned from observing Adelaide. From Adelaide, she has learned all the things she must never, ever do; all the things she must never, ever be. She must not lack in beauty. She must keep her mind whetted like a blade. And she must always be safe around sharp objects. Madness, of all things, is the most unforgivable in a woman.

ON THE FIRST DAY OF her husband's absence, Roscille sits at Macbeth's table and hears the reports of her subjects in his stead. How some of the sheep have suffered a blight and the shepherds will not be able to afford their tithes. How lovers from two feuding families wish to marry each other and hope to get the Lord's permission. How one woman has bedded half the men in a town and caused such an uproar that she must be sent to a nunnery to atone. How, what a pity, none of these young boys can read Latin, can the Lord not spare a Druide or two to teach them?

Roscille says, We will take a smaller tithe from shepherding families this year. She says, These families will no longer feud over petty, ancient offenses or the Lord will come back and splatter the brains of their sons on the wall. She says, Bring this impure woman to the castle, and she will atone by scrubbing my floors and embroidering my dresses. She says, I will have two Druides come on Sunday mornings for school.

Banquho and Fléance sit at her side as she hears these complaints and settles these disputes. When the last man leaves, Banquho says, "You will not send those Druides."

"Why not?"

"Because there is treachery still, in Glammis. You waste time indulging these petty grievances. You should spend your resources seeking out this treachery, rather than coddling these villagers. They are potential traitors, all of them."

Roscille looks past Banquho at Fléance, who dips his head to avoid her gaze. It is too much to expect him to support her openly before his father, but she hopes to shame him a bit, by meeting his eyes. She is satisfied when a flush creeps across his cheeks.

She turns back to Banquho and says, "If you treat every man as a traitor, a traitor he will become, in time."

Banquho's mouth twists. "And this woman you intend to bring to the castle? She may be a traitor, too, ready to misuse her position. You sit here coveting pretty dresses while Glammis turns against its Thane. This is no occasion to fill the halls with empty-headed servants."

"Either this woman is empty-headed or she is a traitor; she cannot be both." Roscille rises from the table. "And this sort of treachery is born from dissatisfaction. The more meanly you treat your people, the most dissatisfied they will become.

These simple justices will inspire love among Macbeth's subjects."

"Why is it love you wish to inspire? Fear will achieve the same."

Perhaps it will, among the brutish people of Scotland. But Roscille will not see more of them punished for her lies. She wonders if her father would see this as weakness; what clever creature would not sacrifice lesser beings to protect itself? She turns it over in her mind. She is not Roscille of Breizh anymore. She is Lady Macbeth, and in her husband's absence, Glammis is her domain to rule.

"This is my purview, Lord Banquho," she says. "The Lord has left these matters to my discretion. If you do not fulfill my wishes, you will face his anger when he returns."

For a long moment Banquho is silent. His fingers twitch at his sides, as if battling the instinct to reach for his sword. His chest heaves.

At last, he says, "There are the King's wishes you must fulfill, Lady Macbeth. He awaits the knowledge you will draw from the prince's screams."

Roscille says nothing in return. Banquho draws himself up, satisfied at her muteness. He thinks they have fought and he has landed the finishing blow. But this is why he is a tactician only, not a strategist. He sees what is before his eyes and in his arm's reach. He has the nobleman's little power and not the emperor's total dominion. He believes the lampreys devour at his discretion, but in truth, they are just dull mouths, and will eat anything their teeth can find.

Roscille gathers her things and leaves the great hall without another word.

THE DUNGEON. SHE HAS NEVER been inside it before. It is not a place for ladies. Her dress drags through filthy puddles, and where she steps, rats shriek and flee into shadowy corners. The torchlight glows wetly on the walls and the grime-coated floor. On the walls there are tools hanging, as if in a garden shed. Long whips, crusted in blood. A cat-o'-nine-tails, gathering dust. Knives in all shapes and sizes, their handles turning to rust. It is a small, oppressive, airless space, like every room of Glammis. There are no resplendent stretching racks. The Duke would find this displeasing. Torture, like all things within his influence, is an intricate, sophisticated thing. Not like these uncivil Scots and their crass, common methods of extracting pain.

Roscille approaches the nearest cell. Its bars are cold, and when she grips them, her skin turns to ice.

"I did not think you would come," Lisander says.

A jolt in her stomach. "Why would I not?"

"Because these matters are below the concern of a queen."

"You are mocking me."

Lisander scoffs, and then he emerges from the darkness of the cell. His face is paler than she has ever seen it, the circles under his eyes deeper and more garish, but his eyes are still sharp and overly green. Even his slow footsteps are graceful; he does not slouch and slog as a prisoner would. It will take longer than a day for a prince to shed his poise.

"What is there to mock? Duncane is dead, at your husband's hand. Macbeth names himself King, and his lady wife Queen."

"He is barely a king," says Roscille, "and I am a queen even less."

Surprise flashes on his face, then amusement. "I see you have lived among the barbarous Scots long enough to understand."

"I do not need to live among barbarians to understand that the greater one's rise, the farther his fall. The higher the tower is built, the more precarious it becomes. Even children with their building blocks comprehend this."

"Now you are mocking me."

"No," says Roscille. "I am not. I do not—I have never wanted this, to be Queen. I am as dull as a dog; I am only trying to survive in this pitiless world."

This confession should be shameful, but Lisander does not look at her with disdain or revulsion. Instead, he approaches her slowly. He lifts his hands and his fingers circle the bars, a mere inch above where she is gripping them.

"All your life you have been muzzled," he says. "So as not to disturb the architecture of the world. But a muzzled dog thinks only of its misery and its shackles. They may rob your body of its power, but they cannot take your mind."

Yet can they not? Roscille thinks of Adelaide, her mind its own tyrant, making her body betray itself, to lust for pain instead of pleasure. This is her deepest fear, beyond the terror of bloodstained thighs and bloodstained sheets, beyond a long fall into the cold sea. Madness. If she cannot think, she will be nothing.

"How do you know this?" she asks in a whisper.

"Because," Lisander says, "I have looked into your eyes."

A stone forms in her throat. She has to swallow hard to keep it from choking her.

"They will come," she manages to say. "Banquho and Flé-ance. I have been given orders to have you tortured for your knowledge. They will use every tool at their disposal to get you to speak."

"They will not succeed." His voice is flat. A fact, not a boast.

"But—" she begins. And then she stops. What can she say? That she owes him a debt twice over, once for not let-ting her die, and then again for not killing her? This thing that binds them does not feel like a debt; there is no ledger, no ink. They are two fish in a pool, circling each other, trapped by the same arrangement of stones. Their rhythms are identical, as they push their silver bodies through the water, in and out, like needles through black cloth. He is the only one who may see her truly. And she does not know why, not yet, but her eyes are two mirrors, throwing his own reflection back at him.

She remembers seeing the notches of Lisander's spine push outward from his skin when he bent over. His flesh, so thin, only narrowly protecting the spreading of veins within; the heart and lungs, so poorly insulated. She wants to retch, perhaps to scream.

"I do not feel pain as other men do," Lisander says, as if he can read her thoughts. "You will have heard that Duncane's line is cursed."

She opens her mouth to reply, but then there is the sound of footsteps on the stairs. She jumps, seized with panic.

"They must not know that I am here," she says, lowering her voice. "They will wonder why I have not ordered the torture to begin already."

Lisander nods. "Go," he says.

So she does, but she cannot help looking back. Roscille imagined she would see him recede again into the shadows of the cell, but even from a distance, his eyes are gleaming in the darkness, two beacons of unnatural green light.

ROSCILLE HAS THE ADULTEROUS WOMAN, Senga, brought to the castle. She is five, ten years Roscille's senior, not old enough to be her mother, but old enough to have fine, delicate worry lines etched across her forehead. These wrinkles emerge more easily on the foreheads of peasants than the foreheads of noble ladies. Roscille is pleased to see that Senga resembles Hawise greatly. Broad-shouldered, with long yellow hair, a serious face that does not show fear. When she stands in front of Roscille, her eyes do not waver, even though Fléance had her dragged through the courtyard by her braid.

Senga does not even flinch while Roscille repeats the rumors she has heard about her, all the lascivious, un-Christian things she has done. She asks if they are true. Senga merely nods.

"Your fellow villagers want you sent away to learn chastity," Roscille says.

Senga's accent is so coarse and provincial that Roscille has a difficult time understanding her as she replies, "If it is the nunnery for me, I will go without trouble."

"No," Roscille says. "You are to be my handmaiden. Do you understand?"

She has to use the Brezhoneg word for "handmaiden." As far as she is aware, this word does not exist in Scots. And if it does, she has never heard it used by the men in Glammis.

"I am to bathe and dress you and darn your gowns? A servant?" she suggests, in Scots.

"You will also be my companion."

Senga's eyes narrow, as if awaiting a trick.

"I would like you to embroider my gowns in the style of Alba. In return, I will teach you to read and write. In your native Scots, if you do not know it already, or if you do, in Latin."

There is something in Senga's gaze that makes Roscille believe she would be amenable to this. A sharp cleverness that was surely not appreciated by the vulgar men of her village. She is brave enough to stand without trembling in front of her Lady, and when her sins were recounted, she offered no apology. Defiant and unruffled, this is the type of woman that Roscille wishes to surround herself with.

"Yes, my Lady," Senga says. "This I can do."

Senga's fingers are rough and callused with farmwork, but they will soon soften with the luxuries of courtly life: three meals prepared by the hands of servants, a feather bed instead of straw, velvet slippers instead of heavy wooden clogs. Even her slight limp will correct itself once her back is no longer burdened with carrying buckets from the well.

As she gives Senga needle and thread, Roscille allows herself to imagine Glammis under her purview, forever. She will have monks sent from an abbey with their books so that a small library can be constructed. She will have musicians play at supper and host tournaments and jousts. All of these are things that Wrybeard did—but perhaps still she can do more.

Perhaps she can bring in more such iron-willed women. She will banish men like Banquho, with their nasty, vain tempers. She will harshly punish any man who shows the flat of his hand to a serving girl. She will only fight wars which are just. When she has such power, she will no longer need to inflict small cruelties in order to survive. She does not need to be the cold creature of her father's conception.

Are these all the dreams of Lady Macbeth? Certainly they are not her husband's desires imprinted upon her. Yet she could only hope to attain this power through his design. *Queen Here-after.* His words. Her fate, arranged only to please him.

But she indulges herself in this dream for several more moments, as Senga settles into her sewing.

SHE AND SENGA ARE TALKING in the great hall when Banquho enters. Rage is all around him, radiating invisible mists. The whites of his eyes are cracked through with red. He shoves past the tables in quick, long strides and then leaps up onto the dais. When he slaps both his hands down in front of her, it makes her book jump and Senga flinch so that she pricks her finger with the needle. A drop of blood squeezes out and falls onto the floor.

"You had this woman brought here against my wishes?" Banquho demands.

Roscille's eyes flicker to Senga. "You are dismissed," she says.

Senga hesitates. Roscille has saved her from the nunnery, and this act has woven a tenuous loyalty between them. The anger in Banquho's voice makes her gaze flash with fear for her Lady. But Roscille only stares at her intently, without blinking, and so Senga hurries out of the hall, trailing her unfinished embroidery.

"And you enlisted my son to do it, without my knowledge? He says he went down to the village and dragged the woman here with his own hands."

"It is Macbeth's will that I should have authority over Glammis in his absence," Roscille says. "If you do not agree, you may take up your grievance with my husband when he returns."

"He left you to keep the castle of *Glammis*," Banquho snarls. "This is not Naoned; you are not a lady of Breizh. You are Queen of Alba. You will not turn this place into a bawdy imitation of Wrybeard's lavish court. That is not the will of Macbeth."

His voice fills up the empty room and echoes around them, pressing in on her. Roscille draws a breath to steady herself, but it is thin and tremulous. She has, perhaps, gone too far.

"I am sorry that we are not aligned in our values, Lord Banquho," she says. She tries to be tactful, tractable even. "I will wait for Macbeth's return before I make any more changes to the castle."

This is very reasonable. Forbearing to his desires. Surely Banquho will see it.

But Banquho does not pause. "You have forced my own son to act against his father's wishes. You have no respect for order or for the ways of our people, Lady Roscilla."

"I am sorry for that," she says. "I will not ask such of Fléance again."

Now, certainly, his anger will pass. She has folded to him entirely, done everything save falling to her knees in repentance. If she misjudged her position, she corrects herself now.

"And you have failed in your one required duty." Banquho

spits the words. "The former prince of Cumberland sleeps easily in his cell. Not a wound on his body, not a scream to be heard."

Roscille stiffens. "He does not sleep easily. He knows he is prisoner. He has been in solitude and total darkness for days; that is a torment of its own."

"That is not the torment our King Macbeth has in mind."

Roscille levels her gaze with Banquho's. She thinks back to the earliest moments of knowing him, when he proudly declared he was Macbeth's right hand and how, since then, his position has eroded like a mudbank in a rainstorm, become slippery and untenable. In no small part because of her. She has even cleaved his own son away from him.

Men are cruelest in their desperation. When they have nothing solid beneath them. Perhaps she should not have been so flippant, in her own precarious position. She is still a woman alone. And all these men around her are blind, roving mouths.

"Fine," she says. But her voice is trembling, and surely Banquho will not miss that. "Let us go, then."

ROSCILLE'S MIND RACES AS SHE enters the dungeon, Banquho and Fléance at her heels. The torchlight gathers on all the room's sharp points and bladed edges. When she descends, she tries to step over the filth-laced puddles, so as not to dirty her slippers, but Banquho and Fléance splash through them carelessly—they wear boots, and the water does not matter to them—so the hem of her skirt is soaked anyway.

She sets the torch into one of the sconces and breathes in

the dungeon's damp, terrible smell. Spreading outward, the torchlight illuminates only part of Lisander's cell, the other half still cloaked in shadows.

He steps into the light. His bone-pale face shows no sentiment at all. "Lady Roscille."

Her palms are drenched and her hands are trembling. "Lisander. You know why I come. I must ask you to tell us your brother's plans. How many men he can rally to his side. The size of Æthelstan's armies . . ."

She trails off. Her mouth feels full of cotton.

"And you know I cannot tell you that," Lisander replies.

"You waste time with words," Banquho hisses. "Make him scream, and he will speak. Give me leave to do it."

Roscille's gaze travels to the instruments on the wall. The bone saw with its rusted handle. She imagines flesh opening up beneath its blade, white parting to reveal vulgar red. And then she thinks of Lisander's mouth on her mouth, her jaw, her throat. The bruises have faded, but the memory is hot, warming the skin that is normally so cold beneath Macbeth's necklace. *I have hated seeing you wear this.*

"No," she says.

Fléance's lips part dumbly, opening and closing like a trout's. Banquho's gaze clouds and then hardens with anger.

"Macbeth should have known this is no work for a woman," he growls, shoving past her. "Weak-minded, frail-bodied, like all members of your sex. Perhaps you have worked some common magic with the beauty of your face, but you have no other value or purpose beyond that. Step aside. I will fulfill the wishes of the King."

He grasps the whip and jerks it from his hook. He turns,

the muscles in his arms and shoulders grinding together like rough boulders in an avalanche. But Roscille does not move from her place between him and the cell.

"Woman I may be," she says, "but I have worked my magic upon you. You have been deceived."

The look in Banquho's eyes. Roscille has seen it often, the bewildered fury of a man who has no experience being defied, whose worldview rests on the axis of his own absolute power.

"What did you say?"

"I said you have been deceived, Lord Banquho." She raises her voice. "There were no masked men. Your son was angry at being left behind, at having no opportunity to prove his worth on the battlefield, so he arranged a plot in which he would play hero."

She tells the story slightly wrong, not because she thinks she will get away with the lie, but because Fléance will not resist jumping in to correct her, and therefore reveal his true part in it.

"She lies!" Fléance does indeed cry out. "It was her plan, not mine—"

But then he stops. He has dishonored himself so greatly that it is enough to stain his whole line; any sons he bears will feel this shame their entire lives, will know why they are passed over, time after time, with curled lips and rolled eyes. He has confessed not only to treachery but also to being manipulated by a woman, some seventeen-year-old foreign bride hiding behind a veil. The shame will even stretch backward, staining Banquho, too.

So then it makes sense what Banquho says next. He has no

other choice except to reply, "Do not protect her honor, Fléance. Obviously she lies. She means to strip your heroism from you. She means to disgrace the name of our family."

Fléance's mouth shrinks into his face. He has been dishonored twice over, for not simply denying her tale. One stupidity layered on top of the other. *My fool of a son,* Banquho must be thinking. If this were a private moment, he would be struck across the face.

But they are not alone, and Fléance merely dips his head, in feigned penitence.

"You are right, Father," he says. "I should not endeavor to shield the honor of a lady who has nothing but evil and trickery in her heart."

Roscille is quicker than Fléance to understand what is happening. They are actors, rehearsing their roles. They will repeat these same words to Macbeth when he returns, in the same low, regretful tones, with hanging heads and darkened brows. They will mime grief, shock. Starting at the tips of her fingers and toes, all her blood begins to run cold.

"My husband left me to keep the castle in his absence," she says, but her voice is rising through its pitches. "He trusts me. He will believe my word over yours."

Yet she cannot even pretend certainty. She is shaking so fiercely that her teeth have begun to chatter.

"Will he?" Banquho's grip tightens on the whip. "There are stories about you, Lady Roscilla. How you drive men to madness with your gaze. Perhaps Macbeth has been struck by such madness, or simply moved by the beauty of your face. But when I have his ear in private, he will know the truth."

Banquho advances. Roscille steps backward, but there is nowhere to go except the cold bars of the cell.

"I offer you this," Banquho goes on. "You will step aside now, and let me proceed with the torture of the prince, and Macbeth will never know of your treachery."

He means to bury his son's truth along with her own. The confession of Fléance's deception is too shameful to be worth what it may offer in return—Roscille's punishment. It is better to keep all the words that have passed within this dungeon a secret from Macbeth.

Because she knows this, she has some power over him, she thinks. They will both be damned by the same confession.

"No," she says. "Your son's fate is yoked to mine. I have nothing to fear from you. Leave this place."

Banquho's eyes are two points, silvery and gleaming, like the ends of a dagger.

"You put yourself between me and this ousted prince," he says, voice low and rasping. "Why?"

Why? Because she is not a cold creature who will see yet another innocent soul bleed for her lies. Because she has stanched the flow of the poison that runs from her father's seed and into her; she is no more his ermine than she is Alba's unicorn. Because Lisander saved her, then spared her, and if it is not a debt that has been woven between them, it is something exquisite, and stronger, a golden rope stretched across an abyss. Because she is the emperor now, and it is within her power to keep men from being devoured by the eels' gnashing teeth.

"Roscille," Lisander says hoarsely, "do not do this."

But she did not account for what she sees, as she stares openly, defiantly, into Banquho's eyes. She did not consider rage beyond reason.

Banquho steps forward, and Lisander reaches through the bars, as if he might be able to grasp him, but it is too far and he cannot—within an instant Banquho has both of her wrists caught in one of his hands. Roscille fumbles to tear off her veil, to catch either Banquho or Fléance in the path of her gaze, but then Banquho's other hand smothers her face, forcing her eyes shut, blinding her. The animal panic overtakes her, and she is writhing, choking out half-formed protests.

She is slippery, like a fish: It takes Banquho and Fléance together to pin her down. There is a table, where the wood is soaked permanently with blood so that it is now a muted red color. They press her upon it. Ropes join her wrists, twisting her arms above her head. Her cheek touches the wood, rubs her skin raw against the lace veil. Her skirts are yanked up, and the sudden coldness of the room on her bare legs makes her shriek.

"Let her go!" She hears, but cannot see, Lisander rattling the bars of the cell. "Flay my skin from my body, I welcome it, just leave her be!"

If Lisander were of clear mind, he would not do this, would not shout. He would not protest the torture of a woman meant to be his enemy. He would watch at ease as she is whipped in his stead. Perhaps he would cringe at the barbarity of it, but he would never object, no. It is a good thing that Banquho and Fléance are too occupied with the task before them to take special note of it. The exuberant spending of such long-hoarded violence smothers all else.

"Here." Banquho's voice is rough. "I will hold her. You take the whip."

At least she hears Fléance exhale, a sound of hesitation. But that is all it is: a short breath into the cold damp air. And then the same air sings as he raises the whip and brings it down against the back of her thighs.

The pain is beyond the capacity of a noble lady's imagin-

ing. Roscille has no reason to have ever felt the sting of a whip
before. That is for servants and slaves and lowborn girls who
forget their place. When the first blow comes, she is still able
to think, amid the haze of red in her mind, *This will be the
worst, and each one after will be more bearable.*

She is wrong. The pain piles up like stones. The lick of
the whip is no easier to bear because she is expecting it; every
time, her skin sizzles, like oil on cooking meat.

She must become an animal in order to survive it. As each
blow lands, Roscille imagines that her body is not her body,
that she is in fact a serpent-woman like the Melusina, and instead of legs she has a scale-patterned tail, thick with muscle
and fat, impenetrable to the weak weapons of men. Fléance
is breathing hard, flushed with this fever-dream of power. She
knows this without even seeing his face.

A scream wrenches its way out of her throat. Her mind
is red, and red, and red, choked with fog and filthy air. Dis-
tantly, she hears the cell bars still rattling. Roscille wonders
if Lisander is thinking of how he stroked his hands up her
thighs, kneading her flesh desirously, and how that flesh is ru-
ined now, flayed into strips and ugly and pulpy with blood.

The pain is huge enough to fill hours, but some small untouched part of her brain knows it has been mere moments.
She begs: *Please stop, please, please,* but perhaps she forms the
words in her head only. She has stopped writhing against Banquho's hands. What is the point of such protests? It will only
delight her tormentors more. This is the greatest of men's aspi-
rations, to—whether through love or through violence—draw
screams from women's mouths.

Words pass between them, gruff and whispered, so she
cannot make them out. But whatever is said makes Fléance

pause. The sudden absence of pain is a gulf that fills instantly with terror, terror that the pain will come again. Like a dim and witless dog, Roscille whimpers at imagining it.

Then Banquho lets go. With her arms released, with nothing to hold her, Roscille's body slides limp to the floor. The cold stone is a relief. It spreads its numbness through her cheeks, her palms, her still-bare thighs. More words pass over her head.

Fléance: Look, she lies as if she is dead. If we have killed her, Macbeth will never forgive it.

Banquho: No, she is not dead. Let us leave her now. She will come to in the morning and we will send for a doctor. It is not so bad. She will walk without limping by the time Macbeth returns.

Fléance: Are you certain?

Banquho: Yes.

Fléance: Then let us go.

THE ROOM SMELLS LIKE A slaughter-yard. Roscille lies belly-flat on the floor. A slippery wetness drips between her legs and onto the stone. To move even an inch is agony. She is barely able to open her eyes.

Through damp lashes, she sees Lisander. He is kneeling on the floor, reaching through the bars of the cell. His hand covers hers. His palm is colder than she imagined it would be, but then everything feels cold now, in comparison to the white fire lacing up and down her thighs.

"Roscille," he whispers.

"It is not your fault. I chose this."

She thinks she says the words aloud, but her voice is so small it scarcely sounds like her own.

"Listen." He speaks in her tongue, in Brezhoneg, even if he has no reason to know it, much less articulate its sounds so tenderly. "I have kept myself from sleep for two days now. I do not have much time before it takes me. So let me tell you all of it before you see."

ACT IV

LES DEUS
AMANZ,
LES DEUX
AMANTS

TEN

"THERE WAS A KING IN ALBA. A VIRTUOUS, NOBLE king, who sought to act as was right, praised handsomely. He wed a worthy woman, fair in looks, and well bred. They loved each other as a fish loves water, a love so deep that the absence of one from the world was inconceivable to the other. So, by the purity of their love, the queen fell pregnant with a son.

"In the flower of his fame and preening with such good fortune, the king went on a hunt in the forest. It was dawn, and they were eager, his knights and huntsmen, joyful in their intent. They were after a mighty stag, one that could be mounted with pride in the king's great hall. The king rode ahead, with the dogs and huntsmen at his heels, and a squire at his side, bearing his hunting bow, quiver, and spear.

"But the king was led a strange way by his horse, wandering from his war party. And then he saw, beneath a spreading tree, a doe with her fawn in company. The creature was the purest white—a doe, yet oddly, it bore horns.

"*Its fur will be a lovely prize,* the king thought, *in which to robe my wife.* He drew his bow, letting his arrow fly. The arrow struck her hoof, so she fell to the ground at once. Yet the arrow turned back in flight, and struck the king on the thigh, so violently that he was filled with a sudden and greatly embodied rage.

"The deer lay upon the grass. She sighed in anguish, and then, astonishingly, her form began to change. She assumed the shape of a woman, beautiful beyond all conception, naked, with hair the color of moonbeams.

"The king did love his wife dearly, and he did so wish to honor her with the creature's pelt. But the nature of man is not such that it can be undone entirely by simple affection. The king still had a man's desires, his hungers, and his vices. And so when he thrust into the bleeding woman, it was not with the point of his sword.

"When he had finished, her blood had soaked the grass. She raised her head, with great effort, and then she gave forth speech:

"'I die here, alas, slain by covetous mortal hands. Sorceress, you will name me, witch; for centuries to come, the birth of your line's firstborn sons will all bear the mark of my vengeful magic. As you have stolen from me my natural form, so too will my power steal the forms of your sons.'

"Then the woman—witch—laid her head back upon the grass and died, and the earth ate up her body, so that by the time the king's squire arrived, there was only the fawn, shivering and bleating for its mother. The squire bore the injured king back to the castle, where his wound was bound and treated. And when he saw his wife with her swelled belly, he fell to his knees in front of her, and confessed all.

"The king had never been an especially pious man. Yet as his son grew in his mother's womb, he prayed and prayed, hoping that he might be released from the witch's curse. He summoned priests, clad them in gold, and kept a dozen at his side always, to pray for absolution.

"Never did he receive God's answer. His son was born in blood and sweat and darkness, and he feared the curse might take his wife from him, too. But she did not die, though the son she gave forth was a strange child, dark of hair where both parents were fair, pale of skin where his mother and father were lively and red.

"For days, the child did not sleep. He wept through all hours of the night, writhing every moment, as if in secret agony. The queen could not settle him. He did not wish to feed. And then, at last, when he slipped into a troubled slumber, the king saw the fruit of the witch's curse: In his crib, while sleeping, his son became a monster.

"In these early days, it was easy to contain him. The creature had a child's body, and a child's strength. He could be strapped down in his bed. But as the boy grew, his monstrous sleep-demon grew as well. A separate chamber was built for him, with no windows, and only a small iron door, too narrow for the beast to slip through. All the servants in the castle were sworn to secrecy, forced never to speak of the roaring they heard through the halls, on pain of death.

"The queen bore another son, this one taking after his parents in appearance and manner, fully mortal, untainted by the witch's curse. But this birth weakened the queen, and soon after she died. In the absence of his beloved, the king sickened, too, though he was not mercifully relieved of his posthumous existence. He aged, every day in diminished agony. His first-born son aged, too, and with him, the monster.

"In his grief and fury, the king sought out all witches and enchantresses in his kingdom, any woman who showed a strangeness. Yet when he questioned them, they all said the same: that the curse of a witch cannot be undone by any except the witch herself. And the witch who cursed his son was dead.

"And that is how the crown of Alba came to be worn by a withering king, and promised by inheritance to a monster."

Lisander's voice grows lower and lower, until it can scarcely be heard at all. As he speaks, his hand grips Roscille's tightly. She lifts her gaze, her unguarded gaze, and meets his eyes. They gleam as if lit from behind by torches. His pupils are so black that she can see herself reflected within them. Her face, revealed at last: bloodless skin and pointed chin and something strange, something *wrong,* that she cannot name. An aberration that runs through her like a crack in the earth itself.

"SO NOW YOU HAVE HEARD it all." His voice is strained, as if something presses down on his throat. "I am Alba's curse, and my father's shame. Any affection he had for me was born of guilt, nothing more. He wished to name me king only be-cause he thought it might absolve him. But he would set loose upon Scotland the cruelest, vilest creature. The beast I am cares nothing for crowns or rites or innocent lives."

With great difficulty, Roscille raises her head. "Do you think this frightens me?"

He does not reply. His eyelids are growing heavy.

"So you are no mortal man. I have seen what mortal men can do. I prefer a monster that shows itself openly."

Her legs feel so stiff she fears she may never move them again. The blood is drying now, sticking her to the floor.

"The bars are flimsy," he whispers. "They will not hold me. I do not know what it will do. What I will do."

Roscille turns up her hand, palm to palm, and laces their fingers together. She says, "Stay. Stay here until you cannot any longer. Please."

"I will." His voice is hoarse. Dim.

Roscille thinks she can prepare herself for what she will see, but her mind has not fully returned to her. It is trapped in the animal of her body, still feeling the sting of every lash. And there is no preparing, anyway. In the half-light, she sees Lisander's clothes rip. His bones press up through his skin. There is the wet sound of tearing flesh—she knows this sound well now—and where he was once pale, unblemished, his chest now ripples with scales. They are the same green color of his eyes, iridescent in the glow of the torch.

It is horrible, beautiful, horrible, then perversely beautiful again. She sees how even his mortal form was made for this, a chrysalis that holds the monster lovingly within it. His face vanishes from the light, and when it emerges again, it is the head of the dragon—she has examined its poor reproduction a thousand times on tapestries, on the proud pennants of the kingdom of Wales, and now it lives and breathes before her. Scales and crescent-shaped teeth, each as long as a dagger.

Its body coils like the serpent it is, and then stretches out-ward, wings unfolding from its back. They seem papery, oddly frail, as if hesitant about flight. The last to change is his hand, still gripped in hers. His fingers tear open with the same violence, showing the claws beneath.

Lisander was right: The cell cannot hold him. The dragon's teeth easily rend the metal apart, breaking the bars like twigs. And then he is free, long body unwinding, scales shimmering. She is amazed by the strength of its body, the thick muscularity of it as it curls over her, almost protective. Perhaps possessive. Dragons are jealous creatures, devoted to their hoards.

Roscille lifts a hand and runs it across the dragon's chest, down the long line of its belly. The scales are rough and smooth at once, like stones in the riverbed, and she is not afraid. If this is her different death, she will beg for it. She would sooner be consumed than taken apart, piece by fragile piece.

She has been turned on her back and the dragon is upon her. Her thighs burn. Despite being a cold-blooded creature, the nearness of its body, the pressure, fills her with warmth. She opens her mouth to speak, but all she can do is moan, half pained, half something more.

And then the dragon lifts off her, and with the beat of wings, it is up the stairs and crashing through the door. There are screams that echo all the way down into the dungeon, the clanging of steel. The smell of fire and ash. It feels as if these sounds pass within seconds, but they must go on for longer, and when it is all quiet, and she knows the creature is gone, Roscille closes her eyes and lets her cheeks run with stinging water.

THE IRONY THAT WOULD MADDEN her, if she let it: Banquho sends Senga to treat her wounds. So he has decided that this is women's work, that it is a good thing there is a woman here after all.

First Senga lifts her off the floor and drags her up the stairs, to her bedchamber. The pain has become a familiar friend. Roscille does not make a sound until she is dropped with little ceremony onto the bed, and then it is only a huff of air, part relief, part expulsion of this overloyal agony.

"Was this because of me?" Senga asks. "Or because of the prince who escaped?"

Roscille presses her face into the mattress. She cannot think of a reply. The question is simple, why, but the answer is depthless. For the first time since arriving in Glammis, her mind does not twist inside a narrowing chasm, trying slowly to release itself. Now she is just meat, wrapped in twine. That is what it feels like, as Senga's tough hands rub cold water and peasant healing salves on her thighs.

They have not sent a Druide or a doctor to do this work because they do not want her to speak with a man whom she might enchant. Women cannot be ensorcelled; Wrybeard declared so long ago, and she has never covered her face in the presence of Hawise. But never mind that Roscille can barely concentrate on not becoming a corpse. Her breasts ache from being pressed first against the floor, and now against the mattress.

So much time passes before the pain withers into something bearable. In aching increments, her mind returns to her. Roscille considers what has gone wrong. She has overestimated her own cleverness. Underestimated the anger of men when their power is taken from them. She has let her heart move her. If she had said nothing while Lisander was on the wheel—if she had held the whip herself—she would be a porcelain-marble queen still, no cracks in her face, no lampreys mouthing her bare ankles and feet. But her greatest failure, perhaps, was believing she might be more: more than her father's ermine, with its pitiless teeth, more than Lady Macbeth, tugged along by her husband's will like a dog on its leash. The arrogance of hope.

She sleeps at strange hours, each sleep threaded through with strange dreams. At first Roscille fears the pain will appear in these dreams, but no—they are mostly scales and teeth. The warmth and strength of the dragon's body over her own. She does not tell Senga, or anyone, this. She does not even articulate the images into words. Does not know how.

In the meantime, Senga brings her food and news from the castle. The food: hard bread, Scottish mutton. She would commit sin for a piece of fruit, fresh with juice, soft enough to split down its center with her thumb. But nothing grows in Glammis. The news: Banquho has taken over the daily affairs of the keep. He has stopped sending the Druides to the villages, but he has let Senga stay, for now.

Macbeth is returning soon.

Fléance comes to visit her, once. He wears a scarf over his own eyes; he is taking no chances. The part of her that is still a seventeen-year-old girl, an animal licking its wounds, wants to insult him—to tell him he looks a foolish woman, shrinking and cringing from her. It is almost worth the promise of more pain, imagining the way his face would curdle with these words.

In the end, she merely says, "What is the state of your honor now?"

He draws a breath, puffing his chest. "You have no leave to speak to me of honor."

"Why not?" Roscille sits up, wincing. The pain still waits inside her like a coiled snake, ready at any moment to strike. "So you have beaten me, like a thousand women have been beaten before. There is no honor in that. And you will tell my husband I begged for it? To be flagellated for my failure? He will not blame me, for to blame me will dishonor him—he is the one who left Glammis in my hands. My failures are his failures. So stick stalwartly to your lies, but they will not save you. If you say I have no honor, I have no honor left to lose."

Fléance is silent. The wound on his neck and shoulder looks glossy, well healed, unobtrusive. It must embarrass him as much as the older wound on his ear. A child's scar. A boy playing at being a man. That is all he is, all he will ever be. Even Roscille could not make him into something more.

"You are a witch," he says at last.

"And yet you played so nicely with me, witch that I am. Eagerly succoring my schemes. That shame will not fade, Fléance, son of Banquho. Whatever lies you tell in this life, poison seeps through the generations. Get out. Let me see no more of you."

SOON MACBETH DOES RETURN. ROSCILLE does not go out to greet him in the courtyard, but she hears the barbican grind open, and hundreds of hooves beat against the dirt. Her room is windowless so she cannot see him, cannot see whether or not he comes back grinning, proudly waving the flag of his clan, dust-caulked and bloodstained but joyous with violent triumph. This is the best she can hope for.

She has had a long time to consider what she will say to

him. But the correct answer is: nothing. This is what men want most of all to hear from women. He will arrange his world, and she will slide wordlessly into the place he has made for her. She feels new to Glammis again, a wide-eyed foreign bride, halting in her Scottish and cowering under her veil. Her thighs are still so raw she cannot bear to sleep on her back. She lies on her belly, gown drawn up over her hips, holding the pain at a slender distance.

Rough bootsteps on the floor jolt her from the bed. They are her husband's footsteps, the treading of a warrior, uncompromising and unfaltering. Softer, more hesitant footsteps follow his.

Macbeth pushes through the door, two attendants at his heels. She raises her gaze slowly, beneath the veil, taking in all of him. There is no blood in his beard, but he is dewed with the sweat of a long journey, his face red and wind-chapped. There are lines etched on his brow that Roscille does not remember being there when he left. As he walks toward her, Roscille realizes, astonishingly, that those arrogant footsteps were not his at all. Her husband is limping.

The shock of this anger makes her forget her previous plan to be silent.

"My Lord," she says in alarm. "You are injured."

"It is nothing," he says.

The attendants are carrying a large trunk between the two of them. By the way their arms tremble, Roscille can tell it is heavy, full. At Macbeth's direction, they set it down on the floor in front of him. Then he banishes them from the room.

"Shall I see to your wound?" Roscille asks meekly. This is a stupid thing to say; she is no Druide, no handmaid either. But she is unmoored. She has never been able to envision her husband as fallible. Always he has seemed as impenetrable as stone.

"Forget the wound," he says. "Banquho has told me what transpired here while I was gone."

Her stomach pools with dread. And then she does the second-best thing any woman can do. She clasps her hands over her chest and says, "My Lord, I am so sorry. I have failed you, dishonored you; there is no punishment I do not deserve."

But Macbeth is not happy with her pleading. She should have known; he may be mortal, but her husband is no ordinary man. He seeks out witches as wives. He wants women with teeth. Not too sharp, of course.

"Forget the honor, too," he says. "I have heard enough of this word from Banquho, honor and honor and honor. Enough. I am weary of it. Honor is an imagined thing, the refuge of weak men. Only power is real. So listen now, Lady Macbeth. I have taken Moray. It is mine. I have cast Duncane's crown into the fire and with its melted remains forged one of my own."

Roscille looks up at him and fashions her face into a mask of admiration. *"King Hereafter."*

"And many of Duncane's allies have abandoned their own vows and fallen into line. The thanes who have not will be destroyed quickly, for Æthelstan will not have them, either. These dumb beasts forget how much the English loathe Alba. The lion and the unicorn will never make peace."

His words rumble like thunder. The hatred between the English and the Scots is as old as the world itself. And with every passing year, more bloodshed waters the roots and makes the animus grow new again.

"That is good," Roscille says hesitantly. "All of Alba will kneel to Macbeth."

He gives a single nod. "That is why I say forget honor. Forget these little wounds. The prince's flight is the greatest boon I could have hoped for. Now the whole island will know that Duncane's line breeds monsters. I have sent messengers in all directions to spread this news. Bards will sing songs of it in every noble's court. Criers will cry it in the street. And the man who brings me the head of the dragon will be rewarded so handsomely that the sons of his sons will want for nothing in their lives."

For a moment, all words are lost to her.

"But how," she manages at last, in a weak voice, "will any man slay such a beast?"

"All beasts may be slain." His eyes fix on hers. "Open the trunk."

She must kneel in order to open it. Bending her legs like this is agony, but she bites her lip against the protest that rises in her throat. Her fingers fumble with the latches. They are trembling, diminished with so many days of disuse where she could not even bring herself to hold a quill. With great difficulty, she unclasps the latch and lifts open the lid.

Inside is a nest of white fur, pale and pure as snow. Roscille blinks in disbelief. Very slowly, she reaches down into the trunk and draws it out: the cloak.

She is holding this dead thing in her hands. Turning it over, she sees the soft pelt of a rabbit, even its small paws intact. Then there is the fox, with its long bushy tail. A bird, a swan, its feathers as sleek as fletching. The shaggy fur of a mountain goat, brushed uncommonly neat. The ermine, the creature from Alan Varvek's coat of arms.

The cloak has a hood, as women's cloaks ordinarily do not. A horse's mane runs up the back, like a spine. She runs her fingers through it, disbelieving, her mind supplying only a single word over and over again: *no* and *no* and *no* and *no*. At the peak of the hood there are two ears, flattened, as if the creature is fearful even in death. And then there is the horn, spiraling, iridescent and conch-like, to its gleaming point.

He has really done it. Fulfilled the condition she thought was impossible, for there are only six white animals that live on the soil of Scotland, and one of them is the unicorn. She did not believe he would dare, that the King of Alba would brazenly slay the symbol of Alba itself. But Macbeth dares anything.

"Blasted creature gored two hounds," Macbeth is saying. "Never hunt with another man's hounds, with dogs you have not fed from your own hand—that was my mistake, which I will not again make. And then with men who are not from your own clan, another mistake. This one was clumsy in his sprinting. Slipped his spear against my leg. I had him stuck in the pillory for two and a half days." He snorts. "Another king might have broken him on the wheel. Let them know Macbeth is a righteous man and capable of mercy."

As he speaks, he begins stripping off his tartan. Roscille is too shocked to move, and his voice passes over her like water. He tosses the filthy plaid aside. Underneath, there is a stain spreading slowly across his wool stockings, blue-black. A wound, unhealed. She can see the spear sliding against the tender skin at the back of his knee—imagine any part of Macbeth being *tender*—the horrified look on the other man's face, the knowledge of his unforgivable error. Her husband, spitting venom and rage.

Ignorant to her horror—perhaps uncaring—Macbeth says, "Put it on."

The cloak. He means the cloak. Roscille slowly draws the six deaths over her shoulder. There is a clasp at the front, where the ermine's mouth joins its tail in a perfect circle around her throat. Above it, the blood-colored ruby gleams.

Macbeth regards her for a long moment. Then he reaches out and grasps her face in his hand. He holds her chin between two fingers and turns her face this way and that, as if she is a piece of pottery he is examining for cracks.

"Beautiful," he declares at last. The pride in his voice—as if he is the first to utter this word, as if the word is a flag he is planting upon her. He has never reminded her of Wrybeard until this moment. But he speaks in the same tone her father did when he proclaimed, *Perhaps you were cursed by a witch.*

"Thank you, my Lord," she says quietly. "You honor me with this gift."

Too late, she realizes she has made a mistake. Storm clouds roll over Macbeth's face. "I told you I no longer care to hear this word. It is a virtue that is below me."

"I'm sorry." Roscille looks at the ground.

Or at least, she tries. Macbeth jerks her chin back up so she is forced to look into his eyes again. He tips his own head, as if in consideration. Then he says, "Show me."

Her mind scrambles. "What?"

"Banquho told me what occurred, in my absence. I should like to see the state of my wife's body."

Briefly, Roscille becomes stone. Her thoughts all turn to nothing, and leave her like smoke. The pressure of Macbeth's fingers on her chin brings her back to herself, enough that she can follow this rote command. With slow, halting movements, she unfastens the cloak. It slips to the floor and piles there, an embankment of snow around her feet. Her feet are bare, have been bare for days, the days in which she has only slept and lived with the pain in her bed like a lover.

Macbeth lets her go and she turns her back to him. Roscille draws her hands to her hips. She is wearing one of the dresses Senga embroidered for her in the style of Alba. A muted, simple pattern that would be regarded as ugly in her father's court. Her fingers shake as she lifts her skirts, baring to Macbeth the backs of her thighs.

She hears the breath he lets out. She hears him shift closer, lowering himself to examine her. She knows he will touch her, but when he does, she has to bite down on her lip to keep from making a sound. He pries at the skin of her thighs, kneading it with a removed scrutiny. Tears gather in her eyes. He must know that it hurts but he does not care.

Macbeth rises again, with another quick breath that this time exposes his own pain, spiraling outward from the wound in his knee.

"Look at me," he says.

Roscille drops her skirts and turns around.

"You should not have allowed this."

Her heart skips its beats. "Why?"

"Lord Varvek swore that the daughter he offered was the most beautiful maiden in the world. You have disgraced your own form, and lessened the value of our marriage alliance."

Roscille's throat closes. She can barely choke out the words, "I am sorry."

"Do not be sorry," he says. "You are a queen."

And then Macbeth closes the space between them and presses their mouths together. He kisses her, through the veil.

The lace rubs her lips to rawness. His arms circle her waist, pulling her against him, and she feels as small as a child, a doll. She manages to twist herself free, breaking his forceful kiss.

"There is one more condition—" she starts. But Macbeth's eyes are black.

"Enough now, Roscilla," he says. "I have indulged this custom and your frivolous wants for long enough. You are my wife and this is your duty. I am your husband and this is my right."

She reaches for her veil, to tear it off, but he has her hands trapped at her sides. It only requires one of his arms to do this. With his other arm, he reaches out and extinguishes the candles between his finger and thumb. The room plunges into darkness.

He shifts her onto the bed and removes the dress from her back. Cold air crackles on her skin. His heavy body arcs over hers. And then Macbeth, Thane of Glammis, Thane of Cawder, King of Alba, the righteous man, takes what is owed to him.

SHE IS SO ANGRY AT HERSELF for this: her silence.

The abbey at Naoned had a book of saints in which all their various martyrdoms were accounted. Roscille remembers reading of one woman who was put to death for refusing to renounce her faith in God. She was burned alive at the stake. The book stated that she did not protest, did not even scream as the flames ate at her flesh. Roscille stole this book from the monks' library and brought it to her father. She was still foolish enough, then, to believe Wrybeard had any interest in cultivating the mind of his bastard daughter.

"What is the point of being martyred if you do not scream?" she asked. "Wouldn't it be thought that you do not care enough about your life to protest its end?"

The Duke looked at her with tepid interest.

"No worldly agony is greater than what our imaginations can conjure," he said. "There was no need for this girl to scream. Everyone who looked on could imagine her pain. The pain is the protest."

ELEVEN

DAWN SLIPS IN THROUGH THE NARROW CRACKS IN the wall. That quiet, gray light. Roscille lies on her side under the covers, palms pressed together under her cheek. Beside her, Macbeth's body protrudes from the sheets. His naked shoulders rise and fall with the long, deep breaths of sleep.

She has had hours now, hours that she could not fill with sleep of her own. Time passed through her like air through an empty shell. Passes, still. Strangely, she finds she is afraid of nothing, not even the pain of moving her limbs. They do not feel like her limbs, after all. She does it in small, stiff increments: Sliding her arms out from under her. Pushing herself up onto her elbows. Then onto her knees. The covers fall off her body. She looks over at Macbeth, to make sure he has not been disturbed. His breaths are steady.

Roscille takes in the room, now filled with light. Her dress on the floor, Senga's careful stitching torn open. The white sheets curving up and down, showing blood in various states of age. The older blood, dried and gritty, like rust. Newer blood, garish and bright, and still wet enough that her finger will turn red if she touches it. When she brushes her hand against the back of her legs, only hard black bits of blood come off. Between her thighs it is newer, still slick.

The cloak is puddled on the floor where she left it. She kneels down—a shock of pain—and gathers it to her chest. It is astonishingly soft and she could spend hours feeling all these various degrees of softness, feathers versus fur, the gloss of the unicorn's horn. The rest of her dresses are in the trunk at the foot of the bed. She is afraid that if she opens it, Macbeth will wake. So she slips the cloak over her shoulders, fastens it at the hollow of her collarbones, and folds her arms across her chest to cover her naked body.

She takes one more thing from the table beside the bed and then slips silently through the door.

DOWN THE WINDING CORRIDORS, the sea rising and falling beneath her feet. Out into the salt-pricked air of the courtyard. Her eyes sting. No one is there to stop her. Not even the horses whinny in the stables, breathing pale smoke from their nostrils. She remembers how cold she was the first time she stood in this courtyard; she does not even shiver now.

The barbican is shut, naturally, so she has to squeeze through its bars. This is easy enough, for no one designs a castle's defenses with a woman's body in mind. Bare-footed onto the rough grass of the hill. Dew makes her exposed skin damp. Behind her is the insistent rush of the ocean, but Roscille does not want its hardness and grit, its crushing, snarling tide. It makes her sick to even imagine. Instead she treads on down the hill, the arches of her feet burning as the ground slopes beneath her.

She stops at the small copse of trees. They are bright and impossibly green, as if fed by a recent rainstorm, though it has not rained for weeks in Glammis.

The clearing is how she remembers it, only Fléance's blood no longer slicks the grass. Last time she was here, she was Lady Roscille, still chafing against her new kingdom, new language, new name. Now it all sloughs off her, like a snake's shed.

The tightly knitted branches protect the glade from the wind, so there is no sound, save her own footsteps, as she approaches the pool. The water is clear, showing her rippling reflection. Roscille watches herself disappear into it. First her ankles, then her legs, her hips, her breasts, until she is drowned up to the throat. Her hair floats out in strands of silver-white.

She feels the blood vanishing from her, but curiously it does not taint the water. The pool remains clear, like a gemstone refracting light. Her legs are slick, and when she reaches down, the ugly texture of the scars is gone. The water holds her in perfect suspension. She does not need to kick to stay afloat.

This moment, too, hangs in timeless suspension. No birdsongs, no early-risen crickets, no scurrying in the underbrush. This is a fairy place, made alive only by unnatural magic. Or so she thinks. Suddenly, the sounds return: birds tittering in the branches, crickets humming, animals blinking their yellow eyes from among the roots. The relief she feels is like a breath finally released. She touches herself. The pain is here again, too. But it is moving away from her with each passing moment, as she sinks deeper and deeper into the water. At last it closes over her head.

So long she has resisted this death by water, struggled and writhed against the fate of Hawise and the First Wife. Now it seems the only power she has left. Perhaps the First Wife thought so, too.

From underwater, there is a muffled sound—large and heavy, and Roscille breaks the surface in a panic. Branches part and twigs snap. She turns around, paddles backward to where she can stand. She is still half drowned, only her head and torso showing, as the serpent winds its way into the clearing.

It looks both greater and less than when she saw it first, in the murk and darkness of the dungeon. Its long body flutters with muscle, stippled with gleaming scales. Its head is enormous, more than half the span of her arms. Its tail cuts the grass as it moves. The scutes that rise from its back make it look more a creature of water than fire, though she smells the smoke that tinges the air a hazy gray color. Among the stone and rusted iron of the castle, this creature was an abomination, an affront to nature, impossible to comprehend. The green hue of its scales was more vivid than anything she could name.

Here, it is the color of leaves that have been nourished by rain, the grass that has been protected from the coarse, stripping winds. It pulls the light of the clearing to it, gathering it and holding it in the long vessel of its body. It fits here, like the arrangement of stones in a streambed.

And Roscille is not afraid.

The dragon approaches her: slow, viperous creature it is. Its huge head tilts, as if to examine her from all angles. Serpents, she knows, see only by movement. Staying still will turn her invisible. So Roscille takes a trembling step forward, moving farther out of the water, until she is only drowned up to her knees, the rest of her body bared, waiting. Flesh and muscle, thick, a meal of milk and honey for this creature, if that is what it desires. She looks into its lidless eyes. Tries to find Lisander there.

But then the dragon is on her, its claws shearing the water. Its muscular body wraps her, constricts it. This is how serpents eat; Roscille has seen it, the adder with its unfortunate mouse. Yet the pressure is not quite tight enough to be painful. It is merely that, pressure, and where its belly scrapes her breasts she feels a throbbing somewhere quite far away from her breast, these two places connected as if by a taut string.

Consume me, she thinks. *Have me, as you will.*

Then, a slipping. The scales turning smooth. The musculature of the creature's body withers, until she feels the tenderness of flesh and the jutting of bones beneath it. The metamorphosis is quicker than nymph to tree, fish to flower. No claws, no teeth, nothing but Lisander's bare skin, his hand fisting her damp hair, and his breath hot against her throat. His chest heaves.

She grasps him by the shoulders, pulling him against her until their bodies seem to bleed together. She gasps out, "You."

He whispers into her neck, "Why did you not run?"

"I choose this death, over any other."

A swallow ticks in Lisander's throat. "I do not think the creature—my creature—would have harmed you. I have . . .

some sense, still. I am changed, not vanished." He draws a breath. "But it is a viler curse than you know, Roscille. My desires are not stolen from me. Rather it is my own basest impulses, transfigured, made monstrous. I am myself, perhaps more truly than any mortal man could ever be."

Lisander leans forward. His head rests against her shoulder. It is a pose of penitence.

"I think I am much the same," she whispers back. "If I have a witch to thank for my curse, she did not change me. She only revealed me."

With a sudden urgency, he takes her face in his hands. His eyes blaze.

"Perhaps you will flee after I confess this," he says, hoarse, tormented. "I did not leave you alone in that dungeon because I wished to abandon you in your suffering. I feared that the creature might inflict upon you a worse fate than what you already had endured. It wanted— I wanted you in the manner a man desires a woman, yet cloaked within the dangerous glamour of claws and teeth."

"Then the beast is more humane than any mortal man," she says bitterly. "To resist such an urge—to flee rather than to feast."

She takes his hand from her face and guides it, slowly, between her legs. He must feel the newer blood there, wounds from the torture he did not have the misfortune to witness. All of a sudden he turns cold, like stone.

But she guides him farther, working his fingers inside her.

"Roscille—" he starts.

"No," she says, her voice breaking. "Please. Let me have this pleasure of my own choosing."

Lisander does not speak. He only swallows again, hard, throat bobbing. And then without a word he kneels.

His hands venture hesitantly, gently over the backs of her thighs, feeling the uneven landscape of scars. For a moment they were gone, the water paring away her ugly flesh and making it new. But that moment was a blink, and they are here again. She is so afraid he will now only see her as this broken, pitied thing. That, she cannot bear.

Roscille kneels beside him in the water. She touches her forehead to his.

Then she kisses him. It is a remorseless kiss. But still she feels his hesitation, the way his lips fumble to open under hers, and he pulls away and says, "Do not make me the monster now, in this human body."

She shakes her head fiercely. "I have vanished from myself. Please help me return."

So when she kisses him again, he does not pull back; without contrition, he obeys her. Their bodies join, knitted at the hips, beneath the surface of the water. It is so easy, the way he slides between her thighs, the way he slips into her: almost formless, a spiritual possession. Any pain that comes is invited. It is her pain, an ache she has welcomed; it belongs to no other creature, no other man. And there is the pleasure to match it, ecstasy running alongside the agony, two parallel cords that knot together in the throbbing place at the bottom of her belly.

When the knot unfurls, it sends tremors through her own body, to the tips of her fingers and toes. Lisander shudders. Below their joined waists, the water blooms pink, like the opening of a rose.

THEY LIE THERE IN THE GRASS, like an oyster shell split open, facing each other as mirrored halves: their noses the point of fastening. Morning light is leaking through the leaves. Soon the castle will be awake, the husband will be awake, searching for her. Roscille closes her eyes and breathes.

"What am I to do?" she whispers, when she opens them again. "I have nothing to return to but chains."

Lisander's lashes flutter. She can see his weariness, how sleep will take him at any moment. Roscille wants to hear him say: *Stay, then.* But even he cannot stay. The creature is a fire, licking at him from the inside out. He says, in a voice thick with exhaustion, "I will be here, as long as I can be myself."

"No," she says, with a bolt of panic. "Macbeth is hunting you. He has spread news of the dragon from the peak of the island to its pit. He is offering untold fortune to the man who brings him your head."

At this, Lisander stirs. Blinking, he says, "Evander will never meet him at the bargaining table then."

"Macbeth does not care about that anymore. He says all of Alba will kneel to him, and then he will beat back Æthelstan without difficulty."

"He will not. Æthelstan's army is larger than anything Macbeth can scrounge together, if he does not die of a blade to the back first."

Roscille is not so certain. Banquho is back at his side, his Lord's right hand. Fléance has escaped the fetters she tried to set upon him. All the machinations she thought so clever have amounted to nothing in the end. Her father sold her as a pleasure slave, and now that is indeed all she is, no canny ermine disguised in bridal lace. How long until she falls pregnant, and Roscille is stamped out beneath the feet of Lady Macbeth?

"This will be the last you see of me." Roscille gathers her cloak to her chest, holds it tightly, though it contains no warmth. "I will follow the fate of his first wife. I know it now."

Lisander sits up, brow furrowed. "How do you know the fate of his first wife?"

"She was a witch-marked woman, too. It is not hard to guess."

Lisander frowns. She is in love with the way he looks almost boyish in these moments, when he confers with himself in his own mind.

"Macbeth was once a forgettable lord," he says. "His father was Thane of Glammis, yes, but he was a second son, unexpected to inherit the title. His elder brother was a warrior, such a one that the Scots respect above all others, battle-scarred and battle-ready. So Macbeth was likely to be passed over, as most second sons are.

"Since he had no status to be envious of, he chose a wife without the king's consultation. This woman was herself a widow—odd, to be a widow so young, and without children from her first marriage, to some other lord of Scotland. She had no particular beauty, nor charm. Her house was not a great house. It confounded many when Macbeth chose her. Even then, though he was to inherit nothing, he was known for being adept in his dealings. The Scots do not respect this virtue so much as Lord Varvek does, of course. Still. It appeared to all to be strange.

"So this woman—she was not well liked, even in Macbeth's own household. She was cruel to her servants; she did not entertain visitors. Macbeth was curiously unperturbed by all of this. He insisted it was a marriage for love. A foreign thing, for Scots. But my father was moved by this sentiment. His marriage, too, had been for love." Lisander smiles crookedly, humorlessly.

Roscille listens, feeling her heartbeat thrum in her chest. "Go on."

"So this woman, this Lady Macbeth, decided to host a banquet for her husband's family, whom she had shown little regard up until then. Macbeth's father came, and of course his elder brother. Wives and children. There was nothing unusual about it, until the food was served. It is said that the stew had an odd taste, but there are few who can even remember such a thing. For anyone who touched that food with their tongue was suddenly overcome with great, heaving coughs. Their faces turned blue; their throats squeezed shut. Lady Macbeth had fed them all poison. The rest of Macbeth's clan, slaughtered. The women and children, too."

Her blood goes cold.

"How?" she manages. "How was Macbeth not executed for this crime? Patricide, filicide. His soul is damned forever. Nothing can wash it clean."

"Because he said it was his wife's doing, his wife's ambition for him to become Thane of Glammis." Lisander pauses. "The king came, and the chancellor. They found poison berries in Lady Macbeth's chamber—how easily she could have snuck them into the food."

Men love nothing more than to be proven right. This strange wife. They were right to suspect her all along. So clever! So perceptive! They must have thought themselves thus, preening in their unstained clothes.

"She was executed for this, of course." Roscille closes her eyes. The darkness of her vision is pricked with red.

"No," Lisander says. "There was a trial organized. My father, in those days, still aping the civilized ways of England and Rome. Lady Macbeth was to be kept in chains until she was summoned before judge and jury. That same old cell, in the dungeon." His gaze travels past her, remembering. "I was a boy then. I saw her only once, a brief passing in the corridor. She was already in her chains. There was little to remark about her, save this—her eyes were very pale. Almost like water."

Roscille's mind, which has been so long asleep, trapped in the tight stricture of pain, smothered, silenced, begins to turn again.

"The morning of the trial two men went to bring her up from the dungeon. But they found the cell empty. Yet the door was not open—it was as though she had slipped through the bars. They sounded the castle's bells, as if there were an enemy's army on the horizon. The search was long and desperate. At last, some keen-eyed servant spotted a woman's dress in the water below the cliffs, churning amid the foam like laundry. The gown was recovered, but Lady Macbeth's body was not."

"And there were no other search efforts? All were happy to believe that she drowned?"

"There was nothing else to believe. She had vanished, like a spirit vacating its vessel."

Roscille stares into Lisander's eyes, letting his green gaze throw her reflection back at her. She sees herself truly, at last. She sees the face that makes men cower and cringe. She sees the shades of her father, in small ways: The pertness of her chin. The high, jutting cheekbones. Wrybeard would never claim this resemblance; perhaps he would be blind to it entirely, as a nocturnal creature is unaccustomed to the light.

"You did not say anything about Macbeth's mother."

"I did not know her," says Lisander. "She was dead, I believe, long before my birth. There were some rumors about strange fates befalling the women of Glammis, but—"

"Surely," Roscille cuts in, "there is some record of her. Perhaps not of the mother. But the wife? At least a name."

He nods slowly. "The name, I do know."

The name rises from Lisander's throat, drifts between his lips, and hangs in the air between them. And then it presses itself upon her, with the heat and heaviness of a brand, marking her naked skin. This pain, this other pain she has chosen, makes her blood run with a vitality she has not felt in so long, as if she is a corpse, revived.

Roscille's limbs unfold. She rises, and with two hands, she pulls Lisander up with her.

"You must go," she says. "Promise me you will stay safe. Far away from here. Free."

"There is no freedom for me when I am absent from you."

"Please."

"What are you going to do, Roscille? Do not ask me to leave you again; I cannot. The longing is with me even when I am the beast; perhaps it is greater, even."

The clearing's natural sounds surround them. Birdsongs, cricket tunes, romping animals. The grass, beneath their feet, damp with the impressions of their bodies. So easily, she could slip back into the water, hold her head underneath until she became a part of the clearing, too, her bones lilting to the floor, silver fish darting through the empty cathedral of her rib cage.

As easily as Lisander will slip out of his human skin when the exhaustion forces his eyes shut.

She considers running, too, of course. But the spear-tips of men would find them before they could make it far. The brightness of her cloak is like a beacon for arrows—there is a reason the weasel only sheds his sturdy brown camouflage at first snowfall.

"You will haunt me, too," she says at last. "We can never be truly apart then, if we are each other's ghosts."

Lisander takes her face into his hands and kisses her. He does not release her until his scales begin to show.

Roscille picks up the heavy cloak and robes herself in it. Tucked cannily into one of the folds, right where the rabbit's fur meets the feathers of the swan, the iron key hums with a mystic warmth.

If she cannot have safety, if she cannot have love, at least she can have this. Vengeance.

MACBETH MUST SLUMBER STILL, because Roscille is able to slide back through the barbican and into the castle without being detected. The light is still the same rheumy gray, as if the sun has been constrained. Perhaps time slowed around the clearing, as river water freezes in winter, ice framing the arrangement of stones. Through the corridors, chasing the sound of the ocean. The key, the lock. The harsh sting of the salt on her skin, its hostile grit. The darkness that is like a wall of smoke. Now Roscille does not hesitate. She steps into the water.

The torch flickers to life. Stretching flames illuminate their white, crooked limbs, which fork the black air. Their wet clothes rise from the water, then descend, then rise again, with the torturous rhythm of the tide. Their feet shuffle against sand and stone. Their chains drag like shells on the seafloor. All the flesh and fabric clinging to their taut bones looks translucent, as the bellies of thin-skinned fish.

Until now Roscille has been stumbling with a mortal's blindness. Now she strides toward les Lavandières without fear. They advance upon her. They circle her, until they are within the reach of one another's arms. Roscille does not need the torchlight to see. In fact, when she closes her eyes, her vision breaks apart with color. Smoke and green and purple miasmas. Memories that are not her own.

She opens her eyes. "I know you."

The center witch responds drily: "It has taken you long enough, to cut off your earthly sight. Roscille. Rosele. Rosalie. Roscilla. Lady Macbeth."

Roscille fixes her eyes on this witch. "Lady Macbeth."

The witch blinks slowly. Like a cat. A serpent. The other two witches continue with their washing. It is only now that Roscille sees the differences between them, where before they were all copies of the other. The right witch is the oldest, wrinkled like aged grapes. The left is second oldest. There are still youthful streaks of black in her hair, braided neatly among the white.

The center witch is waiting. Time slurries around them. The world grows older—or newer—but they do not.

In Breizh, to name a thing is to claim some power over it. They carve runes into the walls of their monasteries—false, un-Christian names, which will fool black-clad Ankou into passing without adding their corpses to his wagon. To banish a fairy, one must only speak their true name aloud. Then they will disappear with a peal of thunder, in a cloud of smoke.

Roscille asked her father once, *Perhaps it is better to have no name at all, so you cannot lose your power to another?* And Lord Alan Varvek, Duke of Breizh, Wrybeard, vanquisher of the wretched Northmen from the narrow channel, replied, *It is not for women to worry about these matters. You will take your husband's name when you wed anyway.*

"Gruoch," Roscille says. "I am pleased to meet you."

At the sound of her name, the witch's eyes crackle with light. Gruoch. It is a name that demands a lot of Roscille's Brezhon mouth, drawing low, harsh sounds from the back of her throat. A name Lisander had to school her tongue in speaking; repeating the word three times over until she could mimic it perfectly. This name is a weed that grows from the rocky soil of Glammis, a plant that, if it is torn up, will merely grow again, showing its vines even in the dry-cracked earth.

"So now you know me," Gruoch says. "What will you ask? Counsel? Prophecy?"

Roscille looks at the other two witches, who have paused in their washing. Still like this, she can examine them: One is squint-eyed. The other has a mole on her cheek. They were wives, too. Ladies Macbeth.

She takes a breath.

"No," she says. "I want to be like you."

Gruoch's white face grows whiter. She scoffs. "You do not want to be like us. Washing clothes for the length of how many mortal lifetimes."

"You are doing his laundry, truly?"

Left Witch: What else are old women good for?

"Yet Macbeth seeks you out for advice, for your farseeing power. If you were truly powerless, surely you would be dead."

Right Witch: What is power, Lady? It is a word that grows more distant from its meaning each time it is spoken. We tell the King what he wishes to hear. And if he does not wish to hear it, he molds it into whatever prophecy pleases him. Bad omens are good omens. The sea is a hellish desert. The desert is a heavenly spring.

Roscille falls silent. She sees the flimsiness of her previous schemes, falling like cut flowers around her. She sent her husband on a deadly mission only for him to come back more powerful than ever. She tried to yoke Fléance to her will, only to have the same ropes turned on her.

Perhaps her greatest mistake was trying to ape the power of mortal men. Now she knows there is another world, waiting beneath the one she knows. Here, in the darkness, she can walk without shielding her eyes.

Left Witch: I see the wounds on you, Lady.

Right Witch: I see the fury behind your silence.

Gruoch says, "I see the protest in your pain."

The darkness around her seems to stretch and ripple. When Roscille looks down, she sees the silver of her reflection, murky and strange, more color than discernible shape. White is bleeding from her body and into the water. As it drains from her, it spills out in all directions, taking on its own forms. Like shadow puppets on a wall, they appear: A bloody dagger and a bloody hand. The crescent-shaped silhouette of a face. And at last, a crown, raised high over this head by a pair of disembodied arms.

When Roscille blinks, all of it vanishes, the dark water sucking the color away.

She lifts her gaze.

"I have a prophecy of my own," she says. "Will you speak it for me?"

TWELVE

I
T IS LUCKY FOR ROSCILLE, THAT TIME HAS PASSED SO SLUG-
gishly, so unnaturally, that her husband does not notice
her absence from their marriage bed. She takes off her
cloak and slides back into the sheets beside him. Every muscle
and bone protests this. It is like returning to a different body,
one that exists in this permanent state of pain, the still-healing
scabs on the backs of her thighs, the tear between her legs,
Forget these little wounds, as if such a thing were possible. As
much as she desires it, her mind cannot have total dominion
over her body.

Macbeth wakes strangely, unlike other men. He does not
roll over, nestling into the sheets, as protest against the rising
sun. He turns onto his back and sits up straight, as though
yanked upward by an invisible chain. His torso, perfectly erect,
is statue-like in its stiffness. His eyes open without blinking
away the bleariness of sleep. Roscille observes this in total si-

lence, as her fear of him resurrects itself. But then a furrow appears between his brows and he lets out a huff of air between his gritted teeth, and Roscille remembers her husband's little wound, which has stained the sheets with a new kind of blood. Black and oozing, dredged from somewhere deep within his body. It must hurt. She cannot see how it would not.

"Wife," Macbeth says, turning to her.

"My lord husband." Her voice is meek, but this is for the best. He will want to know he has broken her. A good punishment; this has been one which mixes pleasure for him with pain for her.

But Macbeth's look of satisfaction is brief. Without preamble, he says, "You will join me in my chamber from this day on."

Roscille watches herself nod, from some distant, disembodied place.

"Banquho told me you brought a handmaiden to the castle."

"Yes." Roscille lowers her gaze. "Senga."

She prepares herself for a new punishment. She wonders if she will be struck, if he will parade her around to his men with a freshly pulsing bruise on her face, proof that Macbeth can indeed keep his wife in line, that he has corrected the error in himself which placed her in charge of the castle to begin with.

But he merely says, "She may have this chamber, then. And she will attend to your bathing and dressing."

She is surprised by this, but perhaps she should not be. Macbeth is King now; he has forgotten these small indignities, he has stamped upon the virtue of honor, snuffing out its noble flame. Some minute defiance of custom on the part of his wife is not enough to chip the great shining armor of his power. And Roscille must not remark upon it, must not call it kindness nor mercy, because such things are below him, too.

So she replies only, "I will tell her."

"It may vex Banquho," says Macbeth. "Perhaps the other men. But that is below my regard."

Macbeth throws off the covers, and Roscille turns away, so she will not have to see the nakedness of his body. She has already felt its strength in the dark. Let it stay there, she thinks. Let the dark swallow it whole.

She hears the grunt of pain as he shifts the heavy weight of his body onto his injured leg. He robes himself in a new shirt and a clean tartan and says to Roscille, "Come. There is a war council waiting."

THAT SHE HAS BEEN INVITED to the council table is a surprise, as well. Yet this time she does not sit at the table. She is instructed to take a seat several paces away, a chair shoved flush against the wall. What purpose does this serve? Surely Macbeth benefits more from hiding her away. Surely Scotland will only allow him so many errant witch-wives. But this, too, she realizes, is another brusque show of his new kingly force. Her presence announces to his men: *I will marry whom I choose. To you, perhaps, she is a witch, but to me she is a wife. Whatever little power she might have is extinguished within the sheets of our marriage bed.*

Roscille feels, somehow, that they can tell, that Winter Fox and Weasel-cloak and Mountain Goat all can tell that her thighs have been newly bloodied. Perhaps it is the way that she sits so shrunken in her seat, more emptiness than form, like a white gash in the world. He has succeeded at last, her lord husband, in misusing her the way a thousand, thousand women have been misused before. He crushed her in his fist, squeezing out all the witchcraft that was valuable to him, and then left her, a husk.

It is the cloak which proves this. Roscille might as well be invisible within its folds. She is Lady Macbeth, and finally she understands what that means: a rung upon which to hang her husband's virtue. The cloak says, *I have conquered Alba; I wear its skin as proudly as my crown. It is my trophy, my treasure, mine, mine, mine.*

"I have left an army in charge of Moray, to quell any potential uprisings," Macbeth is saying. "But I do not think they will uprise. I have slaughtered all of Duncane's most loyal allies—that dumb dog Macduff, his body has been strung up outside the castle walls. Any remaining loyalists will see it and choke on their noble treacheries."

If he has killed Macduff then he has also killed Macduff's wife and sons, so there is no one who remains to someday take vengeance upon him. She imagines her husband tasting this man's blood. She wonders if, after the unicorn was skinned, he butchered the animal and ate it? She finds she can envision this easily.

"Your power has been proven, my Lord," Banquho says. "No one in Alba will challenge you."

Banquho has not looked at her at all. It is Fléance who steals glances, again and again. There is such shame, on his still-boyish face. His shame does not fill her as she expected it to. It is a tasteless meal, like water without wine. Fear is what she seeks from him. And she will not be sated until she gets it.

There is some shuffling of maps and papers, which Roscille cannot see, tokens moving across the table. The low, rough voices of men who all have something to prove to one another. Macbeth murmurs something she cannot hear. The next words that reach her ears are Banquho's, again.

"Now there is the matter of merging households."

"Merging, why?" Her husband's voice. "I do not want Duncane's servants here. Let them grovel and burn in Moray."

"It would be a gesture of goodwill," says Banquho. "To prove you will be King of all Scotland, not merely King of Glammis."

Silence, as Macbeth considers this. Mountain Goat suppresses a cough.

"Fine," says Macbeth at last. "I will take a portion of his household staff, but only those whom I have looked in the eye, who kneel and swear their loyalty to me. There is enough reason to fear treachery already."

"Yes," Banquho agrees. "Which is why you must prove you can do more for these men than any other lord could. That their lives will be better beneath the rule of Macbeth than they were under Duncane, than they would be under Æthelstan or one of those half-Saxon brats."

Roscille's heart stutters.

"On the subject of these brats," says Weasel-cloak, "we have had no success in finding Duncane's monstrous spawn."

A sort of relief fills her, but it is half pleasure, half poison. She hopes he is far away now, safe on English soil. And yet she knows she will dream of him every night, and wake in the cold sweat of a fever.

"That should not be our greatest concern now," says Banquho. "War is coming. Æthelstan's armies will breach the border soon."

"As soon as Æthelstan's army is in tatters and that arrogant *rex Anglorum* is kneeling at my feet, I will slay the dragon myself," Macbeth says. "Until then, let each man of Scotland hope he will be the one to find and kill it, and earn the prize of my unending favor."

It is like the myth of the sunken city, Ys: Give the people something to believe in, no matter if it is impossible. Let anyone with a sword and stupid courage think he may have a chance at slaying the beast. Hope is enough to keep a man clambering up the long dingy rope of his life.

The men all give wordless grunts of agreement. Barbarous as they seem, they are not wholly without reason.

"I return to Moray soon," says Macbeth. "I must be certain no disloyalty lurks there. Æthelstan will try to seize the castle first. He is wise enough to know that Glammis is a fortress which cannot be trespassed. He will think to beat me back to my home and then lay siege there, to starve us to surrender. I will not give him the chance. I will defeat him at Moray."

More nods from his men. Banquho says, "I will be at your side, my Lord."

"No," Macbeth says. "You must remain here. I entrust you not to let this castle fall to treachery or ill management. You may prepare anyway for a siege. It will not come to that, but it is wise still to be ready."

This time, Banquho will take the task eagerly, because of all that is unspoken in Macbeth's words. *My wife failed in this endeavor. Now I trust it again to you—my right hand.* She should have known it. The clever wife who was not so clever in the end; she has been discarded. And the man who was perhaps too hastily dismissed, the man who served his Lord loyally for so many years, he has been elevated again.

"Yes, my Lord," Banquho murmurs.

"Then see to it," Macbeth says.

The men scatter, scraping their chairs against the stone floor, rolling up their maps, slouching out of the main hall. Their gazes do not stop to rest upon Roscille for even a moment. She is wife now, only. She is beneath their regard.

Fléance stays at first, but he is banished by a quick look from his father. He, too, does not glance at Roscille as he leaves. He will go into the courtyard and practice swordplay. Or else he will find some other empty place to rage at this dismissal, at the fact that he has never wet his blade and tasted an enemy's blood. Good. Let each of these injustices wound like the sting of a whip.

With the three of them alone, Macbeth says, "Come with me."

"Where?" Banquho asks.

Roscille already knows.

THROUGH THE WINDING CORRIDORS, following the sound of the ocean. The iron key back on its leather thong, which is looped around Macbeth's throat, and beats against the hollow of his collarbone with each limping step. Roscille and Banquho are careful to slow their paces, to make sure they are never ahead of him. Yet even now Roscille sees the stain of blood on his stockings, a strange dark blooming, like a shape under ice. They stop in front of the wood-rotted door.

"If you are to keep this castle in my absence," Macbeth says, "then there are things you must know."

Banquho's eyes flicker to Roscille. His unspoken question: *Does she already know?*

To answer, Macbeth says, "A husband and wife should keep no secrets from each other."

Banquho says nothing. Macbeth turns the key in the lock and the door opens.

The cold air that awaits them, the godless blackness—all of it is new to Banquho and he gasps. Macbeth pays no mind to his shock. He steps into the dark, his body cleaving the wall of air, clear and straight and unforgiving. He vanishes, and for a moment there is no sound at all, not even his splashing through the water. Then the torchlight flares. Light catches on the crest of each ripple, giving the water that familiar texture of scales.

Banquho looks to Roscille, and makes a strangled noise of bewilderment. But she merely pushes past him, and follows her husband into the dark. Her heart is pounding in her throat. She is close now. She hopes the witches do not forsake her.

Roscille stays on the steps, but the water splashes up, dampening the hem of the cloak, which is so long that it drags behind her like a wedding train. Banquho shuffles to her side. There is a sheen of sweat on his face, the dampness of terror.

The witches announce themselves with the rattling of chains. Their skin is obscenely white against the unforgiving darkness. Their blind fumbling, their visible bones, the clothes that hang off them in tatters: Banquho stumbles on the slick steps as he tries to shrink from them. They circle Macbeth, water rippling out from around them in overlapping circles.

Their voices are like stones scraping the hull of a ship.

Left Witch: Macbeth, Thane of Glammis.

Right Witch: Macbeth, Thane of Cawder.

Gruoch says, "Macbeth, King Hereafter."

Banquho, pressed against the wall, crosses himself, just as Roscille did that first time. "My God—" he starts.

"No," Macbeth says. "Listen. These are not mere epithets; they are prophecies. When they first spoke, I was Thane of Glammis only. I came here and they called me Thane of Cawder. I took Cawder within a week. Then I came and they called me King Hereafter. You know what happened next."

Slowly, understanding overtakes Banquho's face, in an amalgam of revulsion and awe. He has known, of course, that Duncane died through Macbeth's machinations, but to know that his purpose was driven by witchcraft and sorcery is something else. Macbeth has revealed the truth that threatens to transform Banquho's world into something bizarre, unnatural, strange. It has already begun. His vision has been altered, made to see the dark, cold aberration that runs under everything.

"Come," Macbeth says, gesturing to him. "Hear their next prophecy. See what will guide our actions as we stand against Æthelstan."

Banquho exhales. He looks at Roscille again. She is as still and silent as a nymph turned to stone. Yet under the surface, she is alive with feverish wrath.

Banquho takes one step, two. Foot in the water, circles spreading out from around him, his clumsy, too-human movements so obvious in the stillness of the cave. At last, he reaches Macbeth's side. He puts a hand on his Lord's shoulder, to steady himself, forgetting his place for a moment, forgetting the injury that still pulses behind his Lord's knee like a second beating heart.

Quietly, he says, "Speak of my fate, then."

The three women wring out their clothes. They toss the

laundry over their shoulders, so their hands can be free. With their arms outstretched, palms open to the obstructed sky, they speak together, a chorus.

"Banquho. Banquho. Banquho. Thane of Lochquhaber."

"That is no prophecy," Banquho says uneasily.

Left Witch: Banquho, Thane of Lochquhaber. Lesser than Macbeth, but greater.

Right Witch: Not so happy, yet much happier.

Gruoch says, "Thou shalt beget kings, yet be none."

They join hands, and dip them into the water. Where their skin touches, silver spreads in shapes: Banquho reflected back at himself, and back again, and again, faces piled upon faces, and each one wearing a crown.

Banquho cries out, and reaches for Macbeth again, but his Lord is not there. His body is, but his mind and spirit are released. They are out like animals, chewing on the witches' words, tearing them apart with a fury.

Left Witch, Right Witch, and Gruoch all at once: "All hail Banquho! All hail Banquho! All hail Banquho!"

Their voices sizzle in the air, and the water burns green, like a cauldron with its oils. Macbeth turns away from les Lavandières, away from his first wife to face his second. He wears a mask of incandescent rage.

Banquho is already trudging through the water, panting, scrabbling. He clambers up the steps. He is a warrior and can scent blood before it is even spilled.

He shoves past her, hurtling from the dark into the light. Macbeth growls in wordless anger, limping up the steps after him, and the witches do not stop their chanting, and behind her veil, Roscille smiles.

⌒⇜⚜⌒

THE CHASE DOES NOT GO on for long. Banquho's gait is blunder-
ing with terror, and Macbeth limps still, stopping occasionally
to rest with his shoulder jammed against the wall. Roscille can
see smoke rolling off him, from the pyre lit behind his eyes.

He does not even close the door, so the witches' voices
leak out, spilling through the corridors, suffusing the castle
with the smell of salt water. Roscille follows in silence, her
footsteps hushed against the floor.

Macbeth charges into the courtyard, sword already drawn.
His head whips back and forth, searching. Banquho has
reached the barbican, but it will not open for him. He yanks
at the bars like a prisoner in his cell. His face white, he cries
out, "My Lord, please—"

"Lesser than Macbeth, but greater!" his Lord roars. "Not
so happy, yet much happier. Thou shall beget kings! All this
time, the treachery in Glammis has been wearing the face of
my most trusted friend!"

Friend is not quite right. He uses a word that has no equiv-
alent in Brezhoneg. It means "ally, partner, brother-in-blood."
It is a word forbidden to women, a word for warriors only.
There is a closer term in Greek: *hetairos.*

This shouting draws out the castle's other inhabitants.
Servants peek from doorways and windows. Winter Fox and
Mountain Goat and Weasel-cloak all emerge, hands on the
pommels of their swords, ready always to draw. Even the old
Druide shuffles out, Macbeth's Druide, the one who joined
her hand to her husband's on their wedding night.

And then there is Fléance. Pleasure surges through Roscille as she sees the blank horror on his face. *Whatever harm you have done me, it will be repaid now a thousandfold.*

"You believe the word of these creatures over the vows I have sworn to you, many times over?" Banquho asks desperately. "You are mad, Macbeth, to have taken counsel from them!"

Winter Fox blinks. "My Lord, what creatures does he speak of?"

Macbeth turns to him. Blood has spread all the way down his stockings, thick and ugly and black, and dripped into his boot.

He says, "A madness has overtaken the Thane of Lochquhaber."

The words muffle every sound in the courtyard, flattening even the wind, like iron beaten on an anvil. Even Banquho stops rattling the bars, and stands still as the wind sweeps through and ruffles beards and hair, and presses Roscille's veil against her lips.

"No," Banquho says at last. "You are the mad one. Listen! He keeps these women in chains beneath the floors of his castle—no, I cannot even call them women! They are not inhabitants of the earth. They are withered, wild creatures. Witches! And he defers to them, has them speak false prophecies in his favor!"

"Do you see?" Macbeth gestures. "What demonic humors have corrupted our dear friend's mind? To say this, Macbeth harbors witches! He sees unearthly visions before his eyes."

"Lies!" Banquho howls. "I am no traitor, and I speak truly! Go down the longest, lowest corridor of the castle, and see these evil creatures for yourself!"

Winter Fox and Mountain Goat and Weasel-cloak all look

among one another, jaws and lips moving as though they are chewing food, but they produce no words. Roscille will never stop marveling at the stupidness of men when the order of their world is disrupted.

It is the Druide who speaks.

"Perhaps," he says, "we may release these humors from him. Banish the demons, and return our friend to his reasonable mind."

Another beat of silence.

"You do not mean—" Banquho starts.

Two torches burn in Macbeth's eyes. His chest rises and falls with the exertion of the pursuit, but also with the imagination of violence. He is not an epicure, like the Duke. He is a glutton. He has been presented with a grotesque banquet, and he will feast and feast and feast.

"Yes," Macbeth rasps. "Yes, I think that is what we will do."

THE STRUGGLE TO PIN DOWN Banquho and drag him into the great hall is more fumbling than vicious. Macbeth allows Winter Fox and Mountain Goat and Weasel-cloak to do this work in his stead. He limps after them, his face dewed with sweat. Fléance follows pleading, tears at the corners of his eyes.

Roscille is surprised that no one tries to pin him down, too. After all, she was sure to include this in her prophecy: *Thou shalt beget kings.* Damning father and son in the same breath.

But it is better this way, one final insult to Fléance's pride:

They do not believe he can stop them, nor defend himself when blades are drawn against him. He is a boy who will not have the chance to grow into a man.

Roscille thinks suddenly of that other man, Macduff, the dumb honorable dog whose line her husband struck from the earth. The vision she gave Macbeth, of Banquho's sons and sons and sons, his face multiplied through generations, rolling like the tide. This is a man's first, last, and greatest fear: a world that exists empty of him. A world in which his name is never spoken. His blood dried up, his body dissolved into dirt, his grave grown over with weeds. An empty, seedless husk.

Has she adopted the justice of these barbarian Scots? But no, she does not delude herself that this is justice. It is vengeance. A harder, sharper, hotter blade. Driven between the shoulders and twisted.

Banquho is wrestled into a chair. Rope is procured. He is bound, and all the while he is crying out, "No, no, our Lord spouts lies," as if he cannot tell that with each passing moment he seems madder, and the acts against him all the more reasonable.

"Please!" Fléance says. "My father is no traitor. He has been your loyal companion all these years—"

"Years," Macbeth scoffs, "in which his treachery has grown like the rings of a tree."

"I will release him from this treachery, and from the madness that spawned it," the Druide says. "Tilt back his head."

Roscille has never witnessed it before: trepanation. The process of letting out bad humors. She has only heard the distant screams of men and women upon whom this act is performed. Adelaide's horrible, ecstatic wailing.

Banquho's screams are choppy and broken. He chokes on

his own fearful bile. The Druide has the trephine out, a curious little tool, which Roscille always imagined as a blade but is really more like an auger, something which drills, not cuts. She understands now how it creates the distinctive circular scars that burned so bright on Adelaide's forehead. Now the rusted metal borer descends on Banquho.

There is the quick, wet, sucking sound as flesh is pared away from bone. A spurt of blood—it surprises her, how little there is; the Druide is precise in his work and has had many years of practice. Banquho howls.

Roscille cannot imagine this pain, so perhaps it is not perfectly equivalent vengeance after all. And Banquho, in turn, will never know the agony of something torn open between his legs, rudely forced, degraded into silence. But this is close enough.

The next sound is truly terrible: the splintering of bone. Roscille has heard it many times, a too-slow servant clobbered about the face, skewing his nose gruesomely to the left, but the singularity of the noise now, in the otherwise empty silence of the chamber, makes her want to clap her hands over her ears and squeeze her eyes shut.

She feels, suddenly, that she has erred: not in her intellect or her maneuvering, but erred as a Christian, as a soul promised, however obliquely, to heaven. As if she has not already lost her place there for Duncane's murder. As if men do not do worse every day, and still believe themselves virtuous. As if the Duke did not strike down that trembling, unarmed stable boy while Roscille cringed and spoke no words in his defense; surely that was the beginning of her sin, and from there her life has warped and narrowed into an inescapable, damnable blackness.

"Stop," Fléance pleads. "Have mercy."

She should not wear a white garment ever again. At least a dark linen will better hide the blood she sees dripping from her hands, soaking the hem of her dress, and pooling on the floor around her feet.

"This is mercy," says Macbeth. "I am releasing him from his madness and treachery."

But there is no spilling of yellow pus from the wound. No pungent black smoke. Nothing but that first spurt of blood, because there is no treachery, no madness, except the lunacy that will be engendered in Banquho now forever, as he feels that scar on his forehead and thinks of this injustice visited upon him. He will be as mad as Adelaide, confusing pleasure with pain.

Roscille had believed Banquho's death would be cruel but quick. A blade to the throat, opening a second red mouth screaming with blood. A sword through the heart—honor, at least, on his killer's end. She did not imagine this, not ever. Yet surely that is not enough to salvage her soul.

Banquho coughs and wrestles against his binds, his movements savage and jerking, like a man possessed. Perhaps—somehow, the Druide has truly released a long-dormant spirit of madness, one that inhabits every man, curled inside the structure of bones and warming itself against the pulse of his heart. Perhaps Macbeth will see this and say, *Enough*.

But there is only the trephine grinding deeper, and Banquho thrashing more furiously, and her husband looking on with black, pitiless eyes.

At last: Banquho gags on his own blood and spits it up all over the front of his jerkin and then goes limp in the chair. The Druide yanks the trephine free and steps back, letting the tool clatter to the ground. He is saying, "I am so sorry, my Lord, I did not think, I have never, not once in my life," but these words are as distant as echoes to Roscille, as if she is underwater and hearing it all from the world above, separated by an impassable membrane.

Mountain Goat and Winter Fox and Weasel-cloak stand at a silent distance, waiting to be moved into place.

Fléance staggers forward and clutches his father's body. He howls. There is shame in such weeping and carrying on, but that is the least of anyone's concerns, now. *Thou shalt beget kings.* It is hard to imagine how anyone could be persuaded to believe that this sad shuddering boy would someday wear a crown.

Macbeth has his arms at his sides, fists clenched. He has not moved or even blinked for what seems like an eternity. She can see the prophecy playing out in his mind.

Lesser than Macbeth, but greater. He has been lessened, reduced to a corpse.

Not so happy, yet much happier. No red smile on Banquho's face, or on his throat. His mouth is an open cavity, pooling with blood-flecked foam.

Thou shalt beget kings, yet be none. He is nothing now. A cold body. And there will be no cairn to mark his grave.

ACT V

LADY?

THIRTEEN

"WHAT IS YOUR PURPOSE HERE, LADY?"

This is what the man who guards the dungeon door asks her. Roscille did not expect to be confronted at the top of the stairs, did not expect her motives to be questioned. It draws up an uncertainty deep inside of her, one she was content to let seethe and linger without challenge. She is silent. Every time she tries to speak, her tongue feels too slippery in her mouth.

At last, she lifts her head. She meets the guard's gaze—through the veil—and says, "I wish to see the prisoner."

"The Lord forbids it."

"The Lord will not know," says Roscille. "Or would you rather I tell him how you put your hands on me in the hall when no one was there to witness it?"

The guard blanches. It is crude, to manipulate him this way. There is no pleasure or victory in it. If she were a warrior, she would have just struck him the clumsiest, most deathless blow.

In the space between her threat and his answer, the sound of the ocean is strong and insistent under their feet.

At last, with a grimace, the guard says, "Do not be long."

"It will hardly be more than a moment." The guard steps aside, and Roscille descends the stairs.

THE DUNGEON IS A PLACE that fills her mind with fire. She is only halfway down the stairs when a blinding light cuts across her vision, obscuring everything, and in that empty space, memories flower up: her face pressed roughly against the table, the lace of her veil chafing her lips and cheeks. The coldness of the air against her bare thighs. And the pain, always the pain, the coiled viper under the sun-warmed stone, which strikes when it is prodded.

Her legs burn at this reminder. She must keep this fire hidden in her skin; she must feel her pain in silence, or else the men will snarl *madness* and she will be pinned down and a trephine driven through her skull.

But she rights herself and reaches the bottom of the steps. Her cloak drags through the grimy puddles. She keeps her gaze straight ahead, so she does not see the rusted tools on the wall, and especially the whip, still stained with her blood. So that she does not see the mangled iron bars of the cell that once held Lisander inside of it.

She stops before the second cell. Fléance sits flush against the left wall, nearest to the torchlight; he does not hide himself in darkness. When he sees her, he rises to his feet, and his hand sweeps about his hips, as if searching for a weapon. A sword would do him no good, anyway. There is a collar around his throat, and a chain connecting that collar to the wall. Manacled like a dog indeed.

Straining the collar, Fléance turns to look at her. "Why are you here?"

The same question, just as impossible to answer as before. "Did you think you could beat me as you did, and face no recompense?"

His gaze flickers. "Was it worth it, your vengeance?"

If she were a man, he would not ask her this. For men there is no debt of blood which goes unpaid. If the world tips in another's favor, it must be made to tip back again. But the world is never in a woman's favor. She cannot tip the scale. The only choice is: live the same mute, unjust life you have always lived, or tear apart the world itself.

"I feel no satisfaction while you still draw breath," Roscille says, and this is honest, in a way.

A long silence. Fléance's gray eyes burn.

"Did ever a true word come from your mouth?" he rasps. "When you said your husband erred in overlooking me, that my father had done me a great injustice—did you believe it? Or were you merely stitching me into some great tapestry of deception?"

Her fingers curl into her hands. And then the words flow out, before she can stop them.

"I believe my husband errs in many ways," she says. "And your father—he treated you cruelly, without regard. Perhaps I desired your aid, but I never turned you over on your back and made you show your belly. We could have been allies. Friends, even. You name me witch, evil temptress, a thousand spitting insults, but it is you who first forsook me."

There is another long moment of silence. The gray hue of his eyes, once gleaming in the torchlight, now turns matte and churns like the ocean.

"Do not speak of my father." Fléance's voice is near to a whisper. "He was a good man. A just, loyal man. He was not like your father, that false weasel of Breizh, who sold you to Macbeth like a broodmare. Who loved no part of you but the flesh of your pretty face."

A tempest rises in her. Twisting, snarling fury, all of which spirals outward from the hidden eye of the storm. This old pain, in moments forgotten but never truly vanished, rises to life again now.

"This face could be the death of you." Roscille steps closer to the cell, until her hands touch the iron bars. "It would take only a moment. Avoid my gaze like the coward you are, or look into my eyes, and I will compel you to claw open your own throat. To dash your own head against the wall until your brain is pulp. So many agonizing deaths I could give you. My husband will perhaps offer you a painless demise. But I do not think you deserve to be shown such mercy."

Before she can react, Fléance's hands dart through the bars and grasp her by the front of her dress. Roscille fumbles for her veil, but even imprisoned, he is stronger and quicker: He catches her wrists and pins her arms against his chest. His collar and chains rattle.

"Say it again," he snarls. "Tell me you are the maker of my death."

With his grip so tight, this is the first time he has seemed to her like a man. Roscille lifts her veil far enough to spit in his face.

"Kill me if you like," she says, "but I will be the maker

of your own death still, for Macbeth will slaughter you even more savagely."

"He will slaughter me anyway." Fléance blinks her spittle from his lashes. He pulls her closer, until her whole body is pressed against the cold, rust-gritted bars, and she feels the heat of him, the pulsing of hate and anger and perverse desire. "I should have raped you."

Such bald, ugly words make her stomach boil. She does not care if she crushes her own bones to dust, if they push up through her skin and burst through with blood—Roscille wrenches herself free of him. She shoves him backward, hard, and he stumbles against the wall. With satisfaction she notices that, thanks to his fruitless struggling, the collar has badly bruised his throat.

"You men have no imagination," she says.

Incredibly, Fléance schools his face into an expression of cold contempt. Perhaps it is the collar and chains, smothering the flames of rage, but she has never seen him like this before, composed and sneering.

"Perhaps you would not even protest it," he says. "You open your legs eagerly. I do not forget how you took the whipping in the prince's place. This is not something you would have done for a stranger. Does Macbeth know his wife has dishonored him in his own castle?"

Roscille stills. Her blood is cold.

"Adulteress," Fléance adds, as if she is too stupid to understand. "Whore."

But she is stupid indeed, not to have considered it. She is no selfless martyr, not pious enough to protest torture for its own sake. She has never pretended godliness. She has never knelt in this castle, not since the first night when the Druide tied her wrist to Macbeth's. Suddenly all her blood runs hot again and flushes her cheeks a furious red.

"Call me what names you will," she says, "but my husband will not believe them." Roscille does not even know if this is true. Clearing her throat, she goes on, "And you will be dead soon anyway."

"And perhaps you will follow me soon after. There is no dishonor in slitting a whore's throat."

Clever as she has always imagined herself to be, Roscille finds her mind cannot accept this. She must not torment herself thinking of it. The fear will murder reason, wisdom. And then she will fall into the black pit of madness, alongside Adelaide and all the other women who have looked up, like a fish through the surface of the water, and no matter how they flailed, could not stop the thrust of the spear through their bellies.

She rejects this terror. She flees from it.

"Enjoy this posthumous existence of yours," she spits at Fléance. And then she stumbles back up the stairs, nearly falling flat into the filthy puddles, and clinging desperately to the slick wall even when her fingers find no purchase against it.

WHEN SHE REACHES THE TOP of the stairs, Macbeth is waiting for her.

The fear that Roscille only just evicted emerges again with the force of a river at melt. The sudden deluge makes her knees almost crumple beneath her.

"I am sorry, my Lord—" she starts, but Macbeth holds up a hand.

"You will not speak now," he says, and his voice is so gentle that it petrifies her. It is the way one speaks to a lame horse, to calm it before its slaughter. "You will listen."

Roscille drops her head and looks down at the floor.

"No," says Macbeth. "Look at me."

The veil is such a thin barrier between them, as frail as an infant's skin. Roscille lifts her gaze.

"I see now that this treachery in Glammis was following closely behind me, like a shadow. My own right hand, plotting my downfall in secret. I aimed my blade at a target, only to watch it vanish like smoke, all while my enemy's machinations turned on behind my back."

"My Lord—"

But then he reaches up to touch her face and the hardness of his palm, the heat of him, stuns her into muteness. He presses his thumb against her temple.

"This old wound of yours. I do not forget it. Were these masked men real at all?"

Her mind scrambles. She can play the guileless girl, swept up in schemes beyond her understanding, forced at blade-point into silence and obedience. But her husband knows her; at least, he knows Lady Macbeth. She cannot hide within this white cloak of innocence. He has seen the black heart of her. He has stoked this darkness, molded it, used it to his own advantage.

"It was as I said," she whispers. "The men came. Fléance fought them. I did not know it then—it must have been his fellow conspirators, in disguise. I began to suspect it, in your absence. It was Banquho who refused to torture the prince. I thought that they might be working against you. When I confronted them, they beat me."

It is the best story she can manage, in these circumstances. It allows her both innocence—*I did not know; I could not imagine the treachery*—and wiles—*I began to suspect it, that they were working against you.* She occupies the space Macbeth wishes her to occupy. Clever but not too clever. Working always for his advancement, his preservation, his pride. And perhaps when Fléance accuses her of adultery, Macbeth will have her story already in his mind, and reject the tale this chained boy tries to spin.

Macbeth's face darkens. "You should have told me at once. A husband and wife should have no secrets from each other."

Roscille flinches. "I am sorry. I feared their private retribution."

A moment passes, and then Macbeth takes her face between his palms. He turns it over. Like she is a shell tossed to the tide, her skin worn to translucence.

"You have nothing to fear from them," he says. "You are my wife and you are a queen. Fléance will be killed, and this treachery will die with him. You can feed a dog from your hand all your life, and still one day it may decide to bite."

Dogs do not bite without cause. They are thinking, feeling creatures. But Roscille does not dare to say it.

"Well," Macbeth murmurs. "The witches spoke of sons, and this prophecy was not for Banquho's ears alone. It has been beneath my attention until now—but I will not allow my line to end. You will lie with me every night until my child grows in you. If it is a girl, it will be snuffed out before it can make its way into the world. You are to bear me a son only. Do you understand?"

There is not a woman alive who is ignorant to this. Roscille does not know how many times she has watched this play out before her eyes: A woman falls pregnant. Her husband puffs his chest, swanning the proof of his virility around the court. And yet—there is the waiting, the vulture that watches from its remote perch. Everyone sees him but they do not speak of him. The man may choose to turn his eyes away as well, to luxuriate in his pride until the child's birth, when his honor will either be augmented or stripped from him entirely. There is no honor, after all, in a seed that sprouts daughters.

Or he will do this: There is always a woman in the castle who sees things which are beyond the capacity of mortal eyes. She can feel a swollen stomach and know from its shape whether the child inside is boy or girl. And then, the blankness on the would-be father's face, the few long seconds before his body can display his mind's relief or fury, before he either embraces his wife or yanks her roughly out of the room. She will weep, and he will not care. If he is kind, he will merely force the foul-tasting herb mix down her throat, until the girl-child leaks out from her legs like a monthly blood. If he is not kind, he will shove her belly-first down the stairs, an easy dive, a descent smoothed by the thousands of women who have made this same fall. If her teeth or nose break, this is an acceptable casualty. She will wear these wounds shamefully, and the husband will keep his head down, until the memory of this episode fades, until there is another belly, swollen with the hope of a son.

Roscille says, "I understand."

Her husband is not a kind man.

"Good," says Macbeth.

His large hand curls around the back of her skull. He pulls her into him, and then places a kiss on her forehead. Roscille waits there, silent, her skin turning to bark, her arms to branches, her hair to leaves, *Please please please, leave me alone, let me go, I am just a dead thing—living, but dead—and can foster no new life inside of me.* The pain no longer feels like a protest. It is merely pain. She feels as alive as a tree and as dead as a stone.

Her mind is escaping her.

At last, Macbeth lets go. Roscille watches as he limps down the hall, the blue-black stain behind his knee spreading, growing, blooming.

ROSCILLE GOES TO HER CHAMBER—WELL. Not her chamber, anymore. She is her husband's bedmate now. The bear-rug is not her bear-rug. The small narrow bed is where Senga sleeps alone. She finds her handmaiden there now, sitting in the room's single chair, embroidering a bolt of gray fabric.

When she sees Roscille, she rises, dips her head, and says, "Lady."

How quickly she has learned to be deferent, to be a slave. Roscille feels the bile rising from her empty stomach to her throat.

"Please," she says. "Call me Roscille."

Senga's brow furrows as her Scottish mouth forms the Brezhoneg sounds. "Roscille." She pauses. "But you are still my Lady."

"I hoped to be your friend."

What a foolish hope. Roscille has never had a friend who was not tied by duty to her side. The other women in Wrybeard's court cringed from her, as though witchery were catching. Men, of course, do not make friends of women.

They make wives or whores or servants, and since Roscille was a noble lady, the Duke's daughter, she could be none of those. And after the stable hand, the boys were wise to stay away. Hawise, her only friend, yoked to her with a long chain of fear that began with Hastein and flowed through the Duke.

Senga regards her curiously. She stands, laying the unfinished embroidery over the arms of the chair, then sits down on the bed. She pats the mattress beside her. "Sit, then. Friend."

Roscille approaches her. She sits down on the bed that was once her bed, her smallest comfort. Its softness against her skin now feels like a punishment—undeserving skin, still gruesome with scar tissue, black pits of dried blood like a scattering of leeches. She draws in a breath and moves her hand to lift her veil.

"Do not be afraid," she says. "My gaze does not induce madness in women."

"I am not afraid."

Cool air on her cheeks. Relief, like a parched mouth sipping sweet water. She knows she is still trapped, but even horses run in spirited circles around their pens, imagining freedom.

Senga watches her with narrowed eyes, and Roscille watches her back. She is older; Roscille cannot tell by how much. Her hips have the width and laxity of past childbirth. How long ago? Roscille wonders. How many children? She is old enough to have had five or six or even seven children. Roscille, at seventeen, is late to it; she could have filled a lord's castle with sons by now.

Yet this is as foreign to her as the Northman tongue. Her mother died when Roscille slipped, blood-glazed, from between her legs. There was the blind midwife who nursed her, a name Roscille has now forgotten. Hawise was still a girl and virginal.

She thinks of the rumors of Senga, the reason she was cast out of her village, threatened with a shaved head and a wimple and a scapular and ceaseless repentance to God. What did she seek in these couplings—pleasure? What man has ever been punished for that? Love? Is that a sin? Roscille presses her hands flat against her thighs. There is a humming from somewhere deep inside her, the memory of the dragon's strength and muscle as it bore over her body—this is all she has now; the memory.

"Is it possible," she blurts out, "in Alba—a marriage for love? A child born not out of mere obligation?"

Senga's eyes soften, then harden, then soften again. "You are seventeen, yes? Barely more than a child yourself. Your life . . . Well, you are a noble lady, so you know this. Your husband's whims will shape all your years to come. That is the way. I cannot imagine it is so different in your country. But you have a choice. You may pretend love is the reason you submit to him, why you bear his son, and even if it is not true at first, it will be true someday; you have the strength of mind to fashion it so."

"Was it love you sought, when you lay with those men?" Roscille flushes at the boldness of her own question.

Senga's eyebrows dart up her face. A moment passes, then anger. "Have you ever met, Lady, a woman with three children or more?"

Met, Roscille thinks, never. But she has seen them, from a distance. Peasant women, their eyes cast on the muddy ground, ushering their dirty-faced broods. If there is a father, he stands at a distance, observing grimly, then turning to slouch toward the fields for labor. Sometimes Roscille cannot find the father, and the children clamber up their mother, clinging to her hips like growing vines. And there is always the curled lip, the scoffing, why did she not keep her legs closed, she has more children than she can afford, she may as well go peddle herself, now.

"I have not," Roscille admits.

"Well," says Senga, "now you have. There are four, and thank God all are old enough to work, so they do not miss me much. Perhaps they are better for it—their mother, the village slattern. They love me but I shame them. And they shame me, too. You want to know why, but there is no reason that would absolve me. I thought you would have sent me to a nunnery."

"A man would not have to answer for it." Roscille pauses. "He would never imagine being asked *why.*"

"So what does it matter? Love, greed, need, appetite—they are not the purview of men alone."

"Love is not as easy to smother as the rest."

Roscille stares into the middle distance for a long time in silence. She imagines herself lying on that soft grass again, nose-to-nose with Lisander, like an amulet unclasped, two matching halves facing each other.

"I am sorry," she manages. "I do not want this for myself, these stupid girlish hopes."

Astonishingly, Senga takes her hand and brushes the hair back from Roscille's face. So tenderly; she has practiced this gesture many times upon her own children.

"Do men not hope?" Her voice is soft. "They imagine

themselves mighty and clever and virile and powerful. This hope of yours is quite small by comparison."

Small, yes. But it only takes a crack in the foundation of the world to bring careful architecture, strong with centuries, crumbling down. A small blade cuts the water and ripples outward like an echo. And then the world beneath shows itself, first as green shoots in the dirt. And then comes a woman, a witch, tearing her way through the green matter with her teeth.

MACBETH COMES INTO THE ROOM and Roscille immediately dries her tears and puts on her veil. Her husband's face is nothing. The ghostly smudge of a thumbprint on a windowpane. He holds a length of white fabric in his hands.

"Come, Roscilla," he says, in this hollow nothing of a voice. "There will be a council meeting."

She rises and approaches him without a word. The mattress crumples as Senga moves, as if to reach out for Roscille and keep her from leaving. But Macbeth's presence crushes them both into silence. Roscille looks down and waits for her husband to open the door, to turn into the corridor, so she can follow.

Instead, he says, "Wait."

Her mind is a smooth channel through which such brusque directives flow easily. She must keep it empty so she does not think of what awaits her tonight, and the next night, and the next. Macbeth sweeps her hair back from her neck.

Before she can speak, or even think, Macbeth knots the

white fabric over her eyes. Blinding her entirely. When she blinks her crumpled lashes, she sees only a fuzzy blackness.

Panic overtakes her, curdling the words in her throat. When she can still her racing heart, quiet the pounding of blood in her ears, Roscille only manages one word: "Why?"

"I should have done it sooner," Macbeth says, though there is no cruelty in his tone, only the flatness of reason. "My men will not cringe from you so much, or question whether my dominion over my wife is total. And you do not need to see. When you are to leave this room, I will guide you."

And then, true to his word, Roscille is maneuvered through the door, even as Senga makes some inarticulate noise of protest, and into the corridor, all in the rough grip of her husband's hands.

THE FLOOR IS COLD THROUGH the soles of her slippers, and there is the ocean underneath it, surging up as it always does, against the stone barrier which seems thinner with every passing moment. She can sense how far they have gone based on how much their footsteps echo. This is a long corridor, empty. The sound of Macbeth's limping gait fills the silent hallway.

Roscille knows, *Now we are turning a corner, now another one, seven paces and then one more, and then down the longest, narrowest hallway. See,* she thinks with some relief, *my mind has not been lost entirely.* The salt air, as they approach, lifts the skin on the back of her neck. The key slides into the lock. She inhales sharply.

It is the first time she has been here without seeing. Well—

perhaps it is merely the blindest she has ever been. In the beginning, she came only with her paltry mortal vision. She begins to suspect, as Macbeth guides her through the door, that he has not blindfolded her for the sake of his men. She thinks he has some preternatural sense of his own, that he can sniff out the affinity that grows between his wife and the witches. Perhaps he merely thinks she visited them in his absence. Perhaps that is enough to make him take such precautions, to ensure that she is always bound to him first, that she can never look into the milky eyes of les Lavandières and see herself reflected back.

Any light Roscille could glimpse from behind the cloth has now vanished. The blackness is solid and cold. She feels as if she could put a hand to it and leave the impression of her palm.

Macbeth splashes into the water. She hears a low grunt of pain as he does—that wound on his leg. Has he even allowed a doctor or a Druide to see it? He trusts nothing and no one, now. An herbal poultice might be poison. Roscille has stolen this from him, she realizes. Safety. Or perhaps it could be said she has transformed him. A slow metamorphosis, unfolding in stages, like a night-blooming flower. Macbeth, the righteous man. Now he is Macbeth, King of Alba, but bereft of his right hand and unsteady on his left leg.

"Æthelstan and his army come for my head," Macbeth says into the blackness. "Tell me—do I have to fear my demise?"

Slow, dragging footsteps. The chain clattering. The water forced and churned. Once, Roscille would not have been able to tell apart their voices. But now she knows who speaks and when.

Left Witch: Macbeth, Thane of Glammis. Thane of Cawder. King Hereafter. No man of woman born shall harm Macbeth.

Right Witch: Macbeth, Thane of Glammis. Thane of Cawder. King Hereafter. He shall never be vanquished until the wood comes high upon the hill.

Gruoch says: nothing.

Macbeth turns in the water, and Roscille can see it, even without sight: the torchlight freckling the cave ceiling, the deep rise and fall of her husband's chest, the resplendent smile drawing wide across his face, the burning triumph in his eyes.

"I will never fail," her husband says. Awestruck, almost childlike. "These prophecies ensure me. *King Hereafter,* indeed." A raucous laugh that is too loud, that breaks like surf upon the rocks.

Roscille can see three pairs of hands outstretched, palms turned up to the heavens. And then three voices rise, mingling in the pitch-dark air, curling wickedly as smoke: "All hail Macbeth! All hail Macbeth! All hail Macbeth!"

FOURTEEN

IN ROSCILLE'S SHORT AND MOSTLY SHELTERED SEVENTEEN
years, war had never come to Naoned. She always believed it was because the Duke is clever—the ermine
knows how to hide himself from hawks and preys only on
soft-toothed rabbits and mice. War is for arrogant men like
the Parisian prince, or weak men who cannot dissuade their
enemies. Here Roscille cannot think of an example because
the names of weak men are like charcoal to be dusted off your
boot.

Now she thinks war is as inevitable as weather. It has seasons, some redder than others. War came to the other coun-
ties and duchies of France with the riotous color of changing
leaves. Little wars like saplings, easily struck down before they
could flower. Great wars that covered Blois and Chartres in a
hoarfrost of corpses. The pope and the House of Capet prom-

ise a green and eternal summer: peace, so long as they rule this fractious land.

Wrybeard and the other dukes and counts snort into their goblets. But the ermine is a hibernating creature. He grows white fur against the winter; he will stay fat in his den until the air is warm again and hunting is easy. Naoned, a thicket of safety, insulated by her father's wiles.

Here, in Glammis—where Roscille is Lady, even Queen— safety is the bleak and barren landscape. The soldiers which will be spotted from the castle's battlements and then slain with arrows before their war cries even reach Roscille's ears. The rocky hill littered with dashed-open skulls; the yellow grass smeared with brains. And she will be safe in her cloak and her blood-colored necklace and her blindfold, which she must now wear always in the company of men.

She stands on the parapet that faces down the hill, imagining this. Senga is at her side. The slope before her is sheer, dangerous. Beyond it, the copse of fairy trees, protecting that silver pool inside. It is tiny against the vast emptiness of the landscape. A copse. She would not call it a *wood*.

Until the wood comes high upon the hill.

Roscille looks at Senga. "Is your village down there?"

Her village, where her children live still, their love mingling with shame. Old enough to work means old enough to fight.

Senga nods. "It is the last village that Æthelstan's army will loot and burn. Then they will reach the castle."

They will not reach the castle. Because there is no wood and trees cannot uproot themselves and walk in rows like soldiers. Roscille blinks wetness from her lashes. It is starting to rain.

"What do ladies do, in war?"

Senga says, "You tell me. You are the Lady."

"But I have never been in a war."

There is the little furrow between Senga's brows that Roscille has come to recognize. It is familiar, from the first day she came to the castle. All the rest has changed: Her circles and lines have vanished with nights spent on a down mattress instead of straw; she wears slippers now instead of clogs; her hair is combed neatly and tied back in a plait. She raises a newly smoothed hand and touches Roscille's cheek.

"We will both learn together," she says.

THE RAIN FALLS IN HEAVY gouts that turn the window glass marbled and milky. The dirt of the courtyard becomes mud. Tartans grow so wet that their colors and patterns cannot be distinguished from each other. When men stomp into the castle, they shake the water out of their hair and beards like dogs. There are many men now, faces Roscille is not permitted to see, names she cannot connect with those faces. Once upon a time—or if she were Roscille of Breizh, still—she would have memorized them all in an hour, and something about them too, a bit of their soul that shines from them like a slant of light through a crumbling wall.

Now. She sits in her husband's council meetings, blindfolded. The voices run over her like water. Æthelstan's army has taken twelve border towns and burned them to cinders. Pillaged the grain stores and butchered the cows. Raped the women and enslaved the men. The soldiers eat themselves strong on stolen food and stolen wine, and with each passing day, the army grows larger and closer.

Unexpectedly, many Scotsmen have defected to Æthelstan, *rex Anglorum,* king of the English. Perhaps this is because the army is led by one of their own, the late Duncane's son Evander, and they knew Duncane as a fair and honest king, and though he was sickly, their harvests were good under his rule and their land prospered. The same cannot be said for this new Macbeth.

Macbeth, who sequesters himself in this remote castle. Macbeth, who wed a fairy maiden from Breizh, and all the good this alliance has done him, for the Duke sees the largeness of the English army and sends letters to Glammis saying, *It is treacherous to cross the channel now. But my ships will come soon to your aid.*

When Roscille hears this letter read aloud, she curls her fingernails into her palm until small gashes form. She tries to imagine herself in her father's place. The ermine knows when it is time to grow his white winter coat and hide away while the skinny, hungry animals tear the forest apart. But Wrybeard also knows that an alliance cannot be so easily broken. Even if he does not count the loss of Macbeth's army, even if he does not fear Macbeth's retribution, the world still must see that the Duke of Breizh is, mostly, an honest and honorable man. Otherwise, he will never earn the faith of another lord again.

She does not know what would be worse: dying under Æthelstan's blade or her father rescuing her. She envisions Wrybeard climbing down from his carriage, her hurrying to greet him in the courtyard, wearing her garish cloak and her flimsy necklace.

I am Queen now, she imagines saying, chin raised in defiance.

Her father looks down on her, an indulgent contempt on his face. *You are whatever creature I make you.*

Yet still some nights Roscille prays he will come. She prays he will take her away from this gray, evil place where witches live in chains beneath the floor. She wants to ride through the damp green forests of Breizh and cool her feet in the ice-white waters of the Loire. But then when she stands and brushes off her knees she is angry at herself, for missing the home she was banished from, for mourning the father who tossed her away. Nothing more than a lovely face.

A lovely face, and a body that shrinks into the mattress while her husband pries her legs apart and grunts into her ear, *This one will be a boy, an heir.* He would be wiser to father a son on Senga. At least then his line will not be tainted by her Brezhon blood. But Roscille would not wish this fate on anyone, especially not Senga, whom she has sworn to herself she will protect at any cost, who will not be like Hawise— *I promise this.* Senga comes to her in the morning with hard bread and cold milk.

"It will be over soon," Senga says, stroking her forehead. "Your husband does not have the vices like some other men. Once you have fathered him a son, he will stop."

It will never be over, she thinks. Even when he is finished, he remains inside her, her brain streaked through with purple and black vapors, the color of the blood on his knee. The wound that will not close. The wound that stains the sheets so badly that Senga must wash them every day. Roscille wants to tell her to bring them downstairs to the basement. The laundresses will take care of it. They are good for nothing else.

The only way to exorcise her husband's foul spirit is this: Every day, when she sits in the room with the war council, blind, she listens for news of the beast. She almost cannot breathe the whole time, fearing that the doors will slam open, and someone will drag its enormous head inside, leaving a path of blood and entrails. But there is no word of the dragon, and she thanks God—if God could ever be disposed to protect such an appalling creature. And when her husband's body arches over hers at night, sweat from his brow dripping onto her impassive face, she imagines it is Lisander, instead, fierce in his passions, yet less a monster than this man Macbeth.

THE WAR STILL FEELS HAZY and unreal until one morning Roscille awakes to the sound of clanging blades. Her husband has long left the bed. She stands and walks over to the window. The clanging sound is coming from the courtyard, where there are easily a hundred men gathered, more than she imagined the space could hold.

They are pressed shoulder-to-shoulder, most of them on foot, only the leaders on horseback: Winter Fox and Mountain Goat and Weasel-cloak. Macbeth is there, shouting, waving his arms. He is giving instructions, but if Roscille could not make out the words, she would think him a lunatic, the kind that stands outside of taverns and nurses the old wound on his head that struck him simple. It does not help that he limps. He has refused every Druide twice, three times over.

It is almost too far away to see the men's expressions—almost. But their rugged Scottish faces are crimped and twisted into unhappy scowls. Bewildered lines on their brows. Each

one of them has knelt and sworn his loyalty to Macbeth, Macbethad, Macbheatha, Thane of Glammis, Thane of Cawder,
King Hereafter, yet now many look as though they regret it.
The old king was infirm of body. This new King seems infirm
of mind. Madness is not a place, Roscille thinks. It is a long
way down a winding corridor.

One man steps out from his line. He wears a gray-blue
tartan, not clan Findlaích. He is the son or grandson of some
man who promised loyalty to Macbeth, but this promise has
worn thin with the generations. Roscille moves closer to the
window, curling her fingers around the bars.

Man: We will lose our homes and families to Æthelstan's
army if we do not even attempt to make peace. A summit.
There must be some effort—already hundreds are dead. How
many Scots will you accept slain before you meet Æthelstan at
the table? These are not the actions of a king.

Macbeth pauses and his arms drop to his sides. The corner
of his lip twitches—Roscille only knows this because she has
seen the expression on his face many times; she is very distant
from him now, and could not recognize it otherwise.

He approaches the man. He asks, "What is your name?"

The man tells him. Roscille cannot hear it.

Macbeth says, "And what were you promised by that dead,
disloyal Banquho to foment strife here?"

Man: Nothing. I have never spoken to Banquho in my
life. I protest this for the sake of my children and my wife. My
village is next for the slaughter.

A beat of silence. Even the wind quiets itself.

"You do not deserve to wear that battle tartan," Macbeth
says, "or carry that sword. Leave this place. Flee like the traitorous coward you are. You know nothing of Macbeth. I am

King Hereafter. Defeat is impossible—as impossible as the forest rising and marching upon the hill. No man of woman born can slay me."

Man: This is madness you speak. It is no wonder your own right hand turned on you.

Roscille knows what will happen next. She almost does not want to watch, but she finds she cannot turn her head away, cannot close her eyes. Macbeth draws his sword, and despite his wound, despite the madness that makes the edges of him turn fuzzy and strange, the movement is swift. Skilled. Bellona's bridegroom was not an epithet given without cause. The death blow he delivers is as practiced and inevitable as a needle working through embroidery. Blade jabbed in. Blade drawn out. Blood spurts from the wound and from the man's mouth.

He chokes and falls to the ground, where he writhes for a moment and then goes still. The other men do not move as the wind ruffles their hair and beards, their tattered flags, their mismatched tartans. Macbeth raises his sword and licks the end of the blade. Blood glistens on his lips.

"This is the fate that awaits any man who questions my power," he says. "Take this body and cast it into the sea. Let the fish feast on his flesh."

"THERE MUST BE AN EXECUTION."

At the sound of her husband's voice Roscille looks up from her sewing. She has been embroidering a pattern of moonflowers onto a bolt of fabric that will someday be a gown. It is difficult to imitate the tiny, trumpeted petals. She stitches vines that twist and tangle along the border of the frock, serpent-like. She has been hours at this mindless toil. When Macbeth enters, Senga immediately rises and sees herself out, though she casts a worrying glance at Roscille.

Roscille puts down her needle and hoop. "Why an execution?"

"The traitor son of a traitor has been rotting in the dungeon for weeks," Macbeth says. "It would be wise to make an example of him. The other men question my strategies and doubt my power."

Roscille wonders why he is telling her this. Although she has sat in his war rooms, bound and silent, he has not asked her counsel in a long time. Perhaps he merely thinks she will be happy to know how and when Fléance will die. In this, at least, he is right.

"I thought you might help devise a punishment," Macbeth says. "Your father is well known for his prudent violence."

He is going to punish her for Wrybeard's inaction. Maybe that will hurry along the Duke's ships: a blackened eye on his beautiful daughter's face, a bruise pulsing on her cheekbone, a wound that cannot be hidden under her skirts, that will make all men gawk and stare. Or perhaps he has already given up on the alliance and will merely sate his anger on Roscille instead of on her faraway father. She thinks of Agasia, that rudely forced wife, passed between her husband's men like a quaich, a sip for each one. Panic stops her breath.

"What makes you cringe from me now?" Macbeth demands. "Do you not want to play a part in killing this man who is your enemy? Perhaps you have some clever ideas of how to defile his corpse."

Her heartbeat slows, but only just. He does not mean to

punish her, at least not now. He has already gotten his fill of violence somewhere else.

"I have no ideas, my Lord," she manages.

Macbeth regards her in a strange way, his face showing both satisfaction and disgust. "Are you not your father's daughter?"

She does not know how to answer that.

Instead, she replies, carefully, "You should ask Fléance himself, instead. Pretend you are his friend still. Tell him you will be punishing someone else in his stead. Ask him what their punishment should be. He will devise a method of execution that is most abhorrent to him. And that will be your best vengeance."

Macbeth rests a hand against the wall to steady himself, to take the weight off his left leg. After a long beat, he says, "My clever wife."

"A wife is only as clever as her husband permits her to be."

She hates herself for saying this. But every moment she is sitting here, in a chair, with embroidery in her lap, is a moment she is not being whipped or forced or made to kneel. Her life has been cleaved into two simple halves: the time when there is pain, and the time when there is not.

The corner of Macbeth's mouth lifts in a smile. He approaches her, and Roscille holds herself rigid in her chair. He takes her face into one of his hands and leans down and kisses her forehead. He gives a little huff of pain as he does. It sounds just like the way he breathes when he works himself over on top of her. She sits there, turning to stone, until Macbeth rises and leaves her.

THE NEXT DAY, ROSCILLE SMELLS smoke from down the hillside. It is distant, but when she walks onto the parapet, she can see filthy gray clouds blooming just above the line of the horizon. There are many things which could be burning: Grain stores. Houses. Stables. Sheep, cows, horses, women, men. Children made orphans with the wink of a blade. Æthelstan's army is so close.

From the parapet, she also observes the conversations in the courtyard. Men are gathered, but fewer and wearier with each passing day. Their beards are sticky with blood. Their tartans are ragged. Their shoulders are stooped. The rain has come and it has gone, so their horses are ornery and tired looking. Macbeth remains on horseback when he does his rallying. It does not show his limp quite so badly.

Mountain Goat has died in the fighting. His men are jostling with anger over it. Macbeth says, "Are you all chickens? Can you not survive without a head?"

He is not quite making sense. Ripples of discontent pass through the crowd. But no individual man dares to speak against him—not after that first time. Macbeth kicks his horse and urges it to Winter Fox's side. A few inaudible words pass between them. Winter Fox hangs his head. Then Macbeth's horse trots away.

Winter Fox: I will lead today's showing against Æthelstan. Our King has business here at the castle.

The men cannot stifle their murmurs of protest now. Scathing sounds drawn from the backs of their throats. This is not the behavior of a king. Not the behavior of a righteous man. Bellona's bridegroom, who will hide himself in his castle walls while his soldiers die for him? *Reith,* who will keep his sword and beard unbloodied?

Macbeth says, "I promise all who fight today will be honored forever in history. Your sons and grandsons and great-grandsons will remember the nobility of this fight. How you drove the insatiable lion from the unicorn's land. And whoever brings back that green prince Iomhar's head will have a place of honor at my table, at my side, always. I am in search of a new right hand."

The wind howls through the courtyard. It scatters the men like birds.

ROSCILLE SITS WHILE SENGA BRAIDS her hair. They are both on the floor, kneeling, cushioned by the bear-rug. Its fur is still thick and vital, even in death. Its yellowed teeth show no cracks.

Senga says, "I will braid your hair in the style of Alba. Yes?"

"If you like," says Roscille, listless.

"So you will seem more a queen."

Queen Hereafter. King Hereafter. All these prophecies have come true, save for the false ones she stuck into the witches' mouths. Now she thinks of these final auguries: *No man of woman born. Until the wood comes high upon the hill.* She picks the words apart. Perhaps they are like glyphs or pictographs, disguising a code within. The Duke had spymasters who invented such ciphers for him, so that he could hide treacheries beneath pleasantries. These men were always light-footed as mice and spoke in whispers. Narrow men, their shoulders held high and tight. Roscille admired them. They saw what lay beneath the world everyone knew.

She had even entertained the thought of becoming a spy,

as a child, but of course there are no lady spymasters. Roscille looks in the bucket of water she is using a mirror, watches Senga plait her hair. Her skin grows cold when it is lifted from her neck. With its pale color, it looks like she is wearing a coronet of bone.

Beautiful. Lisander's words return to her.

Unnatural, she protested. *Strange.*

No. You have been made to fit a shape that confines you.

Roscille shoves the bucket of water away until she can no longer see. The last person to style her hair was Hawise.

Abruptly, she looks up, jostling Senga's hands. "I will not let harm come to you," Roscille says.

Senga frowns. "What do you mean, Lady?"

"There is no safety here," she says. "Not while Macbeth lives and breathes. And he will always live and breathe."

"How do you know?"

Because the wood will never ascend the hill. Because there is no man who is not born of woman. But Roscille does not say this. Instead, she says, "I will give you what coin I can gather, and disguise you well. In the night, you will slip out of the castle. You will have what clothes and supplies you need. You must find your children before Æthelstan's army arrives at your village, and take them with you. The coin will get you far enough."

Senga drops her hands, and Roscille's hair falls back down upon her shoulders. She is silent for a long moment. "And what about you, Lady?"

Roscille draws a breath. "A queen does not forsake her people," she replies bleakly.

Another long moment passes. Very gently, Senga holds

Roscille's chin and turns her gaze toward her. With a half smile, she says, "And a handmaiden does not forsake her Lady."

Roscille breaks Senga's grip on her face and turns away again. If she looks too long at Senga, she will weep. And she cannot risk her husband seeing tears on her cheeks. He does not wish her to feel any emotion he himself did not engender in her.

As if summoned by thought alone, the door is then forced open. Senga quickly slips the veil back over Roscille's face. Macbeth stands in the threshold, so broad that he blocks the torchlight from the corridor.

"My Lord," Roscille says, and dips her head.

"Lady Macbeth." There is something in his voice. She cannot say what it is, but all the small hairs on her arms stand up, as if prickled with cold. "I have just finished with Fléance."

"Oh." Her cheeks heat. "And did he tell you what you wished to know?"

Senga's hand rests on her shoulder. Her handmaiden's fingernails curl, digging just slightly into her skin. She shifts, an infinitesimal movement, barely detected, the muscles rolling in her shoulders—almost as though she plans to throw herself between Macbeth and her Lady. But Macbeth's stare keeps them both pinned into place.

"He told me very interesting things," Macbeth says. "Come, wife. Let us go."

HE LEADS HER DOWN THE twisting labyrinth of corridors, which Roscille now knows even blind. But he does not force her to wear the cloth over her eyes—why? If once she believed she understood her husband, and his wiles, she now feels as adrift as she did her first day in Glammis, shivering in the heathen cold.

Macbeth limps in front of her; Roscille trails behind. From this vantage point, she can see his wound well: the way it sucks at the wool of his tights, pulling the fabric into the wet, open gash. It seems impossible that he can still support his own enormous body. Sometimes the kitchen boys in Naoned would cruelly tie up a dog's front leg and laugh while it hobbled around, whining at this confusing loss of function. When Roscille saw this it made her angry enough to wish herself a man, so she could enact violence upon them.

The corridor narrows, and the torches on the wall grow dim, showing only black scorch-marks instead of light. At the end, the wood-rotted door with its rusted iron grate. The ocean's gnashing teeth behind it. Did the last prophecy not satisfy Macbeth? What more could he want than the total assurance the witches offered him?

Roscille risks this question: "Has something happened to displease you?"

It could be many things. The seething men in the courtyard. The nearness of Æthelstan's army. The lingering hurt of Banquho's betrayal. But Macbeth scarcely looks at her as he says, "Yes. But it will be righted now."

Then he turns the key in the lock and the coldness captures them both, as though they have been snatched up into the claws of the cruel old goddess of winter. Beira, that is her name here, in Alba. They also call her *caillech,* divine hag. Half woman she is, and half horned beast.

Now les Lavandières shuffle forward, dragging their chains through the water. Gruoch is in the center, holding her laundry, stretching like spider silk between her hands. Their wet white hair clings to their scrawny necks. Roscille cannot imagine what new prophecy her husband wishes to beg off them. What fear does he want them to assuage?

Macbeth stands on the steps; he does not drop down into the water, does not move toward the torch. And, more strangely, he does not say a word. He merely waits until the witches have reached him there, closer to the door than Roscille has ever seen them. The light that leaks in from the corridor shines on their faces, their knobbed fingers. If they lived in the upper world, they would be midwives, wet nurses, widows who bathe the feet of brides.

They stand there waiting, rocking slightly back and forth, as if buffeted by wind. There is no wind, of course, and without their washing, the cave is silent and still. Roscille tries to meet Gruoch's gaze, but she cannot pierce through the milky mortal blindness.

"*Buidseach,*" Macbeth says. The word curves out, cold, in the black air. Gruoch opens her mouth, but Macbeth holds up a hand. "No, do not speak. I do not come asking for counsel or prophecy."

Gruoch's mouth snaps shut. A dog, commanded: *Quiet!*

Roscille looks at her husband. A slow dread unfolds within her.

Very slowly, Macbeth reaches for her. His hands find her shoulders first, and then run down her torso, grazing her breasts, coming to settle at her waist. She is wearing a cloth belt, but this will not stop him. Will he really take her here, in the damp darkness, with les Lavandières as witness? Is this her punishment for Wrybeard's apathy? He does not need to prove his power in front of the witches; already they are shackled and chained, and surely he has already had Gruoch this way, the First Wife. Roscille despises her own cowardice, but she cannot help drawing in a sharp little breath.

"Ah," says Macbeth. "You think me unworthy of your affections?"

"No, my Lord. It is not—it is cold here." Pitiful reasoning. Behind her, the black water bunches and then flattens, like fabric.

"I spoke to the traitor's traitorous son," Macbeth says. "Of course I asked him what you proposed I ask. I said I was seeking to punish another, and what should this manner of torture be? I did not speak of you, Lady Macbeth—no, Roscilla—no, Roscille of Breizh—yet somehow your name was in his mouth. He believed I sought to punish you instead. Why, I asked him. He looked at me almost pityingly, as if I were a miserable fool. To be pitied by a man in chains, with a sword dangling over his head. Why did he speak of you, Roscilla? Why did he look at me this way?"

The question is not a question. It is a snare laid under the false cover of leaves. One incautious step and she will be strung up. "I—I do not know, my Lord."

"You are a liar," says Macbeth. But his tone is light, each syllable like a stone skimming the water. "He unfolded your tapestry of falsehoods, first how you fabricated this attack by masked men, then how you offered yourself, when the whip was raised against Lisander. Your body, stealing the pain from his. I did not understand the reasoning. I do now."

"No," says Roscille. Her heart is beating so fast she thinks it will crack itself open. "He is the liar; he wishes to absolve himself by blaming me—"

"Quiet. You are the Duke's daughter. You learned such wiles at his feet."

"I have no wiles," she whispers. "I am just a lady."

"You have never been just that," he says. "Still, I did not easily believe him, Fléance. He has his own motives, even if his devices are clumsy. Perhaps, I thought, he did merely wish to avoid his own execution. One last effort, raving and wild. But he was perfectly calm as he relayed this to me. As he told me: *You have been cuckolded in your own house, my Lord. Your loyal wife is not so loyal. She hides her true face and her tawdry secrets beneath her veil. She lay with the prince of Cumberland while your back was turned.*"

Every drop of blood in her body turns to flame. The fire rushes to her face, flushes her cheeks.

"No," she manages. "Fléance means to divert from his own betrayal."

"This is what I thought at first, too." Macbeth's hands tighten on her hips, until his fingers are pressing so hard into her skin through the gown that they will certainly leave bruises. "But then I thought—weeks I have been lying with her, every night, and nothing has taken root in her womb. She is long past her first blood and the fault cannot be with my seed. It can only be that another's seed has been planted first. You carry the prince's monstrous spawn."

The words are stolen from her mouth. She chokes on the rising bile in her throat.

"Please," she says, when she can speak. "You cannot believe him. It is not true."

He shoves the flat of his hand against her belly, so rough that it knocks the breath from her. "*Do not lie to me.*"

Roscille stumbles, and barely manages to catch herself before she topples backward into the water. There is something that sounds like the wind, cutting through the salt air, but it is actually a whisper, which passes among the witches, through them, as if they are hollow. Her name, made into a warning.

All three, together: "*Lady Macbeth.*"

"No," her husband snarls. "No Lady Macbeth, never again. And your father will not have you back, defiled by a foreign prince whose body is merely the shell of a monster. You are nothing now. A whore with no name. Nurse your demon child here in the dark."

He pushes her again, and she realizes he was restraining himself, before. Even as he pried her legs apart, even as he ground himself against her hips, he did not show his full strength. His unshackled cruelty now is breathtaking. Though hobbled, nursing this ugly and incessant wound, his power seems beyond that of a mortal man: a depthless brutality, his eyes aflame with anger and hate.

She falls. Twisting back on herself, gown tangling around her legs. Her face hits the water first and plasters her veil to her cheeks and nose and mouth. For a moment, her sodden clothes prevent her from surfacing, and there is a silver bolt of panic, a flash that whitens her vision like lightning, until she is able to claw herself up and onto her knees, and fumble for her veil.

But she cannot catch Macbeth in the path of her gaze. He is already turning. He limps through the door and then shuts it behind him. All light is thieved from her eyes.

FIFTEEN

DARK AND DARK AND DARK. AT FIRST SHE SINKS INTO it, like a sandpit. The air and water seem to be made out of the same stuff, two miasmas of blackness, only one denser than the other. She paddles through the water and swims through the air. Reaching, stumbling. At last, she feels two hard, bony hands grasp her under her armpits. With surprising strength, she is hauled upward, onto her feet.

Left Witch: There you are.

Roscille: No, please. I cannot be here.

Right Witch: This is what we all said, at first. Your eyes will adjust.

Roscille: But what will I do?

Left Witch: Laundry, of course.

Roscille: What will I eat?

Right Witch: You can break the bones of eels between

your teeth. They are softer than you expect them to be. And when you have been long enough here in the dark, you will lose your mortal vision, and you will see only what is to come, not what is or has been. Your mouth will lose its shape and mold to the speaking of prophecy. Have you noticed we no longer have lips? Well, what do we need them for? There is no one to kiss. Ha! Imagine that.

Roscille: Please. I am not like you.

Gruoch: Not now. Not yet. But you will be, if you stay. That is why you must go.

Left Witch: Go? There is nowhere to go! He may not have put you in chains, but you are trapped here, the same as we are.

Right Witch: Fool girl. If we could leave, do you not think we all would have left?

Gruoch: Silence, both of you. Were we not all this girl, once? A Lady Macbeth? Look at us now, nameless. Trapped. We have sat rotting in the dark for too long. Finally there is a chance—we can redeem ourselves in this.

Left Witch: There is no redeeming this. I do not remember my own name.

Right Witch: I can only see in the dark. My hands are made for washing and nothing more.

Gruoch: Perhaps we are lost, fine. But she is not. There is still a chance. If she claims this name, Lady Macbeth, she claims it for us all. Our visions will be her visions. Our powers her powers. Our burdens her burdens. It is not a thing to claim lightly. Do you understand?

Right Witch: Why does she deserve this chance? I have been here a quarter of a century. And you half as long, and you twice as long.

A beat.

Roscille: I do not deserve it. I should stay here, after all.

Gruoch: This is what we were all made to believe. Keep your mortal eyes open. Remember. Think.

Roscille squeezes her eyes shut, not that it makes any difference, in the dark. Yet when she does, her vision explodes in a riot of color. Memories she assumed jettisoned, abandoned like ballast, to maintain the soundness of the ship. It all roars back to her now: the mornings she spent embroidering with Hawise, reading bawdy poetry and smothering their whispers; the evenings turning wide and blue, when they were allowed to wander out of the castle on horseback, Hawise pointing out each animal they saw. The yellow-beaked starlings that blended so well with the bark, the busy red squirrels with their tufted ears, the cormorant perched in the canopy, curiously far from the sea. Hawise knew their names in Norse and Roscille knew their names in Brezhoneg, Angevin, and Saxon. They smeared berry juice on their fingers to coax rabbits from their warrens.

All of these things which have felt so far from her are here now. There was the time one of the Duke's men struck Hawise across the face, for no reason, for any reason, and then grabbed at her breasts, and Roscille was filled with an uncorrectable rage, but she waited. She watched as the man came and went from the castle and always returned with small parcels of goat's milk, such that cannot be made in Naoned for the Duke does not keep goats. Roscille pointed this out to her father and it was discovered this man had dalliances with a bastardess from the House of Capet. Well, there is no place in Wrybeard's court for men who may be swayed to the enemy's side due to matters of the heart. He was gone the next day. To where, Roscille never found out. To hell, she hoped.

Even here, in Glammis: early days, when she sat at her husband's council table and spoke, when she sent him running to Cawder to stain his hands with blood, when she ensnared Fléance in her lie, reading his boyish longings like a cipher. When she came to Lisander's room with a knife and left with a swollen, sweet-kissed mouth. When she threw herself between his cell and Banquho's whip. When she took in Senga, taught her Latin, let her braid womanly wisdoms into her hair. All of these things she did as a girl, as a lady, as a flinching foreign bride, as a witch with death-touched eyes, as Roscille of Breizh. She has believed herself an animal, simple, sharp-toothed, slippery like an eel. But she is both guilty and innocent, both girlish and wise, both witch and woman. Even the dullest creatures in cages dream of freedom. Their desires stretch and flourish, like a tree growing clever branches around the bars of a fence.

She stands in the dark, furious, fearful, thinking, blooming.

Roscille says, "I will take it. I will carry it all."

Gruoch says, "That's a good girl."

She will take everything but this. Roscille reaches up and removes the cloak, letting it slide off her shoulders and puddle in the water. The small waves suck at the furs, drowning it. Then she unclasps the necklace. It makes a small splash as it drops into the water, but then the waves drag it under, too. At last, the veil. She tears it off. Shreds the lace between her fingernails. It is lost to the damp air and darkness. Her cheeks burn with the cold, but she is free.

The witches advance. Gently, they guide Roscille toward the steps, until she can find her own way. She climbs upward, water pouring from her clothes. She touches the door's handle, jiggles the lock. The strength of one woman is not enough to break it. Nor two, nor three. But the strength of four is enough.

The witches wait in their own seething silence. Silver dreams unfold from their milky eyes and lipless mouths.

Roscille cracks the rusted metal under her hand. The door swings open. Light pours in. She looks back once at les Lavandières, to at last see their faces without the veil between them, and then she steps into the torch-warmed corridor, into the glowing, waking world.

SHE HEARS IT RIGHT AWAY, the clanging of blades. Arrows sliding into their notches. Muscles twanging as bowstrings are pulled taut and then released. She hears it with four sets of ears now, as perceptive as a hare. When the arrows hit their marks, there is the fleshy sound, like fruit being cut, the sound of men's lives being stolen from them. Roscille breaks into a run.

By the time she reaches the parapet she is breathing hard, but her legs do not ache—she has the strength of four, now. The archers who are stationed along the battlements do not pay her any mind, even though it is dangerous for a woman to be here, dangerous for anyone to be here. She finds an empty arrow loop and crouches behind it.

There, she watches Æthelstan's army advance up the hill. They are more ragged than she expected them to be: their clothes hanging off them, mud up to their knees. The rain has made the climb even more treacherous, each step risking a death-slide down the face of the cliff. They are so different from the Scottish warriors Roscille has known—no faces painted half blue, no tartans to show the intricate threading of clan loyalties, but the leather of their boots seems tougher and none of their sword-hilts are rusted.

Behind them, the trees of the copse are trees. The bushes are bushes. The animals can smell the blood and fire and are hiding in their warrens and holes. Roscille feels a helplessness overtake her, one that makes her knees tremble. The wood cannot ascend the hill. The soldiers can barely ascend the hill. Most of the arrows land with useless thuds in the grass, but when one does strike, it strikes true. Through the heart, the man falling like a slain deer, twitching and then going still.

No man of woman born. It seems no man at all will even reach the castle. The panic goes through Roscille, sluggish, each beat passing like blood behind a bruise. Where will she go, what will she do, if Glammis does not fall? Forced back into the dark, or back into her husband's bed? The same fate as all women, which she has become an animal to escape—

No. She carries the weight of four now, all their stanched dreams and suppressed desires, and she must not fail.

Five women. *Senga.* Fear laces up her spine. Roscille will not allow her to have Hawise's fate; she will tear apart the stone walls of the castle with her bare hands. This is what propels her back through the parapet, running, her hair coming loose from its braids and streaming out behind her. Her damp gown tangles around her legs but she does not stumble. The sea presses up from beneath the castle, straining toward the surface, and she seems to roll forward, as if carried by the invisible, underground tide.

HER NEW STRONG LEGS TAKE her to Senga's room. Roscille turns the knob but it rattles and will not budge. Something is blocking the door from the other side. She presses her face to the wood and says her handmaiden's name.

A beat. Then there is a scraping, wood against stone, and the door opens just a crack. Senga's face peers through. The lines on her forehead are deep and her eyes are wet and her voice is thick when she says, "Lady—I thought you were dead and gone."

"No," says Roscille. "I am here." And then Senga opens the door wide enough for her to step inside.

When she enters, she sees that Senga has barred the door by jamming the chair beneath the doorknob, clever, as if she has done such a thing before. She has also taken the poker from the fire and holds it in her white-knuckled hand.

She sees Roscille looking, and says, "The soldiers will come. But I will not make it easy for them."

"They will not have you," Roscille says. "Even if your village is gone—your home is by my side, now, as it will always be. We will be free."

Senga's brow furrows deeper. "How?"

She takes Senga's hand. It is warm, rough in places, soft in others, and through her skin, Roscille feels her pulse, throbbing and alive.

THERE IS NO TIME, EVEN, to pack a bag. She ushers Senga out of the room and through the corridors, all while listening to arrows fly and blades clang and men die like cut weeds. Her hope is this: that they will be distracted by the fumes of blood and will not notice as two women slip away.

Their brisk footsteps carry them into the courtyard, which is abandoned because every soldier is crouching in an arrow loop or cutting down his enemies on the hilltop. Roscille's mind is turning and turning as they make their way toward the stable: Take one horse, it will attract less attention, no, take a second, one will tire quickly of carrying two bodies, fill the canteens in the saddlebags, we do not know when we will next find clean water, but then they will slap against the horse's flanks and make alerting sounds.

She lets out a breath. Senga is panting. When Roscille blinks, Hawise's face replaces Senga's, only it is the white, horrified face she has conjured in her dreams, the one that screams silently as she is pushed into the black water.

No. No. This will not be like before. Roscille no longer shrinks beneath her veil. She can enchant and ensorcell her way to safety, to freedom. Her freedom and Senga's and the freedom of three women chained in the dark.

They are halfway across the courtyard when a figure steps out from the shadows. He raises a hand to shield his eyes, as if from the sun or the biting wind, but Roscille knows it is to hide himself from her gaze. She thinks she is witnessing something impossible—a waking dream—until she sees the scar lacing out from beneath his jerkin and up his throat.

Roscille chokes. "You are not dead."

"Nor are you." Fléance steps closer. "Macbeth freed me, on the condition that I fight for him. He knew he would need every man at his side. And yet he swore he sent his harlot, demon-bearing wife to hell."

"Perhaps hell could not hold me." Her blood is hot. The scars burn on the backs of her thighs, the pain striking as if it were new again, the viper flashing its silver teeth.

But she is not now what she was then. Her flesh has thickened. She may look a fragile flower, white-petaled, but this merely conceals her; it does not bind her.

"You have again given me a good chance to prove my honor," Fléance says. "What titles and favors will Macbeth bestow upon me when I deliver him the corpse of this unworthy witch, this hagseed whore?"

Beside her, Senga flinches at the words. Roscille grips her handmaiden's arm.

"Come closer, then," she taunts. "Or are you too much a coward to look into my unclothed eyes?"

"I am no coward," Fléance snarls. Even now, it is so easy to rile him, this boy playing at being a man.

And then he draws his sword, which cuts the air, and Roscille darts forward to catch him in the path of her gaze, but he is just half a heartbeat faster. She feels the heel of his hand crush her temple, and her vision sparks, and when she manages to recover her sight Fléance has his arm locked around her throat and his sword pressed flat against her belly.

Roscille writhes against him, spitting her fury. Senga falls to her knees.

"Please," she begs. "Please, my lord, do not do this."

"Your handmaiden pleads so nicely," Fléance rasps, breath in her ear. "When I am finished with you—"

That is when Roscille screams: loud enough for four voices. So loud that the sound seems to ripple out from around her, like water. Even Senga claps her hands over her ears. And Fléance winces, which gives Roscille a chance to bite down, hard, on the hand that constricts her. He shrieks. Blood spurts.

His sword digs a little bit into Roscille's side and the pain streaks through her. Everything is blurry and held at a distance, as if behind a translucent veil. *This will not be my death,* she thinks, furious, *but if it is, I will fight until my last breath, and take every piece of him that I can with me.*

And then Senga cries out, not in horror, but in pure shock, her mouth rounding into an awestruck *oh*. She is staring up at the sky.

The dragon's long green body unfurls like a ribbon, knotting and then stretching. The sky is rough and choky with storm clouds, but what little light there is pools within its scales, turning them iridescent. The suddenness of it, the impossibility, and the great creature's obvious strength make Fléance stammer out a wordless noise of fear.

The creature is the same—Roscille remembers the crushing might of its body around hers—but different, in ways that are not obvious to her until it draws closer.

Its thick tail is banded with thorns. Between its claws are weeds that it has ripped up from the earth. The underside of its enormous body is slicked with mud, lily pads and petals pasted on, and clinging to various scutes and appendages are tendrils of vines, sticky pine needles, and fragile ferns, as if it has just wrested itself free from a large thicket. Moss drips from the peaks of its wings.

For weeks the creature has twisted in some distant forest, hiding itself among the oily shadows and the dark leaves. It has taken this dark matter with it, and as the dragon lowers itself into the courtyard, the words of the prophecy fall into place like a key in a lock: The wood has come upon the hill.

Roscille dives away from Fléance as the dragon descends upon him. She skids on the dirt, palms burning. But she recovers herself quickly enough to turn around. And so she has the privilege and the pleasure to see this: a young man, dying in agony.

AFTER ITS CLAWS HAVE RIPPED flesh and its teeth have snapped bone, the dragon vanishes. It happens within the span of moments; if Roscille had blinked, she might have missed it. There was the creature's sinewy body, stretching across the dusty courtyard, and now there is only a man, curled in on himself, naked, vulnerable. Fléance's blood stains his sides; his arms are red up to the elbows. There are still weeds and thorns tangled in his hair, braceleting his wrists and ankles. He is breathing hard.

Roscille rushes to his side and collapses there, forehead resting against his shoulder, hands clutching at his beautiful, familiar face. Air rushes out of her and so do her words. She presses herself to him and tries not to weep.

Slowly Lisander raises his head to look at her. His green eyes are wavering, inhumanly bright. At first she fears there is no recognition in them. Perhaps the dragon has at last consumed the man; perhaps he is now nothing more than the shell which holds the monster within it. But then he exhales and his lips turn up faintly at the corners and he says in a low, tired, loving voice, "Roscille."

"Lisander," she whispers. "I thought you had gone."

He shakes his head. "All this time I writhed inside the monster's body, in the woods. But even the dragon knows your face. Your voice. If such a creature has any desire greater than blood, it is to protect you."

A dragon does not have many qualities to admire, but it cannot be said that it does not want, and that it does not guard its treasures jealously. Roscille lifts one of Lisander's hands in her own. The blood is caulked deep beneath his nails. She thinks of how they must look here, kneeling in this mess of mangled flesh, two unnatural creatures who are so natural in each other's company.

Senga is watching with wide eyes and a white face. Roscille rises, and she pulls Lisander up with her. He is still weak, unused to his human body. It has been so long since his feet have touched the earth.

"Don't be afraid," she tells Senga.

But when she reaches her handmaiden, Senga merely pulls Roscille into an embrace, pressing their faces close. She holds Roscille for a long time, even while the sounds of war skid past them like rocks down a mountainside, and while the storm clouds gather. At last, she lets go. She says, "Not afraid of you, Lady, never."

Lisander, who is still holding her hand, says, "We must go. If any more of Macbeth's men spot us, we are dead or in chains."

"No," Roscille says. "This fight must end with Macbeth. There can be no other way."

"The men see this as a fight for Alba, not merely a fight for their Lord or for Glammis. It is the English who come to suppress them, again, to dilute their Scottish bloodlines. Even if Macbeth is dead, they will not stop."

"They will not stop for Æthelstan, true. But they will stop for Duncane's chosen heir, the son with the blood of Alba in him. If they see you are alive, they will know Æthelstan is not here to trample them, merely to depose the traitor and restore Duncane's line."

Lisander turns his face away from her. Shadows pass across it.

"You would ask them to kneel before a monster and place a crown upon its head," he murmurs.

Roscille tips his chin up, forcing him to meet her eyes. "You are more than the creature your father has made you. Perhaps you are not mortal, not entirely—but I have felt the tenderness of your flesh; I have seen the nobility of your nature; I have been blessed to know your selfless spirit. Still you are a man."

"Kiss me, then," he says, "and prove it."

She grasps his face, without reluctance, without contrition—just as she did that first time, his hand tangled in her hair, his hips rolling against her. His mouth opens to meet hers, the ask and the answer. He bites her lower lip, the faint surfacing of the monster, but his tongue is gentle, soft with mortality, and his arms are endlessly tender. When she breaks the kiss at last, their hearts beat furiously in tandem.

Without letting his arms drop from her waist, with their foreheads still close, Lisander whispers, "I will show myself, then. I hope they will see what you do. I hope it will be enough."

Wind sweeps the courtyard, blowing in the storm from the sea, where lightning has already begun to crack the air and waves are rising in great heights. On the other side of the wall, men are falling like struck trees. And reluctantly, Roscille removes herself from Lisander's embrace.

"If you are to show yourself," Senga says drily, "perhaps it should not be *all* of yourself."

Lisander, as if he has only now remembered his nakedness, flushes.

To Senga, Roscille says, "Find him clothes. I will go after Macbeth."

"No," Lisander says at once, seizing her again by the arm. "He has no honor left in him; only ambition and rage. He will think nothing of striking you down. At least let me—"

"You cannot," says Roscille. "There is a prophecy. No man of woman born can slay him." She does not have to say the rest. The thoughts drift out from her like silvery visions, like spirits escaping their vessels. *I am not a man. Not quite a woman, either. Roscille of Breizh, beautiful, witch-kissed, witch.*

Soldiers beyond the wall roar and choke on the blood in their mouths. Evander is among them. Perhaps slain already. For all the men who drop to their knees when they see Lisander alive, there will still be more who rally behind their limping, diminished Lord.

It will not end, truly, until Macbeth is dead. Roscille releases Lisander's hand, and she goes into the depths of the castle.

ROSCILLE KNOWS WHERE TO WAIT for him. When Æthelstan's men are bashing in the barbican, when Evander's head is brandished on a pike, when the battle is either lost or won, Macbeth will come here. The iron door is behind her, cold air slipping through the cracks in the wood. The torches gutter against the wall. Beneath her feet, the ocean roils in its endless rhythm.

She hears him coming before she sees him: that shuffling gait, the hot breath exhaled through his flared nostrils. As he grows closer, around the last bend in the corridor, she sees a hand shoot out and grip the wall. It is streaked with blood both old and new, bright red and rust-hued, announcing all the deaths he has made. And then he comes, his enormous body penetrating the narrow hall, his shoulders so broad he can barely fit through.

He towers like a giant. This was Roscille's fearful first impression of him, his preternatural largeness. Yet she is not afraid like she was then, kneeling before the Druide, letting him yoke them together with his bristly rope. All her chains have been slashed, all her vows broken.

Macbeth's eyebrows leap up his face when he sees her—a brief moment of shock, and then his lips pull back in a snarl.

"You should not be here. You should be growing ancient and blind in the dark."

"And what prophecy would you hope I speak?" Roscille draws herself up. He is not quite close enough to meet her eyes. "Your doom is written already, and it is close. The wood has come high upon the hill."

"Liar," he says. "It is impossible."

"You yourself have witnessed many impossible things come true."

"Impossible for ordinary men," he says. "I am not so constrained. No mortal means can fell me. The only impossible thing is my death."

"If you are so certain," Roscille says, "then look into my eyes."

Macbeth smiles cruelly. Blood is so wet on his face that it glistens still.

"You have always thought yourself too clever," he says. "Roscille of Breizh. You have never kept to your place. I should have tied you to my bed the moment you stepped upon Scottish soil. You have worked in the shadows, fooling all with your innocent face, hiding your secrets beneath your veil. Well, it is off now. And I can see you truly. Your father is writ all over you. He has crafted this tale, that you have been cursed, that you hold this power of compulsion. And perhaps for those who believe such superstitions, it is real enough. But had he not spread this story in Breizh and beyond, you would have no power at all. The only real power you have ever had is the dagger I placed in your hand."

Roscille stands marble-still. Indeed, her father was the first to speak the words aloud—*perhaps you were cursed by a witch*. Before, it was no more than whispers and rumors; her beauty was strange enough to make men shiver, but she never compelled, enchanted, ensorcelled. It was just the stable boy, and could his own lust not have moved him? Then there were Duncane's guards—but there she had acted only at Macbeth's direction. Her magic, blooming only at the cultivation of men. Could it be so, truly?

A coldness creeps into her bones. Doubt, boring like a trephine.

Macbeth sees this doubt and his smile deepens. "So come then, Roscille. Roscilla. My dear wife. Lady Macbeth. Other men may have cringed from you, but I never have. Look into my eyes. I will look back and I will not tremble."

He slouches toward her, lumbering like an unwieldy creature half turned to stone. Roscille takes a stumbling step backward. The animal fear returns to her. Her own ghost inhabits her body—that girl, cowering in her bridal lace, is here again now. And Macbeth, Bellona's bridegroom, Thane of Glammis, Thane of Cawder, King Hereafter, is reaching for her with his blood-slicked hands.

Her back hits the door and the salt air winds around her ankles. Chains, she thinks, there are always more chains. But then she thinks of the three women on the other side, seething in the dark. They broke the lock, the four of them, together.

Her chest swells. And then she rises to meet Macbeth's eyes.

She has never looked into them before—the irony; she never dared. They are blue, and clear enough that she sees herself reflected back, like a fish darting through a small pool of water. At first nothing shifts in their surface. There is only the same fierceness and fury and preening victory, the certainty that she will fail. But Roscille keeps staring.

Slowly, a cloudiness overtakes him: The whites of his eyes seep into the irises, then the pupils, until his gaze is milky and matte, and she sees nothing reflected back. Macbeth gives a throaty cry and tries to turn away, but Roscille grasps his face in both of her hands and forces his gaze back to hers.

He falls to his knees. She stands over him. His veins bulge, and their color changes to a dense, tarry black. His skin, by contrast, grows paler and paler; it is the bone beginning to show through, his flesh wasting away, until there is only the meat and muscle of him, and a naked skull. His scream dries up in his throat.

And then there is no sound but that skull striking the stone floor. Roscille steps away, hands dropping to her sides.

Voices behind her, breaching the door. Three of them braiding together, like a tangle of weeds showing their shy heads in the soil, breaking apart the hard, cold earth, and straining upward into the light.

CODA

HAIL, KING, FOR SO YOU ARE: THE USURPER IS DEAD and gone. Standing in Glammis's blood-soaked soil, let the crown be set upon your head. A king of Scottish extraction, a king for all of Alba, the heir to his ailing father's throne. And of the fiendish creature within? Well, the man who acknowledges his monster is always wiser, kinder, nobler than the man who does not. These men fester with ghoulish wounds. All hail the king who shows his demons openly, and thus is not consumed.

Hail, Queen, who is known by many names: The cruel Lord is dead and gone. Show your eyes and speak your will. Let it carry across the green hills and the low valleys of Alba, across lakes and rivers and the narrow channel where your father lies. Henceforth you will be known in all lands for your cleverness and your justice. And of your unnatural stare? Let them call you witch, as they do any woman who professes power. All hail the Queen who shows the dark threads beneath the world to which the mortal gaze is blind.

And now, we secret, black, and midnight hags: Our toils are ended. Our chains may rattle, but they do not bind. At last, we sleep. We dream.

ACKNOWLEDGMENTS

To my agent, Sarah Landis, who has never once failed to perform magic when I needed it most; to my editors, Tricia Narwani and Sam Bradbury, whose insights and passion for this book have shaped it into the best possible version of itself; to the teams at Del Rey and Del Rey UK, who I have been tremendously lucky to work with: My gratitude is endless.

Thank you to the Bard for his verse, of course, and to Marie de France for her lais.

ABOUT THE AUTHOR

AVA REID is the #1 *New York Times* bestselling author of the gothic fantasies *A Study in Drowning, Juniper & Thorn,* and *Lady Macbeth.* She lives in California.

Instagram: @avasreid

ABOUT THE TYPE

This book was set in Bembo, a typeface based on an old-style Roman face that was used for Cardinal Pietro Bembo's tract *De Aetna* in 1495. Bembo was cut by Francesco Griffo (1450–1518) in the early sixteenth century for Italian Renaissance printer and publisher Aldus Manutius (1449–1515). The Lanston Monotype Company of Philadelphia brought the well-proportioned letterforms of Bembo to the United States in the 1930s.